Until She Is Safe

A Blair Emerson Novel

Linda Amey

TREATY OAK PUBLISHERS
AUSTIN, TEXAS

PUBLISHER'S NOTE

This is a work of fiction. Names, characters, places, and incidents either are the product of the author's imagination or are used fictitiously. Any resemblance to actual persons, living or dead, events, or locales is entirely coincidental.

No part of this book may be reproduced or transmitted in any form or by any means, graphic, electronic, or mechanical, including photocopying, recording, taping or by any information storage retrieval system, without the permission in writing from the author.

Published in the United States of America
TREATY OAK PUBLISHERS
Austin, Texas

Cover Design by Kimberly Greyer

Library of Congress Cataloging-in-Publication Data
ISBN: 978-1-959127-26-0 (print)

Available in print and digital on Amazon

DEDICATION

To compassionate people,

Who extend second chances.

CHAPTER 1

Rylie Thorp raised binoculars to his eyes. Cigarette smoke coiled around the brim of his cap and snaked out the car window into the thick October air. Kyla Phelps crouched in the back seat, evening shadows and anxiety giving her young face a haggard look. The two had been watching the mall exit for an hour, parked in the middle of a crowded row of cars, unnoticed by security cruising the sprawling asphalt acres.

The perfect circle of the high-powered lenses snared an Asian woman emerging from the mall alone. Clutching a shopping bag in one hand and her purse in the other, she crossed the wide, well-lit sidewalk, but then hesitated before stepping off the curb. Working her head from side to side, the woman seemed to search her mind and the near side of the crowded lot.

"Trying to remember where she parked her car," Thorp muttered, lowering the binoculars long enough to take a drag off his cigarette and to sweep strands of oily blonde hair from his forehead. "Just hang a victim-sign around your neck, idiot."

With visible uncertainty, the petite woman stepped off the curb, and then crossed the traffic lanes, her approaching image grainy and indistinct through the binoculars. Thorp chuckled at the way the woman craned her neck, peering around cars angled on both sides of the aisle like bones on a spine. "I could have sworn I parked on this aisle," he mocked, thumping his cigarette out the window.

Standing under one of the lot's powerful lights, the woman dug in her purse. Deliberately, she extended her right arm, fist closed. The headlights of a Honda sedan parked two aisles away blinked on, drawing the woman's quick, relieved attention.

"Dammit." Thorp lowered the binoculars, letting them dangle from the neck strap. Lighting another cigarette, he picked up his cell phone, and then exhaled a smoky greeting to his friend Nesto, parked on the far end of the lot. "Just checking in, man."

"Nothing yet?"

"No, but there will be. I counted five Toyotas on this side of the building." Thorp ended the call, and then lobbed the phone over his shoulder. Kyla ducked, banging her head against the window.

"Jackass," she muttered, hurling the phone into the front passenger seat.

Thorp grinned with satisfaction, training the binoculars on the mall exit again. A trickle of people flowed out the door, crossing the traffic lanes in pairs and threesomes, heading for their cars. Resting his elbow in the open window, he sharpened the focus on a young couple holding hands as they walked. The two appeared to be in their late teens, each wearing boots, jeans, and quilted vests. With his free hand, the boy carried a garment bag over his shoulder. Even from two aisles away, Thorp could see smiles on their young, unsuspecting faces.

"That's right, cowboy," Thorp coaxed. "Just keep right on walking. See that white Camry down there?" Again, Thorp sharpened the focus, chuckling as he watched the couple lean close to each other. "Oh, now ain't that sweet? She just needed a little smooch."

"Dammit, Rylie." Kyla kicked the back of the driver's seat. "Stop with the play-by-play. You're making me nervous."

Thorp turned with a quick twist of his head and shoulders, his right arm crooked over the seat back. With vicious swiftness, he struck Kyla in the face with the back of his hand. Her head snapped, fanning her mahogany-colored hair across her face. "Mouth off again and you'll be spitting teeth."

Shifting in the seat, Thorp located the young couple with bare eyes, and then raised the binoculars. They were nearing the end of the row now, still walking hand in hand. Three cars remained. If Nesto, and not Kyla, were sitting in the back seat, Thorp would bet the man fifty bucks that the kids would leave in the Camry.

Thorp liked working with Nesto. The two of them had snatched several vehicles using only Thorp's Mazda, but then they had failed several times too. City drivers were not as careless as they used to be, not as naïve. The advantage of a box-and-bump was that it eliminated the target's option of driving to a public place to exchange information. The disadvantage was that it required two vehicles and three people. The only reason Thorp had agreed to involve Kyla Phelps was that the good-for-nothing girl owed him money.

Thorp's pulse quickened. "I knew it."

The kids had released each other's hands and were standing at the rear of the white Toyota Camry. The boy slid the garment bag off his shoulder into the trunk, and then pressed down the lid. The girl gave him another quick kiss, and then got in the car on the passenger side.

Thorp dropped the binoculars on the seat, and then snatched up his cell phone. Nesto answered in the same eager way as before. Thorp spoke with steely calm. "Finally snagged one. It's a white Toyota Camry. You know what to do." He locked eyes with Kyla in the rear-view mirror. "You sure you can do this?"

"I'm sure." She nodded her head in quick little bobs. "Just like we practiced."

Thorp thumped his cigarette out the window, started the engine, and then turned on the headlights. He backed Kyla's old Taurus out of the parking space, keeping his eyes on the Toyota as it reversed, and then rolled up the aisle. "There's two people in the car, Kyla."

"Right. Got it. I know what to do."

"You'd better," Thorp warned, turning right onto the traffic lane. The Toyota was several car lengths in front of him. "With me, it's one strike and you're out."

"I can do it. Just be sure to—"

"Shut up." Thorp spoke into the cell phone. "Nesto, there's two people in the Camry. They're heading toward the south exit. You got them?"

"Got my eyes on it right now. White Toyota Camry."

Keeping a safe distance from the Toyota, Thorp pulled his cap brim low. Headlights appeared in his rear-view mirror and blinked. "I see you, Nesto. Stay right behind me."

The south exit emptied onto a four-lane side street. Traffic was light. The signal at the intersection ahead glowed green. The Toyota sped through in the outside lane, the Taurus and Nesto's Ford truck following inconspicuously. Thorp had checked the traffic lights the night before and found them well synchronized. Chances were good that the cowboy would sail through the next intersection too.

"Nesto, I want to catch him at a light, but we're gonna have to slow him down." Thorp spoke calmly, but his pulse was racing. "Make your first move."

The Ford truck eased into the left lane, passed Thorp in the Taurus, and then pulled alongside the Toyota. Thorp changed lanes, taking up his position behind the truck. Again, he found Kyla's image in the rear-view mirror. Her eyes looked frantic. "You ready?"

"I'm ready."

The three cars breezed through the second intersection. "Let's block him in, Nesto. Claim your spot."

The truck gathered speed, and then eased in front of the Toyota. Thorp positioned the front of the Taurus opposite the Toyota's rear fender, trapping the vehicle in the outside lane. The speedometer read twenty miles an hour. "Slow him down, Nesto. This is good."

The cars were in the middle of the block now, the boy's darkened profile visible through the window of the Camry. He looked straight ahead, giving no indication that he wanted to change lanes.

"Looking good, Nesto. Just keep it steady." Thorp slowed the Taurus, easing behind the Toyota again. "Stay where you are, cowboy," he growled. "Stay right where you are."

Single file, the vehicles approached the third intersection. Thorp gripped the steering wheel, his pulse soaring. "Get ready, Nesto." He narrowed the gap, his gaze darting between the rear of the Toyota and the traffic signal. "Three. Two. One. Now!"

With impossible suddenness, brake lights glared. Tires squealed. Nesto's truck skidded to a noisy stop. The front of the Toyota pitched down, wheels locked, tires screeching. Thorp locked his grip and stiffened his arms. He hit the brake just hard enough to screech his tires. At perfect speed, he eased the Taurus into the rear of the Toyota, tapping it forward, well clear of Nesto's truck.

"Hold your position, Nesto," Thorp ordered. "Go, Kyla."

The rear door of the Taurus flew open, and then slammed shut. Kyla stumbled past Thorp's door. Fear and her slumping posture made the girl look pitifully gaunt.

"Come on, cowboy," Thorp muttered, his throat tight with tension. "Get out of the car. Do the right thing."

The driver's door of the Camry opened slowly. The boy emerged, squinting in the glare of headlights. Thorp snatched up his cell phone. "Good job, Nesto. Now get out of here." The engine roared as the truck sped out of sight.

Thorp watched as Kyla stumbled to a halt at the rear fender of the Toyota. Frantic, she shouted, "Get away from the car!" The boy's young face twisted in confusion. "Do it!" Kyla demanded. Her right hand shot out, raising a nine-millimeter shoulder high.

Stunned, the boy backed into the open car door, his panicked gaze locked on the gun. "Okay. Okay." He stepped cautiously to the side, keeping his hands chest high, palms revealed. "It's yours, okay? No problem."

Kyla waggled the gun at him, the soles of her shoes scraping the pavement in a frantic dance. "Get over there," she ordered, wobbling the gun toward the sidewalk. "Hurry up."

Thorp watched the scene unfold, his chest heaving. The boy stumbled around the front of the Toyota. Headlights illuminated his silver belt buckle. It was large and oval, a rodeo trophy buckle. "Get your girlfriend, cowboy. All we want is your car."

Kyla lunged for the open door, the gun banging and scraping. She dropped clumsily into the driver's seat as the panic-stricken boy yanked at the passenger door. "Get out, Hannah. Hurry!"

The passenger door flew open. The girl, throwing herself out the opening, battled with the shoulder harness. The boy scrambled to free her, shouting and pleading.

Suddenly, the Toyota lurched forward. Thorp yelled. "What the hell are you doing, Kyla?"

The force flung and jostled the panicked girl. Her arm was bent behind her at an impossible angle. Screaming, she dropped to the pavement, disappearing for an instant from Thorp's view. Her writhing form reappeared as Kyla sped away, the right rear tire of the Toyota grinding over the girl's thrashing legs.

Thorp jerked the steering wheel left, and then jammed the accelerator. One final look over his shoulder captured the cowboy waving frantically at an approaching car, and the girl lying lifeless on the pavement.

CHAPTER 2

LIVE OAK, TEXAS

A damp November wind whistled around the secluded cabin, its persistent gusts stirring branches of ancient live oaks. Weary leaves, brown and brittle, fell silent to the ground below. Some skittered along a recently constructed flagstone path leading from the detached garage directly to the door of Blair Emerson's roomy new bathroom. When she had handed Manny Taggert the detailed drawings of the addition, the befuddled carpenter's expression had said, "Why in Sam Hill do you want an exterior door to your bathroom?"

Fitted with a stackable washer and dryer, the costly new bathroom was but one of the creative accommodations Blair had made since uncovering her daughter's painful secret. For now, Brandi's obsession with germs was in check. Not having to share a bathroom with her mother would surely help keep it that way. The exterior door, should Brandi's OCD take hold again, would permit Blair to shower and change clothes before moving about the cabin at the end of her workday.

Frosty air whistled around the bathroom door. Blair shivered, found a thick wool sweater in her closet, and pulled it on. Again, she checked her watch. Manny was late. Her patience was growing decidedly thin by the time his truck rumbled up the gravel driveway leading from Southworth Road, and then lurched to a stop near the garage.

Through the bathroom window, Blair watched Manny shrug off his plaid jacket, and then toss it onto the lid of a dented toolbox stretching across the bed of his truck. The man had lost weight during his brief jail stay, but Blair guessed he still weighed well over two hundred pounds. He really was a decent sort, but even in his early forties Manny was as susceptible to peer pressure as any kid at Brandi's school. Last year, he had gotten caught up in another guy's vendetta against an environmental activist, long gone from Live Oak now, and the two men had found themselves in jail. Upon his release, Manny had returned to the only skill he had, in his words, swinging a hammer.

Watching Manny now, Blair could not help but grin. The man had buckled a tool belt around his waist, and then adjusted it as if he might need to quick-draw his hammer. Then, with the ease of lifting a six-pack of beer, Manny hoisted a gray steel toolbox from the truck bed, and then snagged a coil of weather stripping.

Blair opened the bathroom door and stuck out her head. A gust of wind whipped strands of straight brown hair across her face. The air smelled of cedar and the damp debris of fall. "Not a minute too soon, Manny." She pointed at a pile of old rags on the floor, as he crossed the threshold. "I was stuffing those around the door at two o'clock this morning."

Manny grinned, his face not nearly as round as it used to be. "Bet you was cussing me with every breath."

"It wasn't your fault. How could you know that the hardware store would be fresh out of weather stripping."

Manny set his toolbox on the floor. He had begun the bathroom addition weeks ago, but now he surveyed the room as if for the first time. "Sure like this tile you and Brandi picked out. Looks just like old stone. If money ever gets tight at your funeral homes, you two could hire out as decorators." Chuckling, Manny picked up the roll of weather stripping. "You two done a real good job."

"So did you, Manny." Blair patted the man's thick shoulder. "I'll get out of your way now, and let you finish."

"Before you go, Blair. I want to thank you again for letting me do this job." Awkwardly, he shifted his considerable weight from one booted foot to the other. "Because of your recommendation, looks like I'm going to get to replace the roof on Miss Lindquist's front porch."

Blair gave Manny a thumbs-up. Leaving him to his work and the unwelcome chill of her bedroom, she walked down the hall to the family room.

The Texas-rustic cabin, situated on fifty acres only minutes from the small town of Live Oak, was not particularly old, but it appeared to be. Its heavy-grained oak floors were richly stained. Walls of smooth, unknotted pine contrasted pleasingly with the floor's dense texture. The fireplace, built of San Saba sandstone, dominated one end of the room. The mantel, skillfully carved from a single oak slab, held an oak-trimmed clock and a gallery of family photos.

The studio portrait of Blair's parents had been taken just before her father's death. She had always treasured it, but even more so now that her mother was gone too. Blair had taken particular care to interrupt the chronological photos of her sister Charlotte's two children. The strategy was meant to divert attention from the glaring gaps within photos of Brandi.

The mantel clock chimed. Five o'clock. Brandi would normally be home from school by now, a fact not lost on Nixon. The Boston terrier had taken up his post at the front window. He watched the driveway with keen anticipation.

"Poor, Nixon." Blair tickled the soft skin behind his erect ears. "Brandi really is having dinner with her dad tonight. I wouldn't tease you about a thing like that." The dog cocked his head in canine skepticism, and then resumed his duties as sentry.

The land line rang. Blair took the call from a phone in the kitchen, smiling instantly at the singsong greeting in her ear. "Hello, Aunt Blair. It's your favorite niece."

"You're my only niece, Alli," Blair teased. "But even if you weren't, you would still be my favorite. How was school today?"

"So-so," Allison answered. "I got in a little bit of trouble. I had to smack Chandler on the arm. He called me skinny. Is Brandi at home?"

"She's having dinner with her dad. Myles picked her up after school."

"And Nixon is standing at the window watching for her." The child spoke with exaggerated resentment. "Mom still won't let me have a dog. She says she has too much on her plate."

"Your mom is right, Alli. A dog can come later."

"Why later? I've been in remission for six months, Aunt Blair. Surely Mom's had time to scrape some stuff off her plate in six months."

Remission. Though not synonymous with cured, the word meant hope and health. It meant palatable pills, not the ravages of chemotherapy and radiation. Despite all that, hearing her nine-year-old niece utter the word sent Blair tumbling back to the moment she heard Charlotte say. "It's leukemia, Blair. Allison has leukemia."

Blair heard Manny's heavy footfalls behind her. She turned and pointed to the coffeepot. Manny declined with a waggle of his hand. "Alli, I've got to run. Mr. Taggert is here. I'll tell Brandi to phone you later." She replaced the receiver, noticing that Manny was grinning, as if he had a joke to tell.

"That was Allison, right?" he asked, chuckling. "I ran into her at Al's the other day. Her and Charlotte was sharing a banana split. Know what she said to me?"

Blair cringed. "There is no telling."

"The cute little thing smiled real big and friendly and said, 'Hi, Mr. Taggert. It's good to see you again. How was prison?'" Manny's broad shoulders bounced with each burst of laughter. "You should have seen your sister's face."

Blair chuckled mischievously. "I would have paid good money."

"You would have got your money's worth." When Manny's laughter subsided, he raised his empty hands, palms up. "Well, if there's nothing else you need, I guess I'm done."

The two walked through the dining nook, and then onto the screened back porch. The door to the original laundry room stood ajar. A washer and dryer occupied one wall. Last week, Manny had asked Blair if she wanted him to move the appliances for her. "Oh, no. I have new ones coming for my bathroom," she had explained. "Those are Brandi's." Jokingly, she had added, "If you were raising a teenage girl, you would understand the need for two sets."

Manny closed the door to the cramped, dank room. "I'll bet one thing, Blair. On cold, windy days like this one, Brandi will be sneaking her basket into your laundry room."

Blair laughingly agreed, but she knew Manny was wrong. Brandi would sooner lug her clothes down to the creek and wash them on a rock than share a washer and dryer with her mother—a mortician of all things.

An unfamiliar car pulled to a stop at the side of the house. A young man emerged. His jeans were wrinkled, his blue cotton shirt rumpled and askew. He looked as if he had slept in the white compact. As he neared, the young man seemed familiar to Blair, but she could not place where she had seen him. Realization dawned when he stuck out his hand.

"Hello, again, Blair. Remember me? Jason Hammond. *Austin American-Statesman.*"

Blair ignored the man's offered hand. "What are you doing here, Jason? I've told you that I don't want to talk to you. I've ignored your phone calls and emails for weeks. Are you incredibly dense or just rude?"

"Neither. I'm a man doing a story. Like it or not, you and Senator Lakeman are major players. And so is your daughter."

"Well, I don't like it, Jason." Blair uttered the young man's name with noticeable condescension. "Quit harassing me and get off my property."

"Blair, please," Hammond persisted. "I just want ten minutes of your time. Five, even. What could it hurt? Wilson Rule's book will be in the bookstores any day now."

"Are you sure?"

"I got the press release." Hammond took another step toward Blair, his expression pleading. "I'm not asking you to go into detail about Brandi's abduction and recovery. I just want to quote you in my story."

Was it possible? Blair worried. Had Wilson Rule's book been published already? She had learned through her ex-husband that the true-crime author was writing a book about Brandi. Rule had requested an interview, first with Myles, and then later with Blair. He had been flatly turned down by both. Myles had threatened to sue if Rule persisted, but ultimately the man could not be stopped.

To Blair's knowledge, no one in Live Oak had spoken with Rule or his researcher, despite their repeated efforts. People in Blair's old neighborhood in Austin had been pursued too. She still owned a home in Barton Hills and had rented it to one of the funeral directors who worked at Emerson Funeral Home in Austin. Kent had been outraged when Rule's researcher had asked if Blair had left behind any personal items, inquiring specifically about photographs.

Blair had vowed to ignore the unprincipled publicity monger and his book, but how could she? The man had written about her child. Keeping silent about her objections—no, her disgust—conceded that the man had a right to relate and comment on what Lenny and Jewell Bond had done to Brandi.

"All right, Jason," Blair snapped. "I'll give you a quote, and it darn sure better show up in your article."

Instantly, Jason Hammond produced his cell phone, and then tapped the screen. Blair snatched the device from the man's hand and jabbed RECORD. "Wilson Rule and his ilk are child abusers," she began. "Rule probably wouldn't strike a child with a fist, or a belt, or an open palm. His weapon is a keyboard." Blair's pulse raced and her voice rose. "Rule violates children by making their personal pain a public topic. He invades their privacy and threatens their security." She gripped the phone so tightly that her hand shook. "Worse yet, the man is making money off the trauma inflicted on children, such as my daughter. What he is doing is cruel and evil. It ought to be against the law."

Sensing Manny at her elbow, Blair tossed the phone back to the reporter. "There, Jason, you've got your quote."

Manny stepped into the gap between Blair and the much smaller man. "And if you don't put every word she said in your newspaper, you're gonna have to answer to me." Manny rested his beefy hand on the claw hammer dangling from his tool belt. "Now get the hell off my friend's property."

Hammond jammed the phone in his pocket, and then raised his hands shoulder high, palms toward Manny. "I'm already in my car, big guy." He backed away. "Firing up the engine right this second."

As the car bounced down the lane toward Southworth Road, Blair choked back an angry outburst. Pretending not to notice, Manny touched her shoulder, tugged on his plaid jacket, and then dropped his tool belt noisily into the bed of his truck.

CHAPTER 3

SAN ANTONIO, TEXAS

The job interview took place in what Tommy Lee Worsham called the conference room. Lenny Bond had arrived ten minutes early and was now seated in a folding chair at a long, narrow table. Worsham sat opposite him, a man to his right, and a woman to his left. Worsham was what Lenny called a man's man, with the body of a running back and shoulders so wide they blocked light from the window behind him. Lenny wished he had bulked up with his quilted jacket. His skimpy windbreaker made his sloping shoulders all but disappear.

Pete DeLeon had called this morning's interview a slam-dunk. As much as Lenny wanted to believe his buddy, he was having doubts. Since walking into the room, Lenny had felt the woman on Worsham's left glaring at him over her goofy looking half-glasses. Her pale, green eyes reminded Lenny of Thompson seedless grapes. Her lumpy jowls look as if she had stored a few next to her jawbone. The scowl on the woman's face said that the only thing likely to get slammed or dunked was Lenny's hopes of landing a job there.

Worsham looked like a running back, but when the man spoke, he sounded like a news anchor. "Mr. Bond, thank you for coming. You've met my attorney, Ed Monaghan, and my human resources director, Hortense Holder." He pulled a folder off a stack and opened it. "Fifteen years ago, I was convicted of armed robbery and served three years in prison in Illinois. When I got out and moved back here to San Antonio, no one would hire me. I did the only thing I knew how to do. I borrowed a lawnmower from my father and went to work. Today, Worsham Services employs sixty people. We specialize in commercial property maintenance. At all times, I have ten people on my staff who have been or are currently involved in the criminal justice system. Some have completed their sentences. Others are out on parole. All receive the same benefits as my other employees, but they can only work for me for a year. Starting in month nine, Ms. Holder sets up job interviews." Worsham motioned with his thumb toward the window behind him. "The building you see back there is a dorm. I don't charge rent, but the residents pay all utilities, food costs, and keep the dorm as spotless as a barracks." Worsham removed a prepared packet from the folder, and then handed it to Lenny. "That packet contains more information about Worsham Services. You can review it later." He closed the folder, and then set it aside. "Now, Mr. Monaghan has a few questions."

"Yes, sir," Lenny answered, improving his posture. "Thank you, sir."

Ed Monaghan was a tub of a man with a red face and front teeth like Chiclets. When he looked down at the file before him, the folds of his chin obliterated the knot in his tie. "Mr. Bond, begin by recounting the events surrounding your incarceration."

Lenny stirred. "Recount? You mean figure up how many years ago this all started?"

"Recount," the man repeated impatiently. "Summarize from the beginning."

"Oh, gotcha." Lenny licked his thin lips, but his mouth was so dry he had no spit. "It all started when my wife Jewell got to wanting a baby real bad, but she couldn't have one. This went on for a long time, and then one day—We was living in Dallas at the time.—she drove down to Austin on her day off from the liquor store."

"You didn't go to Austin with her?" Monaghan inquired.

"No, sir." Lenny shook his head emphatically. "I had no idea what Jewell was up to until I come home that night. She was acting real nervous and took me into the back bedroom. There was a baby asleep in the bed."

"Did your wife tell you at that point that she had abducted the child?"

Lenny nodded. "Yep. She sure did."

From the corner of his eye, Lenny watched the grape-eyed woman—Damn. He had forgotten her name.— pick up her pen and write. Monaghan then told him to relate what Jewell had said about the abduction.

"Well, she said she went down to Austin with that plan in mind, drove around for hours, and then ended up in west Austin. She saw a car parked in a driveway with one of those child seats in the back, so Jewell parked on a side street and watched a while. The backyard was fenced but, being in our old truck, she could see over it. Before long, a woman came out the back door carrying a little girl in her arms. The kid was wearing a swimsuit. The woman picked up a water hose, but the little girl got in her sandbox instead. Jewell said the woman sat on the patio watching the kid play. Then real sudden like, she went inside. I got no idea why." Lenny paused, brought his hand up to his nose and rubbed it hard with his finger. "Jewell was so desperate, you see."

"What did your wife do, Mr. Bond?"

"She got out of the truck real quick, opened the gate, walked across the backyard, and then lifted the baby right out of the sandbox." Lenny's thoughts stalled, as they always did, when he tried to picture Jewell doing such a thing. She had been a good woman, not a mean bone in her pitiful body.

"Mr. Bond, when you knew the child had been abducted, why did you not call the police?"

Lenny had his answer ready, figuring the question was sure to be asked. "Jewell was my wife. I couldn't just rat her out to the cops. She begged me to keep quiet, so what could I do?"

"But what about the baby's parents?" the man asked, glancing down at the yellow pad in front of him. "Myles Lakeman and Blair Emerson. Did you think about them?"

"We didn't know for days who the baby belonged to, not until it hit the news. But, no," Lenny answered honestly. "When my thoughts started going down that road, I kinda headed them off."

Staring at Monaghan's yellow pad, Lenny wished he could read upside down. He had not expected to be grilled like a rack of ribs. What had Pete gotten him into?

Lenny's thoughts were scrambled when he heard the word *died*. He unsnarled them, deciding that Monaghan had asked about Jewell. Hard to believe, Lenny thought. It was only two years ago that she died. Seemed like a lifetime.

Buying time, he asked Monaghan to repeat his question, and then answered it. "About eleven years later, Jewell had a car wreck. Right before she died, she told April that if she ever wanted to know who her biographical mother was, she could ask me, and that I would tell her."

"April. That's what you and your wife called Brandi Lakeman?"

"Right. You see it was in April that we got her."

"So the child grew up thinking she had been adopted." The man kneaded the flab under his chin like biscuit dough, looking perplexed. "What happened after your wife died?"

Again, Lenny felt the burn of the grape-eyed woman's glare. "Jewell left me in a mess. I had this twelve-year-old kid that I didn't have the foggiest idea what to do with. One thing led to the other, and I decided the best thing for the kid was to give her back to her parents."

"Give?" Monaghan cocked his head, reminding Lenny of a bulldog listening to a peculiar sound.

"Honest to God, Mr. Monaghan. Giving Brandi back was my first thought. If I would have stuck with that, then we wouldn't be having this nice meeting today." Lenny chuckled. When no one smiled, he rambled on, relating how he had contacted Blair Emerson and demanded a hundred fifty thousand dollars for Brandi's return. "I got part of the money, but then things got all gummed up. I'm proud to say, though, that Brandi ended up where she belongs."

"And what did you do, Mr. Bond?"

"I headed south to Laredo, changed my name to Lee Pickens, and laid low." Lenny's thoughts stalled again. He pictured himself in the Cadillac Bar talking to that snake Victor Rizzo, margaritas making his tongue as loose as the flesh under Monaghan's chin.

"My notes indicate that you made a second attempt to extort money from Blair Emerson."

The room turned suddenly warm. Beads of sweat formed on Lenny's upper lip. "That's not exactly right. One night when I was drunk, I mouthed off to an old boy named Rizzo about the money Blair owed me. There was some talk about trying to get it, but I backed out. Problem was, Rizzo didn't back out. When I got wind of what the guy was planning to do—You know, make Blair think I was after the rest of the money.—I followed him to Live Oak where Blair and Brandi live."

"And then you shot Mr. Rizzo, correct?"

Lenny made solid eye contact with Monaghan, just as Pete had told him to do. Then he locked square on at Worsham. It seemed to Lenny that the man's brown eyes had just turned black, daring Lenny to lie.

"I did shoot Rizzo, but it was a accident." The room was now as hot as the prison laundry. Lenny wiped sweat from his brow and upper lip. "The Hays County grand jury didn't indict me for nothing. They just turned me over to Travis County. I pleaded guilty to aggravated kidnapping of Brandi and got sentenced to two years."

"I have no further questions of Mr. Bond." Monaghan closed his folder, and then leaned back in his chair, his shirt buttons straining against the holes.

The grape-eyed woman inched her chair forward, resting her large forearms on the table. Soft flesh inside the sleeves of her sweater flattened on the tabletop like a deflated tire. "Mr. Bond, I have but one inquiry."

Lenny twisted in the metal chair, forcing himself to face down what had to be the scariest looking woman in south Texas. He realized he was holding his breath, bracing himself for her question. *Mr. Bond,* she would say, *do you know that if I had my way, that chair you are sitting in would be plugged into that socket over there?*

Lenny forced himself to breathe. "I'll do my best to answer your question, Mrs. Thompson."

"Holder," the woman said. "Hortense Holder."

"Sorry." Lenny's stomach churned.

"Mr. Bond, if Brandi Emerson-Lakeman were sitting here beside me, what would you say to her?"

Lenny burped, a small but audible little burst of air. "Excuse me." He swallowed hard, and then exhaled loudly. He had expected a Clayton Kershaw fastball, but he could handle this toss without a glove.

"Well, I would ask Brandi what she thinks about being a senator's daughter. Then I'd tell her to hang in there when that dang Wilson Rule's book comes out. In case you didn't know, that greedy dog wrote a book about Brandi, and what Jewell and me did. Then I'd ask her how her little cousin Allison is getting along. She come down with leukemia last spring, and Brandi's been real worried about her."

"Wait. Excuse me, Mr. Bond." Hortense Holder frowned, corrugating her forehead. "How do you know all that?"

"Brandi told me."

"You have contact with her?" the woman asked, puzzled.

"Once a month," Lenny answered proudly. "She writes me a letter once a month, and I get to write back once a month. So I guess that would be two contacts, depending on how you look at it."

"The child's parents allow you to correspond with their daughter? For how long?"

"Since right after I went to prison." The woman was not nearly as scary now, enabling Lenny to look into her pale, green eyes. "Blair visited me there one day, saying that Brandi was dealing with a lot of, you know, emotions. Then she said that Brandi's therapist thought that it might be … uh … therapatic for her to write to me, get some things off her chest and all." Lenny went on to explain that Blair had laid down some rules. "She said I could write once a month, that I better not use no prison lingo, and that no bellyaching was allowed. Plus, Blair made it clear that she was gonna read every letter before giving it to Brandi, and that if I broke the rules, she would send the thing right back to me." Lenny raised his right index finger and waggled it in the air. "In all that time, Blair has only sent one letter back to me. I grumbled about not getting enough sleep because my cellblock was so dang noisy. Blair considered that bellyaching, so she drew a big red circle around that part. Under it, she wrote, 'Too damn bad.' Then she wrote that she had suffered through eleven years of silence when she should have been hearing her child's laughter."

Lenny's narrow shoulders slumped. His chin sank. For a long time, he stared at a small oval stain on a floor tile. When he looked up again, his eyes were clouded with tears.

CHAPTER 4

HOUSTON, TEXAS

Taylor McFadden steadied himself on the second rung of a ladder, and then realized he had arrived there empty-handed. Over his shoulder, he called to his frustrated helper who was grumbling at the tamper-proof packaging designed for a dozen innocuous screws. "Hannah, toss me the screwdriver."

"Phillips or flathead?"

Taylor chuckled at his girlfriend's response. How many nineteen-year-old girls even knew the difference?

"Phillips. And I have all the screws I need now."

Hannah tossed the stubborn package into the air. Screws rained onto her bed. "Now he tells me."

Taylor poked a screw into a pilot hole, gave it a few quick turns with his fingers, and then took the screwdriver from Hannah's extended hand. Installing wood blinds was the final step in the process of converting the Rennicks's downstairs guest room into Hannah's bedroom.

Her parents had been determined to finish the change-over before Hannah was released from the hospital. Well into his daughter's three-week stay, Dean Rennick had prodded his wife regularly, each urging growing in impatience. One day, Taylor had stopped by the Rennick home on the way to the hospital to get Hannah's iPad. From upstairs, he had overheard Dean Rennick raise his voice to his wife. "What are you waiting on, Olivia? Do you think if you leave all Hannah's stuff in her room that she'll have no choice but to get out of her wheelchair and climb the damn stairs?"

In the end, Olivia Rennick had compressed the gut-wrenching process of sorting, packing, and organizing Hannah's belongings into a single, miserable day. Taylor and Dean had given the guest room a fresh coat of paint, and then switched the furniture between the two rooms. They had moved Hannah's clothes, electronics, books, photographs, and her favorite barrel racing trophies. Except for the hardwood floor, Hannah's new room was identical to the old, even the coat of pale, green paint.

With the project at last complete, Olivia had begun to cry. "I want Hannah upstairs. I want her down the hall from us where she has always been."

Taylor knew with absolute certainty what Olivia Rennick had really wanted to say to her husband. "I want everything like it was before Taylor let a maniac steal Hannah's car and nearly kill her in the process."

More than a month had flown by, or dragged, or vanished since the night Taylor and Hannah had gone to a monogram shop at the mall to pick up her father's birthday gift. The images tattooed in Taylor's memory were horrifyingly vivid. Hannah struggling with the seat belt. The red-haired woman yelling, shouting orders. The man in the cap staring as he tore away in the Taurus. The tire of Hannah's Toyota chewing her foot and ankle.

Dean and Olivia Rennick had said all the right words to Taylor. "It wasn't your fault. Hannah doesn't blame you, and we don't either. Don't blame yourself."

But how could he not? Taylor knew carjackers faked accidents. Only an idiot would have gotten out of the car. Why hadn't he warned Hannah the instant he realized what was happening? Why hadn't he jumped back in the car and gotten the hell out of there?

Taylor still tortured himself with those and a dozen similar questions. The rock bottom truth was that he had not realized they were being carjacked until the woman pointed the gun at him. By then, it had been too late.

Twisting the final screw into the last bracket, Taylor turned to Hannah. "We're good to go."

Hannah gripped the ends of the headrail, lifted it off the bed, and then rested it across the arms of her wheelchair. Taylor ached inside as he watched the girl he loved maneuver around the foot of the bed. Hannah was five-foot-six and had weighed a hundred-thirty pounds at the time of the carjacking. She was down to a hundred seventeen now. Her slimness accentuated every facial angle and enlarged her round green eyes. Her thighs, once strong and toned from a lifetime on horseback, looked fragile under the thick knit of her sweatpants. The bottom of the right leg dangled limply over the empty, metal footrest. "Hannah is in recovery," the surgeon had said, his mask dangling on his chest. "She came through fine. As I warned, the trauma to her lower leg was massive. I'm sorry, but I was unable to reattach her foot."

Hannah rolled her chair near the ladder. She lifted the headrail with both hands, straining to place the heavy blind within Taylor's reach. He grasped both ends, positioned them between the two brackets, and then snapped them shut. "All right. Let's see how this puppy works." He backed down the ladder, collapsed it, and then set it in the corner. "Give that cord a yank, babe."

Hannah grasped the wheels of her chair, turning them with ever decreasing awkwardness. At the window, she pulled the cord to the side. The heavy slats dropped slowly, her hand rising as the cord withdrew. The plastic pull slipped from her fingers. The slats fell noisily, banging the panes and the window trim. The bottom whacked the sill before coming to a rest. Hannah tugged on the high end of the cockeyed blind, but it would not budge.

Frustrated, she spun her chair away from the window, rolled to the foot of the bed, and then began raking her hand across the comforter, gathering screws into a little pile. "I can always get my Mommy or Daddy to help me," she whined, childlike, "if I want to look out the window."

The doorbell sounded. The diversion gave Taylor reason to leave the room, and the chance to ignore the sarcasm in Hannah's tone. Limitations frustrated her. Not knowing what lay ahead scared her. Taylor knew that, but he had no idea what to say. He had concluded over the past month that saying nothing was surely better than saying the wrong thing.

Standing in the foyer, Taylor had not expected to open the front door to Ted Bellinger. The mild speaking man was a lieutenant with the Houston Police Department. He had become something close to a family friend since the carjacking. Taylor invited him in, explaining that Dean and Olivia were running errands.

Hannah joined them in the living room, her expression telegraphing her surprise to see the man. The two exchanged warm greetings. Bellinger said Hannah looked better every time he saw her. "You'll be back in the saddle before you know it." Hannah shrugged indifferently, and the three gathered around the coffee table.

The detective announced that he had some news about the case. "Crime Stoppers got a call from a two-bit used car dealer. The man said that the day after the carjacking, he bought the Taurus we've been looking for."

"That's fantastic." Hannah reached for Taylor's hand. "Are you sure it's the same car?"

"We're sure. The man described some minor body damage. It was a piece of information that we withheld when we asked for the public's help in locating the car. There's no doubt he bought the Taurus the day after the carjacking, and then sold it a few days later."

Taylor's heart and his thoughts raced. "Who sold the car to him?"

"The seller's name was Kyla Phelps, at least that's what she told the guy."

"Have you arrested her?"

"No. We're still trying to track her down. The tip only came in a few days ago."

"Why did the man wait so long to come forward?" Taylor demanded. "He must have known you were looking for the Taurus, otherwise he wouldn't have called Crime Stoppers."

"I don't know, Taylor. A thousand-dollar reward, maybe." Bellinger smirked. "He's a sleazy operator. He has a copy of the car title, but he failed to get a copy of the woman's ID. He claims to have seen it at the time of the purchase, but who knows?"

Hannah released Taylor's hand, and then knotted her fingers in her lap. "Kyla Phelps. So she is the woman who ran over me?"

Taylor and Bellinger exchanged somber looks, and then the detective patted Hannah's forearm. He spoke firmly, yet tenderly. "I can't say for sure. But we won't stop looking for her, Hannah. I'm not giving up on this." Tears gathered in the girl's eyes, but she blinked them back. "And when we find that woman, I guarantee you she will tell me who was driving the Taurus that night."

CHAPTER 5

LIVE OAK, TEXAS

Dressed for work in a black wool suit, Blair Emerson stood at a mirrored dresser, listening with limited interest to an early morning television news show. She pushed her brown, shoulder length hair behind her ears, smoothed her bangs to the side, and then clipped on a pair of pearl earrings. Her schedule was full today, and she was grateful. Focusing on another person's loss helped to put her own problems into perspective. She was particularly aware of that reality when she waited on parents who had lost a child to illness or accident. As heartbreaking as Brandi's absence had been, at least it had not lasted a lifetime.

Blair was closing the clasp on her watch when the news show ended. She picked up the remote, pointed it at the set, and then froze.

"Tomorrow on *Good Morning, Central Texas!* Wilson Rule discusses his book, *A Stranger's Eyes,* an in-depth look at the kidnapping and recovery of Brandi Emerson-Lakeman, daughter of newly appointed Senator Myles Lakeman and local funeral home director Blair Emerson."

A shout from the kitchen sent Blair rushing down the hall. She found Brandi standing at the counter with a paring knife in one hand and a half-peeled carrot in the other. Her face was pale, her eyes wide. The girl jabbed the knife at the small television mounted beneath the upper cabinets.

"Did you hear that?" she screeched. "That book." She whacked the carrot against the cutting board. "And that man. That Wilson Rule. He's going to be on television tomorrow."

"I know, honey." *Why didn't I warn her last night? Blair fretted. I should have known this could happen.* "Brandi, I know this is terribly upsetting, that you feel exposed and embarrassed. But we knew this day was coming. You're prepared for it."

"No, I'm not," she snapped, her eyes shining with sudden tears.

"Just remember what you and Dr. Westinghouse talked about." Blair plucked a tissue from a box on the counter, handing it to her daughter. "If anyone mentions the book, you're going to say something funny. That's the way *you* decided to deal with the embarrassment. With humor, Brandi."

"That's not *dealing* with it, Mom." Brandi snapped the carrot in half, and then jammed the jagged pieces into a Ziploc bag with ones she had peeled and cut into perfect sticks. "I hate this. And I hate that man."

Blair longed to embrace her daughter, to cup her face, to kiss away her tears. She never knew, though, when such gestures would be welcomed. "I wish I could say that this will all be over soon, but I doubt that it will. You can count on that idiot Rule to get his mug on every show he possibly can."

"But it's my life." Brandi wiped the paring knife clean, and then slid the blade forcefully into the slotted block. "He shouldn't be able to write about my life."

Blair said nothing. They had talked about Wilson Rule's legal right to capitalize on Brandi's story. They had also talked about the man's despicable moral code. None of that mattered, though, to a vulnerable young girl whose privacy was being stripped away.

♦ ♦ ♦

THE CHAPEL AT Emerson Funeral Home in Live Oak overflowed. The room's sturdy oak pews seated more than two hundred people, but at this morning's memorial service, guests crowded the outer aisles as well. At the front of the chapel, Blair had placed a narrow, linen-draped table. On it stood a simple arrangement of yellow roses and a bronze cremation urn. The urn contained the cremated remains of Dr. Beatrice Paige, a prominent obstetrician who had practiced in nearby San Marcos.

The prelude of classical selections concluded. While the minister stumbled through a particularly ill-suited psalm, Blair's thoughts strayed, settling as they so often did on Brandi. Reluctantly, she revisited the image of her daughter's stricken face after hearing her own name on television that morning. How was she managing at school? Had anyone mentioned Wilson Rule's book? Had Brandi managed a clever comeback? Or was she struggling through her day, counting the minutes until it was over?

Reclaiming her concentration, Blair focused on the minister who had concluded his reading and was introducing the second speaker. The man scheduled to deliver the eulogy was not another pastor. The eulogist was one of Dr. Paige's sons. In no time, he had spurred the mourners to laughter.

"When I was in high school, Mom had one unyielding rule. 'If you're going to be late, phone me. Don't make me worry about you.' At first, I religiously obeyed her rule, but one night I slipped up. I was an hour late and had not phoned her. Well, Mom was waiting for me, but not on the sofa with her arms crossed over her chest and a scowl on her face. No. She was waiting for me in my bedroom, specifically my bedroom closet. When I sneaked into the dark room, Mom jumped out and yelled, 'You're late!' She scared me senseless." The crowd roared. "Mom had only one thing to say before going to bed. 'Fear. It's not a fun experience, son.' Needless to say, I never made that mistake again."

The forty-plus man then read a letter his mother had written him on his twenty-first birthday. He closed by reading another letter, one that he had penned to her last night. Friends and relatives fought back tears. Most lost the fight. During the postlude, the minister rose, dismissed the crowd, and then approached the family, smiling as he offered words of comfort. The service had been a celebration of a successful life joyously lived.

Blair returned to her office, speaking to guests along the way, many of whom she knew personally. Fewer than a thousand people lived within the village limits of Live Oak. Blair had grown up there and, as early as elementary school, had helped her father at the funeral home.

At the University of Texas, she had earned a degree in business while working part time at Emerson Funeral Home's Austin location. Upon graduation, she had moved to Dallas to study funeral service and mortuary science. After the yearlong program was completed, she returned to Live Oak to serve her internship under her father's supervision.

Displaying her licenses as a funeral director and embalmer next to those of her father had been one of the proudest days in Blair's life. Texas administrative code required that licenses be conspicuously displayed. With his arm around Blair's shoulders, her father had said, "Whoever wrote that part of the code must have had the two of us in mind."

At her desk, thumbing mindlessly through mail, Blair looked up when her office manager, Lillie North, appeared at the door. Lillie was a cherished fixture at Emerson Funeral Home, competent and dependable. A handsome woman, as Blair's father had described her, Lillie had a soothing voice and unlimited patience.

"A reporter from KVUE just phoned," she advised Blair. "I told him you had no comment on that man's book." Without waiting for a response, she continued. "I scheduled a prearrangement conference for tomorrow. Nine-thirty. Bill Weekly. He asked to see you specifically."

Blair took the pink message note, and then laid it on her desk. Bill Weekly's wife had died last year of cancer. Blair had made the death call herself. She recalled the dear man's reminder as she rolled the cot bearing his wife's sheet-draped body from their home. "Take good care of her, Blair, just like your father would have."

The chapel, when Blair returned there, was empty, the narrow table stowed. She had instructed an employee to take the urn containing Dr. Paige's cremains to the dressing room when the service concluded. Turning off the chapel's numerous lights, Blair was mindful of one critical task remaining before her responsibilities to Dr. Paige's family were met.

At the rear of the building, Blair walked down a wide corridor, and then pushed open a door marked with a hazardous-chemicals sign. The dressing room had once been part of the preparation room where embalming was performed, but her father had remodeled the space. Bringing the old building's preparation room into compliance with state and federal laws, he had added an improved eyewash station, shower stall, and a powerful ventilation system. The remodeled dressing room was well lit, its walls and floor a pastel blue. It was there that bodies were cosmetized, dressed, and casketed. *Bodies.* The term was routinely used by her staff, but the word was forbidden in the presence of families and friends. "This person is dead," Millard Emerson had instructed his daughter. "But he still has a name. Use it when you refer to him."

Blair found the bronze urn locked inside a cabinet alongside an identical urn still empty. The doctor had two biological sons, each with different fathers, both deceased. Each son wanted his mother's ashes buried with his own father, a request easily met. Blair unscrewed the lids on both urns, and then set them aside. Cautiously, she poured half the cremains into the empty urn. The dense, grainy substance was nothing like ashes and had a distinctive charred odor.

When the transfer was complete, she returned the two urns to the cabinet and locked the door. Tomorrow, Dr. Paige's sons would sign for the urns containing near-equal portions of their mother's ashes, and the doctor would have fulfilled both her children's wishes.

At a small sink in the dressing room, Blair picked up a plastic bottle of Safe-T Soap. The common act of lathering her hands, rubbing them together under the flow of warm water, triggered thoughts of Brandi. Her obsession with germs was a tightly guarded secret. Not even her dad knew how she struggled.

Blair had received a text from Myles that morning with news about Lenny Bond. Contrary to what Myles had expected, Lenny Bond had not been paroled to Webb County in far south Texas. The man had been paroled to Bexar County, and Myles was seething. Lenny Bond, convicted of Brandi's aggravated kidnapping, was now living in San Antonio, little more than an hour away from Live Oak.

♦ ♦ ♦

THE SCHOOL COUNSELOR stopped Brandi in the hall before classes started. Clint Blanchard motioned for her to take one of the gray metal chairs in front of his desk, and then he took the other. Brandi shrugged off her backpack but kept it in her lap, gripping the straps to steady her shaking hands. To conceal the sudden onslaught of nervousness, she forced herself to slouch a little and casually crossed her feet.

"Brandi, I have a confession to make." The man leaned toward her, his expression exaggeratedly solemn. "I've been participating in a conspiracy, but my conscience will not let me continue."

Acquainted with the counselor's sense of humor, Brandi relaxed a little. "What kind of conspiracy?"

"It involves you." Clint Blanchard glanced over his shoulder, and then spoke in a whisper, as if someone in the empty hall might overhear. "In fact, my co-conspirators have assembled in the gym to carry out the final stages of their scheme."

Brandi giggled. "What are you talking about?"

Blanchard's teasing tone changed, and he smiled reassuringly. "I'm talking about your friends here at school. The word has been out for a while now about Wilson Rude's book." He emphasized the deliberate mispronunciation of the author's name. "All the kids feel so badly for you. So do the faculty and staff."

Brandi maintained her casual pose. Her feet were still crossed, but now her ankles were stiff. Her upper body slumped, but her stomach muscles were tight and knotted. What was Mr. Blanchard talking about? What was going on in the gym?

"My job as co-conspirator this morning is to keep you here for another few minutes. Then my intercom will buzz. I'm supposed to tell you that Mr. Dixon has called a special assembly, but that I don't know what it's about. Then you and I will casually walk down to the gym." Clint Blanchard screwed up his face in disapproval. "But, Brandi, my guess is that you have had it up to here with surprises." He raised a hand to his thinning hairline. "So unless you want me tagged as the school traitor, don't ever let on that I gave you this heads-up."

Tension constricted Brandi's throat. When she spoke, her voice sounded high-pitched and childlike. "But what are they going to do?"

"Show their support," Clint Blanchard answered earnestly. "I know that attention can be embarrassing, but at least the whole thing will be over in a few short minutes. Then you can go about your day without worrying about what people are thinking. And everyone else can go about theirs without wondering if they should say something to you about the book that is coming out, and would it be the right thing if they did."

The intercom sounded. While the counselor spoke, Brandi's thoughts raced. Every student, all the teachers and staff were assembling in the gym. Would she have to stand up before them and say something? *No.* She could not do it.

Clint Blanchard stood, and then touched Brandi's shoulder. "The plan is in motion. Now, please. Save my reputation. Act surprised."

Brandi's heart hammered during the brief but agonizing walk to the gym. Feeling sick to her stomach, she sat next to her best friend on the front row of the bleachers.

After a brief welcome, principal Thomas Dixon began his remarks. "Far too often, we hear about problems in America's schools. Harassment. Bullying. Even violence. We rarely hear about the many admirable acts of students, but that is not the case at Barton Middle School. Recently, several students approached Mr. Blanchard with the idea of expressing support for a fellow student who is facing a particularly difficult challenge."

Brandi felt the reassuring pressure of Nekisha's warm hand on her icy one. "He's talking about you. So hang in there."

Dixon looked at Brandi and smiled. "It is impossible for us to know, Brandi, what you are going through, nor is it easy for us to put into words how much we care. But your fellow students were determined to try. I think they have succeeded. Now, Brandi, if you will come forward, we have something very special for you."

Brandi's legs were so weak she could hardly stand. She looked at the counselor with jittery, brown eyes.

"You can do it," he whispered.

Feeling weak and wobbly, Brandi made her way to where the principal stood. Stephanie Patterson, a fellow classmate, joined her, carrying a large yellow gift bag. Every inch of its shiny surface was covered with students' signatures.

Stephanie grasped the two handles of the bag, and then spread open the top. "Brandi, everything Mr. Dixon said is true. We're really sorry about what you're going through. We know you've got a lot of courage, but if there are times you feel a little down, look at this and think of all the people who care."

Brandi stuck her trembling hand down into the masses of tissue paper. She felt the hard edge of something in the bag and grasped it. The object was heavy, so she reached deep into the bag with her other hand. Every eye was on her, and her face burned. Still, as nervous as she was, she could hardly wait to see what was in the bag. Tissue paper floated to the floor, as she withdrew the gift. When at last it was visible, Brandi gripped its frame with both hands, and then held it in front of her. "Oh, my gosh. It's me."

Barely conscious of a ripple of laughter, Brandi studied a framed drawing of the athletic field and the school mascot standing under the goal post. The bobcat's arms jutted into the air. Its powerful right paw gripped one of Brandi's sneakered feet. Her arms, too, were extended overhead, elbows bent, clenched fists gripping the crossbar. The amazing likeness of her face had a fiercely determined expression. Her neck craned. Her tilted chin cleared the crossbar by inches. At the bottom of the drawing, in large block letters, were the words, CHIN UP, BRANDI! YOUR FRIENDS AND FELLOW STUDENTS AT BARTON MIDDLE SCHOOL.

"We hope you like it," Stephanie said eagerly.

"I love it," Brandi answered, her voice decisive and strong, her eyes moist with gratitude. "It is so cool. I can't believe this." Not knowing if the others had seen the sketch, she turned it toward the assembled students. "This is awesome. Thank you so much." Satisfied laughter and applause filled the gym. Brandi hugged the gift to her chest. "I can't believe they did this," she said, as Clint Blanchard approached her.

"They care about you, Brandi. We all do."

When the assembly was over, Brandi stood near the door, showing the drawing to departing students, and saying thank you, over and over. Suddenly, the fact occurred to her that someone had drawn the sketch, had painted it, someone she needed to thank. She asked Stephanie about the artist, and then supplied the answer herself. "Carlos did it, didn't he?"

Stephanie nodded, and then pointed at the tiny initials nearly hidden in blades of grass on the athletic field.

"I have to thank him." Brandi scanned the thinning crowd. "Will you find him, Stephanie?"

The shy young man was half-dragged to where Brandi stood, as embarrassed as she had been by the attention. Carlos explained that he had started to draw the mascot supporting *both* Brandi's feet. "But then I decided not to. You're a strong person, Brandi. You can keep your chin up without anyone's help."

Brandi left the amazing gift in Mr. Blanchard's office, but her thoughts returned to it throughout the day. She thought about what Carlos had said, about his reason for drawing the sketch as he had. Not for a moment had she considered disagreeing with him, but Carlos was wrong about her keeping up her chin with no one's help at all.

CHAPTER 6

SAN ANTONIO, TEXAS

Tommy Lee Worsham hired Lenny Bond the day of the job interview. Lenny had moved out of his friend Pete's home off Wurzbach Road and into the dorm at Worsham Services. The only reason he had signed up to work in the kitchen was that the line next to that particular job on the duty sheet had been blank. The other option had been cleaning bathrooms. Now, Lenny wished that the box of Morton's salt he set aside was a can of Comet. No question it would be if he had understood what his bunkmate had meant by "Gordon Ramsay with a prison tat."

Dub Black's movements were as quick as his temper. Orders shot from the man's mouth like bullets, whizzing past Lenny's ears. His hands were machines—grabbing, chopping, pouring, stirring. The recipe for beef stew Lenny struggled to decipher was scrawled on a brown paper bag. The instructions included words such as handful, tad, and dab. Even Dub Black's verbal instructions sounded like a foreign language to Lenny.

"Hey, Dub," Lenny said, gun shy. "What did you mean by drag the meat in the flour mixture?"

Dub Black stomped across the kitchen to the center island, his stocky legs pumping. Peering through bifocals, he stabbed the paper bag with a meat fork. "Dredge, you moron. It's dredge."

With that, the man tossed a few cubes of beef into a bowl of seasoned flour. Stubby fingers twirled the pieces around a few times, plucked them out again, and then dropped the dusted cubes into an empty bowl. After a long and deliberate glare at Lenny, the man carried the bowl to the stove. In a gesture resembling a dice toss, Dub Black flung the meat into a Dutch oven. Hot oil sizzled and popped ignored onto his hand. "Do I need to explain what I mean by cook until golden brown?"

Lenny shook his head, and then began dredging, regretting again that he had sentenced himself to thirty days of working with this guy. Of course, if there was one thing Lenny considered himself good at, it was winning people over. For a long time, his sister Arlene had shunned him like a leper, refusing to visit him in prison and rarely answering his letters. It had taken Lenny a while to figure out that repentance carried a lot more weight with Arlene—tons more, in fact—than an admission that he had really screwed up. Without the smart lady lawyer Arlene had hired to win over the parole board, Lenny would still be cooling his heels as a guest of the Texas Department of Criminal Justice.

So, Lenny figured, if he could drag Arlene over to his side, then he could at least start tossing the rope over Dub Black's way.

Dredging the last batch of beef, Lenny dug around in his mind for a conversation topic, while keeping a careful eye on the batch already browning. To win over Arlene, he had shown interest in her husband the banker and their daughter Eden. Lenny had detected that his twenty-something-year-old niece had some problems of her own. He decided to use a similar tactic now, showing interest in his boss for the next few weeks . "Is Dub your real name or a nickname?"

"Nickname." Dub spoke over the rapid-fire click of a chef's knife against a chopping board, the blade a hairbreadth from his immaculate fingernails as it sliced through a yellow onion. "Real name is Johnny Walker Black."

While Dub ripped the paper-thin skin off another onion, Lenny pondered the man's answer. How did a fellow get Dub out of Johnny Walker Black? And where had he heard that name before? A country music singer, maybe?

"That meat's brown," Dub barked, his voice raspy from years of smoking the cigarettes bulging his shirt pocket. "Take a slotted spoon and get that batch out before it burns. Drain it on those paper towels there."

Lenny wiped his hands on the crisp white apron tied about his narrow waist. What looked like a hundred utensils dangled from a long metal strip on the wall. Lenny's mind went suddenly blank. He was fairly sure that Dub had told him to use a spoon, but four hung in front of him. Each had a long handle, so that was good. Dub hadn't let on, but Lenny knew that hot oil popping onto bare skin had to smart.

The first of the spoons had a curved handle, the kind used to serve soup. Dub had used the second one that morning to stir a pan of scrambled eggs. As far as Lenny could tell, it ought to work fine to scoop meat out of a pan of oil. The third spoon was an odd-looking contraption with a little mesh basket attached to a long handle. He was wondering what in the world Dub used the thing for when the man stomped across the kitchen.

"Slotted spoon." Dub Black snatched the fourth utensil from the strip, and then whacked Lenny on the chest with it. "What's up with you, Bond? Does your mind empty every time you blink?"

The slotted spoon worked well, and in no time the first batch of beef was draining on a sheet pan lined with paper towels. At a safe distance, Lenny tossed the second batch into the oil, using the slotted spoon to separate the pieces. He thought about what Dub had said and smiled. "You know, Dub, my mind must not empty itself every time I blink, because I'm still trying to figure out how you got your nickname."

Dub Black plopped a bag of carrots onto the island. Ignoring the twist tie, he poked a thumb through the plastic, and then ripped open the bag, dumping its contents onto the counter. "My mama didn't like my old man naming me after a bottle of Scotch whisky, so she started calling me J. W. My buddies shortened it to Dub, and it stuck."

"Aww, I get it." Lenny grinned, his narrow lips almost disappearing. "Dub. Short for Dubya." He chuckled again, realizing now why the name Johnny Walker Black had a familiar ring. "I like it, Dub. Real original."

Dub Black disappeared into a long, narrow pantry, and then reappeared with a sack of red potatoes. When he put the bag next to what looked like half a cord of carrots, Lenny pretended not to notice, busying himself with the slotted spoon, moving the meat around in the sizzling oil. When the second batch was a dark, golden brown, Lenny reluctantly started removing the pieces from the oil. He was almost finished when his bunkmate appeared at the kitchen door.

Jamar Warfield was medium height like Lenny, but muscular and a good twenty pounds heavier. His black hair was cut close to the scalp, and his moustache was pencil thin. The pink scar starting below his ear looked like an earthworm crawling just under the man's dark skin, inching its way down his face, disappearing under his jawbone. How Jamar had gotten the scar was still a mystery to Lenny. It was one thing to ask a fellow about his nickname, but another altogether to quiz a guy about how he got his face sliced.

Jamar Warfield, still dressed in the black shirt and trousers he had worn at a job interview that afternoon, told Lenny he had a phone call. "The woman says she's your sister."

Lenny frowned. He had talked to Arlene last night. Why was she calling now? "Hey, Jamar, can you help me out here, man?"

When Jamar started across the room, Dub Black motioned him toward the sink with a peeled carrot. "Hands, Warfield. Soap and water."

Lenny scooped out the last of the batch, gave Jamar instructions, and then hurried to the room the men called the office. The spacious room was as tidy as Tommy Lee Worsham's conference room. Most of the space was occupied by two gray metal desks equipped with phones and two computers that Lenny had no idea how to operate. Even the Tracfone that Jamar had made him buy gave Lenny fits. He would give Arlene the number, if he could remember what it was.

Without sitting down, Lenny pressed a blinking red light, and then picked up the receiver. "This is Lenny. You there, Arlene?"

"Oh, yes. I'm here."

"Whatcha know?"

"What do I know?" Arlene sounded angry, a tone familiar to her brother's ears. "I know you deserve to be right back in prison if you had anything to do with Wilson Rule and the book I'm holding in my hand."

CHAPTER 7

HOUSTON, TEXAS

A television played in apartment two hundred, but no one answered the door. Taylor McFadden knocked again, rapping the surface harder this time, but still got no response. Determined, he reached past the rail skirting the second-floor alcove, and then knocked on a windowpane. Taylor had driven twenty miles in Houston traffic and lied to his girlfriend Hannah about where he was going. He was not leaving Wood Shadows until he talked to the person who lived in apartment two hundred.

Taylor knocked again, and then saw movement behind the window curtain. "Hello. Could I talk to you a minute?"

Orange-stained fingertips emerged between the sheer panels, separating them slowly and cautiously. One side of a child's face appeared in the narrow opening, his chin resting on the windowsill. The boy's sandy brown hair was a mess, the part a random zigzag. His freckled cheek was rosy, and his upper lip puffed by a cold sore. The boy studied Taylor with a wary brown eye.

"Hey, there." Taylor rested his forearms on the rail, and then leaned toward the window. "Are your mom and dad at home?"

"I'm not telling you." The boy's voice, muffled by the glass, was decidedly defiant. "Do you think I'm stupid?"

Taylor chuckled. "No, I don't think you're stupid."

"If you don't go away, I'll call nine-one-one."

"I just have a quick question." Taylor motioned over his shoulder with his thumb. "Do you know who lives next door?" When the boy nodded, Taylor asked for their names, but the glass muted the child's response. Taylor pointed to his own ear and said, "Sorry. I can't hear you."

The curtains fell together as the boy withdrew from the window. Seconds later, the deadbolt lock scraped, and then snapped back. The door inched open, pulling the chain lock taut. The boy peeked around the door, looking up under a flop of sandy hair. Taylor backed away a step, not wanting to scare the child into closing the door to call the police.

"Sorry. I couldn't hear you through the window," Taylor explained. "Who lives in that apartment?" Again, he motioned over his shoulder with his thumb.

"Just Kyla."

Taylor tensed. He had obtained an address for Kyla Phelps online, hoping the information was current. Now he was standing ten feet away from her door. This little boy actually knew the woman who had run over Hannah.

"Are you a police officer?" the child asked, lisping because of a gap in his lower front teeth.

Taylor weighed his response. If he claimed to be a cop, would the kid be helpful, or would he threaten to call nine-one-one if Taylor didn't produce a shield? He opted for the truth. "No, I'm not a cop."

"My mom said to say police officer, not cop."

"Sorry." Taylor grinned. "Your mom's right. Why did you ask me if I'm a police officer?"

"Because they've already been here looking for Kyla. She wasn't home though."

"Has she been home since then?"

"Nope. But I'm keeping an eye on the place." The boy paused a moment, and then spoke in a grave, but somehow satisfied tone. "Kyla's in big trouble. My dad said she made a check bounce. The police want to know the minute she shows up."

Taylor wondered who was withholding the truth about Kyla Phelps—the police or the little boy's dad. "Is your dad going to help the police?"

"No way. He said if the police want Kyla, they can find her theirselves. He likes Kyla, but me and my mom don't. My mom is a soldier." The boy's smile was wide and proud. "She's far away in Ger … Ger … namy."

"Germany, huh?" Taylor nodded with earnest admiration. "That's awesome. Why doesn't your mom like Kyla?"

"She hangs on my dad."

Taylor squatted by the door, one knee to the concrete floor. "Truth is, I don't like Kyla either." Eye to eye with the little boy, he unzipped the pocket of his windbreaker and removed a pack of Big Red. The jacket actually belonged to his friend Adam. Taylor had found it in his truck. Kyla Phelps had been nervous as hell the night of the carjacking, waving the gun around, shouting orders. Taylor hadn't shaved for two days, but he worried that she might recognize him if he showed up at her apartment in broad daylight wearing boots, jeans, and a white shirt.

Taylor thumbed two pieces of gum from the package and passed one to the boy. "I've got an idea." Casually, he peeled off the foil wrapper, folded the gum in half, and put the piece in his mouth. "What's your name, by the way?"

"Benjamin James Walters." The boy unwrapped the gum with fingers stained the same orange as the streak down his knit shirt. "Ben for short."

"People ever call you Benjy?"

"My mom does." Ben chuckled. "But not when she's upset with me."

"How about I just call you Ben? My name's … Mac." Taylor withheld his real name without knowing why. "I'm wondering, Ben, if maybe we could team up and help the police find Kyla." The prospect of asking the boy to keep a secret from his dad didn't set well with Taylor, but the man had no intention of turning Kyla Phelps into the police. Ted Bellinger had guaranteed that the woman would be arrested, but cops couldn't watch her apartment twenty-four-seven. Taylor had stood by and let Kyla Phelps nearly kill Hannah the night of the carjacking. He would not stand by now and let her get away with it. "What do you say, Ben? You think we could work together and help the police? It would have to be our secret, of course. You couldn't even tell your dad."

"No problem." Ben squatted next to the door, mimicking Taylor's posture, even folding the gum in half before putting the piece in his mouth. "I'm good at keeping secrets. I promised my dad I wouldn't tell Mom that Kyla wants to keep her bed warm while she's gone."

Taylor's reluctance to ask the boy to keep a secret from his dad vanished. Kyla Phelps was scum. She belonged in prison. Somehow, he and Benjamin James Walters would see that she ended up there. "Okay, Ben, this is the plan. I need you to phone me the minute Kyla comes home. Can you do that?"

"You bet."

"First, we need to exchange phone numbers. Do you have a cell?"

"No. But I have … uh … a digital phone."

"Does Kyla ever call your dad on that phone? On your phone?"

"Nope. Only my dad's cell."

"When you receive a call on your phone, does the caller's number or name show up on your tv?"

The child screwed up his face, obviously puzzled. "My tv? Why would it do that?"

"Never mind. I was just making sure, in case I call you sometime. Our plan must be a secret, you know." Taylor grinned at the boy. "I'll bet you know your number." When the child nodded, Taylor produced a pen from the pocket of the windbreaker, and then scribbled the numerals on the heel of his hand. "Now I'll give you my number." The boy stuck his hand out the opening, palm up. "We'd better not write it on your hand." Taylor considered his options. He could write the number on a piece of paper, but then the little guy might misplace it. "Give me the gum wrapper, Ben, and one of your shoes."

The child sat on the floor, and then removed a worn sneaker. He passed it and the crumpled wrapper through the opening. Taylor wrote his cell number on the inside of the foil, and then folded it neatly. Peeling back the sneaker's soiled inner sole, he slid the wrapper beneath it, and then pressed it back in place. "How's that?"

"Cool." The boy spoke conspiratorially. "No one will ever know, but you and me."

"Ben, phone me the minute Kyla comes home." Taylor exaggerated the urgency of the instructions. "And if she phones your dad, try to get me the number. Can you do that?"

"No problem." The eager child reached past the door and retrieved his shoe. "I know how to navigate my dad's cell."

"You do, huh?" Taylor chuckled. "You're a smart kid."

"I'm six and a half." The little boy pointed to his neck. "I have strip-throat. I can't go back to school until I'm a hundred percent."

"Great. Not that you have strep throat, but that you'll be around to keep an eye on things." Taylor stood. When the boy followed suit, Taylor reached through the opening and tousled his hair. "Thank you for your help, Ben. Your mom would be really proud of you."

CHAPTER 8

AUSTIN, TEXAS

Emerson Funeral Home in Austin employed five funeral directors and embalmers, two provisional licensees, and twelve other full or part-time employees. Allan James had been promoted to manager after Blair made the firm's Live Oak location her primary focus, but the man insisted that Jane Prescott was the manager-in-fact. The woman was more than the office manager. She was the staff's rudder.

After a lengthy meeting with her staff, Blair left the funeral home in time for lunch with her best friend. Liz Elrod and her husband lived in Barton Creek, a country club community where Blair, too, was a member. The home's country French décor suited Liz perfectly. The kitchen was light and airy, with granite countertops and washed oak cabinets. French doors in the living room opened onto a terrace overlooking the green expanse of a fairway on one of the club's courses.

For lunch, Liz had brewed iced tea and made a platter of nachos. As was her routine, she asked about Frank Traxill. "How much longer will he be in Montana?"

"He's decided to stay until … until his dad dies."

Liz nodded knowingly. "That sounds like Frank. I know you miss each other."

And they did. Frank and Blair had found their way back to each other almost a year ago. Their love had deepened in the months since then. Brandi adored Frank. In time, they hoped to be a family. But now, Frank's parents needed him. He had taken emergency leave from the Austin Police Department. "My career will always be there," Frank had said, "but my dad won't." Blair had promised that she would be there too.

Liz changed the subject, asking how things were going at the funeral home. Blair told her about the death of a young college student who died in a car wreck. "We're shipping his body back to Beirut." She took a nacho from the platter, pinching off a string of melted cheese and licking her fingers. "I'll be on the phone for hours with the consulate. I think the office is in Washington."

Liz picked up a fork and raked a jalapeño slice from a nacho. "Speaking of Washington, when do Myles and Charmaine leave for Virginia?"

"They're already gone." Blair anticipated Liz's scowl. It was quick to come.

"That man. Brandi hasn't even been home two years, and he's already moving halfway across the nation." Liz deepened her voice, mimicking Myles. "People have an obligation to serve their country, sweetie. I hope you understand." She rolled her eyes. "Who is he kidding?"

Blair picked up another nacho, adding the piece of jalapeño Liz had rejected. "I had a text from him. He had some astonishing news. Lenny Bond is out on parole. He's living in San Antonio and working at a place called Worsham Services."

"No way." Liz peeled sticky cheese from the edge of the platter and piled it on a nacho. "What does Myles intend to do? Hire a private investigator to follow Lenny Bond around, praying he'll violate his parole?" She twisted her mouth in exasperation. "Does Brandi know?"

"Not yet." Blair nudged a few errant beans onto a nacho. "I'll tell her soon."

"Better you than Myles."

Liz was right. If Myles were to tell Brandi that Lenny was living in San Antonio, he could not possibly resist voicing his outrage that the man was seventy-five miles away from Live Oak. Brandi would say that she understood, all the while fighting the internal battle between disloyalty to her dad and sympathy for Lenny. In sum, Blair knew that such a conversation would only add to the stress her daughter was under.

"Oh, Liz," Blair said, suddenly excited. "You should see what the kids at Brandi's school gave her." The description she offered fell far short of the caricature's charm and the artist's talent. Blair wished that she had taken a picture of the gift.

"Sounds adorable. Text me a picture of it," Liz said, reading Blair's mind. "Was it Wilson Rule's book that inspired the kids to do that?"

"It was. Brandi was so touched."

The conversation grew suddenly still. Liz seemed to ponder a blue pitcher in the center of the table and an airy arrangement of white carnations it held. Blair studied her friend's expression. "Enough of the furrowed brow. What's on your mind?"

Liz pulled the platter of nachos out of Blair's reach, her green eyes wary. "Promise you'll stay calm. There is a sleeping child down the hall." She left the table, and then quickly returned, holding something behind her back. "Blair, there is no question that Wilson Rule is an arrogant, reprehensible toad, and I hate the fact that he's written this book."

"*This* book?" Blair set her glass down hard on the woven placemat. "Liz Elrod, do not tell me you bought a copy."

"Shhh." Liz protracted the warning. "If you wake Clay, the rest of these nachos go down the disposal."

Blair lowered her voice. "Why did you do that? How could you pay good money for that trash?"

"I considered shoplifting the thing, Blair, but that didn't seem right either." Liz sat, and then laid the book face down on the table. "I had to buy it. I had to buy it for you."

"For me?" Blair's voice rose. Liz glared another warning, and Blair lowered her voice again. "I wouldn't read that book if the man paid me by the word."

"You don't have to read it." Liz slid the book across the table. "But you must look at it. It has pictures, Blair. Pictures of Brandi."

♦ ♦ ♦

Live Oak, Texas

THE STONE HOUSE at the corner of Southworth Road and FM 149, with its handsome stone columns and sweeping front porch, belonged to Ethel Lindquist. Blair tapped her horn, catching the attention of Manny Taggert propping a ladder against the porch roof. Smiling to herself, she remembered how Manny had rested his hand on his claw hammer the day Jason Hammond showed up at her house. Odds were that her entire quote would appear in Jason's article. Who would risk getting on the considerable wrong side of Manny Taggert?

The Range Rover rolled along the blacktop road, taking gentle curves with ease. At home, Blair parked in the garage, made her way across the backyard, and then unlocked the door leading into her new bathroom. The beep of the alarm reassured her. Hazel never failed to arm it before leaving, even when she knew Blair was on her way home.

The first year after Brandi returned, Blair had hardly been able to let the girl out of her sight. Lenny Bond had lurked in every shadow, waiting for Blair to lower her guard. Nothing—not Brandi's reassurances, not months of counseling, not ridiculous efforts at thought control—had kept Blair's fears at bay. As was too often her habit when all else failed, she had turned to prayer, pleading with God to take away her fear that Brandi would vanish again. Oddly, the vehicle God had used was Blair's critical screening of Lenny Bond's prison-cell letters to Brandi.

Showering quickly, Blair pulled on jeans and a sweatshirt. Knowing that Brandi would think nothing of the passing minutes, she retrieved the book from her satchel. *A Stranger's Eyes*. She opened it to pages of black and white pictures included midway in the book. Ignoring the first page, she turned to the second. She only glanced at the pictures on the left. The captions were painful to read, triggering guilt that would never go away.

The side street by the Lakeman home where Jewell Bond parked, watching, waiting. The privacy fence around the backyard, its gate unlocked.

Her right thumb rested on a picture that, according to the caption, had been taken two months before Brandi's kidnapping. Jewell and Lenny sat on a sofa. Lenny's right arm rested on the sofa back and his left hand held a long-neck beer bottle. Jewell looked away from the camera, her chin tucked, a half-smile on her lips.

An adjacent picture showed Jewell standing by an old truck. Dressed in dark slacks and a loose-fitting shirt, she was pitifully thin. Dark crescents showed under her eyes. Her shoulder-length hair looked hardly combed, thin wisps blowing across her unsmiling lips.

Two pictures of Brandi were positioned on the lower half of the page. Blair wished for a magnifying glass so that she could see even the tiniest detail. The caption indicated that the snapshot had been taken three months after the kidnapping. Blair agreed. She knew the baby in the plastic swimming pool with a sailboat, a yellow duck, and a plastic shovel. Blair had brushed the thin, loose curls hanging around the child's oval face, had smoothed locks off her forehead. She had rubbed sunscreen on those thin shoulders and arms, dabbed it on her cheeks as she squirmed. And to her utter amazement, she recognized the swimsuit the child was wearing. Gray in the photograph, the suit was actually pink. Blair had bought it herself just before Brandi disappeared.

It was astonishing to Blair that Jewell had taken a snapshot of Brandi in that swimsuit, but in the long run it had not mattered. No one had put two and two together. No one had concluded that Jewell's adopted baby was the child abducted from her home one April afternoon in Austin.

The second image, according to the notation, had been taken when Brandi was three. Except for the brick sidewalk where she stood, all around her was white with snow. The coat she wore, red Blair imagined, was shorter than the knit dress she wore under it. Dark tights warmed her legs but made them look as thin as sticks. The coat should have been buttoned on such a cold day, Blair thought, and gloves should have warmed her little hands. A wool hat, pulled low and snug, hid all but a few stray curls. Its narrow brim shadowed Brandi's eyes, but the rest of her face was visible. It was a thinner face, Blair realized. But why? Because she was perhaps ten months older than when she had disappeared? Or had she suffered and grieved after being torn away from her mother?

Blair banished the thought and turned the page. The picture by her left thumb was a stab in her heart. Jewell and Brandi in front of a Christmas tree. The shadows around Jewell's eyes were gone, and the smile on her lips was full. April, according to the caption, sat on the floor next to her. Her hair, appearing to be light brown, was parted on the right and brushed in loose curls that reached the middle of her ears. The corners of her lips were tilted in a shy smile, the lower one puffy and chapped. The stripes in her cute cotton dress were shades of blue, Blair decided, and the buttons on the front were dark blue balls.

Just as before at Liz's house, Blair was mesmerized by the intensity of the enormous brown, almost black, eyes looking back at her from the photograph. They were unmistakably Brandi's eyes, but no other features belonged to her child.

Cheekbones and hints of dimples were unfamiliar features, just as the sound of her voice would be if only Blair could hear it.

Blair laid her head back against the chair when her eyes began to sting. She fought the ache in her throat by taking deep, slow breaths. Without looking down again, she closed the book and brought it to her chest. "Oh, God," she moaned, clutching the book tighter. She was so grateful to see the pictures, but she hated Wilson Rule for seeing them first.

Flicking off the lamp, Blair sat still and tense in the sudden dimness. Anger tightened her chest. She squeezed the thick book hard with her hands. Lenny Bond did this. That con man sold pictures to Wilson Rule, but he would not get away with it. Blair would see to it. If she had to threaten to lie to his parole officer, she would get her hands on every single picture that two-bit loser had of her child.

CHAPTER 9

SAN ANTONIO, TEXAS

Lenny Bond and Jamar Warfield sat at a small table in the sleeping quarters at Worsham Services. Wilson Rule's book, *A Stranger's Eyes,* lay on the table between them. Just looking at the book made Lenny's stomach churn. It was as thick as a Bible, and covered with what Jamar called a dust jacket. The background color was black. Wilson Rule's name was printed at the top in large, red letters. The title, *A Stranger's Eyes,* was printed toward the bottom. Between Rule's name and the title was a pair of lonely brown eyes staring back at Lenny.

His sister had been quick to decide that Lenny had sold his story to Rule, and then thrown in the pictures to boot. It had taken Lenny the best part of an hour to convince Arlene that she was wrong. It was just a matter of time, he figured, before he got a letter from Myles Lakeman's lawyer, a call from his parole officer, and a severe tongue lashing from Blair.

"Jamar, I admit it. I've seen these pictures of me and Jewell. She kept them and a bunch of others in an album. I've probably seen the ones of Brandi, too, but I swear on my mama's grave that I didn't sell them to that guy Rule." Lenny slapped the book, and then slid it across the table to Jamar. "But I guarantee you, mine is gonna be the first name that pops up when Blair and Brandi's dad start putting two and two together."

"Myles Lakeman." Jamar twisted the corner of his mouth, shaking his head. "A United States senator. Heavy weight enemy you got there, Bond."

"Yeah, and he's really got it in for me."

"You stole his kid, man." Jamar spoke to Lenny as if he were demented. "What do you expect?"

"She's Blair's kid, too, but she cut me some slack."

Hoping for the best, Lenny had mailed Blair a letter with his new address at Worsham Services. Would she allow him to stay in touch with Brandi now that he was out on parole? The only reason she had permitted contact in the first place was that the kid had worried about him being in prison.

The instant Lenny had slammed the mailbox lid, he had known that the letter might just close the door on any more contact with Brandi.

Lenny groaned. "Blair cut me some slack before, but when she sees them pictures, she'll be wanting to cut my throat." He screwed up his face, shaking his head in desperation. "All I can do is hope that Jewell's album is in the boxes Arlene is sending to me."

At the time of Lenny's arrest in Live Oak, what little he owned had been in an apartment he and his friend Pete had shared in Laredo. A few months ago, when Pete and his girlfriend had split up, Pete had moved to San Antonio. Before moving, he had written to Lenny in prison, asking what he should do with Lenny's belongings. Arlene had agreed to store the boxes at her home in Amarillo.

Last night, Arlene had agreed to send the cartons to Pete's house right away. Lenny had considered asking his sister to go through the cartons herself, but not knowing what all might be in them, he had thought better of it. All he could do now was hope that when he tore back the flaps, he would find Jewell's album with every single picture of Brandi still in it.

Jamar picked up the book, and then opened it to the pictures. "The album you're hoping to find … When was the last time you saw it?"

"I been trying to remember." Lenny squinted, his blue eyes narrowing. "I definitely remember seeing it two years ago when me and April was in Dallas."

Before leaving Virginia Beach after Jewell died, Lenny had hurled into a dumpster garbage bags full of junk his pack-rat wife had held onto. In Dallas, he had dug around in the trunk of the old Buick, looking for proof that April was Brandi. Blair would have been a fool to turn over a hundred and fifty thousand dollars without it. And Blair Emerson was no fool.

The proof had been in the trunk of the Buick. Jewell's treasure chest. A carved wooden box he had bought for her in Mexico. In it, along with the album and a bunch of other junk Jewell had saved, Lenny had found the swimsuit April had been wearing the day Jewell snatched her, and the red plastic shovel she had held in her hand. It had been a colossal stroke of luck that he hadn't thrown the things away.

"Yeah, Jamar, I definitely seen the album in Dallas two years ago." Lenny waggled his head in resignation. "But there's no telling what happened to it after that."

Jamar studied the pictures in Wilson Rule's book. *A Stranger's Eyes.* His expressionless gaze lingered on the snapshot of Brandi and Jewell in front of a Christmas tree. "Your wife just snatched the kid and never looked back, huh? Didn't you worry about getting caught?"

"Not that I remember. We moved around a lot back then, and I was stoned half the time."

Jamar frowned, the crease between his black brows deepening. "And nobody suspected a thing?" he questioned. "Your family? Your friends? Nobody?"

"Jewell was real convincing. They all thought we adopted April just like she said. Hell, after a while, I almost believed her myself."

Jamar pressed on, his tone disbelieving. "How did you enroll her in school without a birth certificate?"

"Jewell made her one," Lenny answered proudly. "She took some other kid's birth certificate and used Wite-Out on some names. Then she made a few copies. The school never gave it a second look. She even forged some adoption papers just in case she needed them, but she never did."

Jamar closed the book, and then slid it across the table. Lenny turned it over when he noticed Wilson Rule's piercing eyes staring at him from the back cover. "What am I gonna do, Jamar? If Lakeman makes up his mind, the man can cause me some serious problems."

"There's not a parole officer in the country that wouldn't sit up and take notice if he got a call from a United States senator." Jamar leaned back in the chair and crossed one leg over the other. "If you don't want to get yanked back behind the walls again, you'd better keep your nose as clean as Dub's kitchen floor."

"Then you gotta help me, man," Lenny pleaded. "I don't remember rules as good as you do."

Jamar chuckled. "I heard Dub yelling at you in the kitchen the other day. 'What's with you, Bond? Does your mind empty every time you blink?'"

"That old man rides me like a Harley," Lenny complained. "I keep my cool, though."

"You better. Otherwise, Worsham will kick your ass out of here."

Lenny stared at the book. Jamar was right. He couldn't risk trouble of any kind, not with Dub Black, and not with Myles or Blair. "How am I gonna convince them that I had nothing to do with that thing?"

"How about telling them the truth?"

"The truth?"

"Yeah, Lenny. Pictures didn't just materialize in the book like magic. Somebody gave them to the man. If not you, then who?"

"Beats me."

"Well, think, man." Jamar's deep voice rose in exasperation. "This is important. You'll have a lot better chance proving your innocence if you can put the blame somewhere else. Defense attorneys do it all the time."

Jamar was right again. When Blair or Myles started accusing him, and it was only a matter of time, he had to convince them that somebody else sold Rule the pictures. "If the album is in one of the boxes Arlene is sending, and if all the pictures are there, then that proves I didn't do it, right?"

"No, it doesn't," Jamar snapped. His tone said his frustration with Lenny had peaked again. "You could have made copies, and then put the originals back in the album. The fact is, assuming you didn't lie in that oath you made on your mama's grave, this deal went down one of two ways when word got out that Rule was writing the book." Jamar uncrossed his leg, put his muscular forearms on the table, and leaned toward Lenny. "One, somebody dug out some old pictures of their own and sold them. Or, two. Somebody that had access to your stuff ripped off your wife's picture album while you were behind the walls."

Lenny groaned, his shoulders slumping. "Two weeks out of prison, man, and trouble has already tracked me down."

CHAPTER 10

HOUSTON, TEXAS

Taylor McFadden pushed his girlfriend's wheelchair along the uneven gravel path leading to the corral at Lazy K Stables. Today was the first time Hannah Rennick had been there since leaving the hospital a month ago. "If my dad put Ivan up to telling me something is wrong with Castaño, I'm going to be so mad." Hannah's voice vibrated with each jolt of the chair. "I'm not ready to ride Cass."

Taylor spoke before thinking. "You ride with your thighs, not your feet." Hannah's back stiffened. She muttered something without looking at him, but the creak of the corral gate and Ivan's greeting drowned her words.

"Hey, Hannah. I'm so glad you're back." Ivan, a trusted hand at Lazy K, said hello to Taylor. He quickly turned to the issue of the horse as they entered the barn, and then approached the stall door.

Castaño, Spanish for chestnut, was Hannah's barrel-racing horse. The gelding was a tall, muscular quarter horse, with a deep chest and powerful hindquarters. He had clean limbs, a single white sock, and a spirit as competitive as his owner's.

"Like I told Mr. Rennick," Ivan began, "Cass doesn't seem to want to put weight on his right hind foot."

"When he's standing or walking?" Hannah asked, stretching to stroke the horse's velvety nose.

"I noticed it when he was standing in his stall."

"Cass has a habit of resting a hind leg, but usually it's his left."

Hannah rolled away from the door. Taylor assumed she wanted him to lead Castaño out of his stall. All he could do was assume because she hadn't acknowledged him since his remark about Hannah not needing feet to ride a horse. He hadn't said the right thing since the night of the carjacking. God, Taylor agonized, how did I let that happen? That lunatic ran over Hannah, and I just stood there and watched.

Taylor pulled back the spring-loaded latch, and then opened the stall door slowly. The air inside was cool. It smelled sweet with clean straw and feed supplemented with molasses. "Hey there, big guy." He patted the horse's broad cheek. "Look who's here. It's Hannah."

Ivan handed Taylor a leather halter, which he pulled into place over the horse's muzzle and behind his ears. When the headgear was buckled snugly around Castaño's head, Taylor attached a lead rope, and then led him out of the stall. He noticed that Hannah was studying the outer surface of the horse's hooves, looking for horizontal ridges or vertical cracks.

In the corral, Taylor trotted the horse in a straight line, parallel to the fence, so that Hannah could watch Castaño in movement.

"Give him a looser rein," she ordered. "Let him move his head freely."

Taylor trotted alongside Castaño, Ivan standing beside Hannah. To Taylor's surprise, Hannah soon asked them to switch places. Relinquishing the halter rope to Ivan, Taylor walked across the corral and stood next to her.

"Taylor, see how the hindquarter on the left side sinks when the left foot hits the ground."

"I see that." Taylor frowned. "But didn't Ivan say it was the right leg bothering Cass?"

Hannah was quiet for a moment, still watching Ivan lead the horse away. "And it would be the right leg," she said, a conclusion realized. "The left hip sinks a little because the left leg is having to take extra weight."

"So that means the trouble is in the right foot." Taylor signaled to Ivan, and then asked him to take Castaño into the barn. Pushing Hannah's chair, the black rubber wheels gray with dust, he watched the horse closely, detecting a slight but consistent horizontal unevenness in his hips.

Inside the barn, Hannah told Taylor to use a quick-release knot when he tied the halter rope to a metal ring. "If Cass gets frightened, he might jerk back. He's not used to you."

Hannah rolled into the tack room, and then returned with a hoof pick, positioning her chair in her horse's line of sight. Taylor, facing the horse's tail, stood close to the right flank, a relatively safe place should Castaño decide to kick. He ran his hand down the hindquarters and lower leg, and then lifted Castaño's foot. Holding it well clear of the ground, he checked the horse's balance, looked for any sign of discomfort, and then took the blunt-end hoof pick from Hannah.

Checking for injuries as he worked, Taylor cleaned the grooves beside the frog, and then the sole of the foot while Hannah watched. He knew what she was thinking, that this was her job, not his. Taylor removed mud, debris, and flaking horn. When the pick prodded a certain area of the sole, Castaño tensed and tried to free his foot.

"Easy, boy," Hannah ordered. The horse quickly calmed. "A little tender right there, is it?"

With no injuries apparent to the eye, Taylor and Hannah agreed that the problem was likely a bruised sole, probably from stepping on a rock. In Hannah's absence, the stable owner had agreed to exercise Castaño everyday until Hannah could resume riding. Taylor wondered now if that day would ever come.

"You need to rest your foot for a few days, Cass," Hannah said, able now to stroke and pat the gelding's head. "Do you think he needs a protective pad, Taylor?"

"I don't think so, but let's check on him again tomorrow." Taylor led Castaño into his stall, and then removed the halter. "If he's not better after two days of rest, I'll make a pad for him."

Ivan retrieved a small container of treats from a bin, and then gave it to Hannah. Taylor smiled as he watched. Feeding a horse by hand could be dangerous, but long ago Hannah had taught Cass to use his lips, rather than his teeth, when taking a treat from her hand. Without fail, Hannah offered the treat with a closed hand, knuckles up, fingers protected. As soon as Cass sought the treat using only his lips, Hannah flipped her hand over, and quickly opened her fist. Cass nibbled the treat from her palm, and then nudged her for another.

The sound of footsteps on the gravel path preceded Dean Rennick's appearance in the barn. Hannah's father, clearly glad to see his daughter out of the house, asked about Cass. Hannah explained the likelihood of a bruise, and then said, "You didn't have to drive out here, Dad. I told you I would check on him."

"Actually, I'm on my way to a meeting," Dean Rennick explained patiently. "I have some encouraging news. Ted Bellinger phoned."

A question tore from Taylor's mouth. "Have they arrested Kyla Phelps?"

"Not yet, but they may have found her accomplice. His name is Rylie Thorp. Detectives were at the man's apartment investigating another crime. You won't believe what they found. My birthday present."

"Your jacket?" Hannah asked, incredulous.

"KDR monogram and all."

"That's fantastic." Hannah reached for Taylor's hand and squeezed it. "Now what happens?"

"I don't know exactly, but your mom and I are headed to the police station to identify the coat."

"What about Kyla Phelps?" Taylor pressed.

"Thorp said he's never heard of her, but he's probably lying. The guy is a two-bit criminal with a lengthy arrest record. He claims to have bought my jacket from some dude at a bar. Ridiculous."

"Is he in jail?"

"Not yet. All they could charge Thorp with is possession of stolen property. Just a misdemeanor." Dean Rennick leaned down to kiss his daughter on the forehead. "You and your mom should have bought me a more expensive coat." Then he patted Taylor on the shoulder. "They'll get him, son. Don't worry."

"But what about Kyla Phelps? She's the one who——" Taylor could not bring himself to complete the sentence. "She had the gun. She stole the Toyota."

CHAPTER 11

AUSTIN, TEXAS

Liz Elrod arrived at Blair's office in Austin with cheese, crackers, and fruit. On a comfortable sofa at the window, she peeled back the plastic lid of a divided tray. "I thought about bringing a bottle of Merlot," she said, removing the lid from a thermos. "You're going to need something to mellow you out before you head to San Antonio."

Blair had received a letter from Lenny Bond, providing her with his new address. She had phoned him at work, demanding to meet with him this afternoon, but not saying why. The man couldn't have been more nervous if Blair had told him that his parole had been revoked.

"How's Brandi taking all this?" Liz asked.

"She's really upset about the book," Blair answered, layering a cracker with thin slices of cheddar. "And she is furious with Lenny for selling pictures to Wilson Rule."

"How sure are you that he did it?" Liz asked. "The man had to have known that you and Myles would come after him."

"But who else would have had access to those pictures?"

"Did you ask Brandi?"

"Reluctantly, yes." Blair set aside the untouched snack. "She said Jewell kept pictures in a little album. Apparently, after Jewell died, Brandi put the album inside a wooden box that Lenny bought for Jewell in Mexico. Jewell called it her treasure chest." Blair gazed out the window, feeling her spirits sink. "I hope Brandi is okay. Can you imagine, Liz? Despite it all, she handles things like a trooper."

Liz poured glasses of tea from the thermos. "Maybe the pre-emptive strike made by the kids at school took the edge off. The caricature of her is adorable. What do you hear from Myles?"

Blair squeezed lemon into her tea. "I phoned him. I had to warn him that Rule's book has pictures of Brandi in it."

"Which tirade lasted longer?" Liz asked. "His outrage or his threats?"

Blair frowned in mock disapproval and was ignored. In every other respect a compassionate person, Liz was unsympathetic when it came to Myles. There had been so much to alienate her. His affair with Charmaine and the divorce that followed. His refusal to see Lenny Bond through Brandi's eyes. And, most recently, what Liz called his sanctimonious prattle about why he took the senatorial seat, and then moved halfway across the nation from his daughter.

Picking up the cheese and cracker, Blair told Liz that Myles and Charmaine would be home that weekend to pack. "Seems they found a house in Virginia."

Liz ignored the domestic update. "Did you tell Myles that you're seeing Lenny today?"

"No. I thought I would wait until after I got the pictures from Lenny. And I *will* get them, one way or another. Then Myles won't second-guess why I confronted him."

Liz fell silent, her gaze lingering on the thermos lid. "I think you should have told Myles." She spread another cracker with Brie, and then laid a thin apple slice atop it. "Think about it, Blair. By now Myles has bought the book, seen the pictures, and exploded. Before the redness in his face can recede, the lawyer in him will take over. If he hasn't already done it, he'll call Lenny and threaten some kind of legal action."

Blair carried the argument to its logical conclusion. "Then guilty or not guilty, Lenny will get scared and deny having pictures of Brandi." Liz was right. Lenny could not hand over to her what he had already sworn to Myles that he did not have.

After their brief lunch, while Liz packed the remnants, Blair sent Myles a text asking him to phone her, adding that she was meeting Lenny today and insisting that Myles have no contact with him.

♦　♦　♦

SAN ANTONIO, TEXAS

WORSHAM SERVICES operated out of a narrow building with a brick façade and corrugated metal sides. The rear of the structure was accessed through a gate in a chain link fence, leaving the front office accessible from a nicely landscaped parking area where Blair pulled her Range Rover to a stop.

The front door opened immediately. Lenny Bond emerged. Blair sat staring at the man, her heart throbbing with angry anticipation. She had seen Lenny Bond only a few times before. In some ways, he looked far better than he had then. He was dressed in jeans and a red polo shirt with the Worsham Services logo stitched above the pocket. His hair was very short, the remnants of his prison cut, Blair assumed, and his face was clean-shaven. He was noticeably thinner. His face appeared almost formless, and his narrow shoulders fragile.

He approached the Range Rover like a valet, eagerly opening the door. His greeting was decidedly nervous. "Hi, Blair. I see you found the place." Standing aside, he allowed her to get out of the vehicle, and then closed the door with little more than a click. He motioned to the building with a knuckle-nicked hand. "We can talk inside. Would that be all right?"

The lobby was tastefully furnished, with upholstered armchairs against one wall and a console flanked by two more chairs on another. On the wall behind the desk hung a portrait of a man about Blair's age, early forties, with thick, wavy hair, as dark as his deep-set eyes. The photographer had captured an expression that was neither stern nor welcoming. Determined, Blair decided. The man looked decidedly determined.

"That's Mr. Worsham," Lenny said, motioning for Blair to take one of the chairs in front of the window. "He built this business hisself. Started off with nothing but a borrowed lawn mower. Now he's got sixty people working in the field and four here in the office." Lenny sat beside Blair and continued his obviously prepared speech, tapping his thumb against his thigh as he spoke. "We specialize in commercial property maintenance, but we're getting ready to expand into landscape installation. That's why Mr. Worsham hired me. We'll be building plant beds, and paths, and retaining walls. I've been laying brick for years, so he's looking to me to do a lot of that work and train some helpers too. This is the first time Mr. Worsham has let a parolee head up a crew."

Blair laid her handbag on the table between them. "I was surprised to read in your letter that you live here on the property."

"Rent free." Lenny's pale eyebrows arched. "Right now, there's seven of us parolees in the dorm. No women. I work in the kitchen with my friend Dub Black." Lenny's speech screeched to a stop. "But you didn't drive down here to hear about me."

Struck by the sudden silence, Blair said, "No, I didn't, but I suspect you know why I'm here. It's about the pictures in Wilson Rule's book, and don't tell me you haven't seen them."

"But I ain't seen them," Lenny insisted. "I wouldn't look at that low-life's book with somebody else's eyes."

Blair almost chuckled, but she doubted that Lenny would have noticed. The man was pathetically nervous, more so than when she had phoned him. If he were someone other than Lenny Bond, she would feel sorry for him. But this was not someone else. This was the man who had participated in the kidnapping of her child. He had attempted to extort money from her just two short years ago. A man who had terrorized her with his threats to disappear with Brandi if she went to the police.

"Lenny, you took me for a fool once, but don't try it again," Blair warned, her tone and expression stern. "You sold those pictures to Wilson Rule, and you might as well admit it."

"When in the world could I have took pictures of Brandi? I been in prison for over a year."

"They're childhood pictures," Blair snapped, "and you know it."

"Wait a minute." Lenny frowned and shook his head hard. "I don't know nothing about this. Now it's true that Rule contacted me, but I never talked to him. Never. I sure didn't offer him pictures of Brandi. Why would I do a thing like that?"

"For money, Lenny. It wouldn't be the first time you've made money off my child."

The comment went either unheard or ignored. "I promise you. I don't know what pictures you're talking about."

Blair removed the book from her handbag, and then opened it to the pictures. *A Stranger's Eyes.* Showing it to Lenny, she watched his face closely. His gaze locked on a picture of his wife. He took the book from Blair, and then laid it on his thigh.

"I haven't seen that picture in years," he said wistfully. "It was took outside our apartment in Dallas." He glanced at the one of Jewell and him on the sofa, and then at the images of Brandi. "How did Rule get his hands on these?"

"You tell me," Blair ordered. "Brandi said Jewell kept her pictures in an album. After Jewell died, Brandi personally put that album in a wooden box you bought in Mexico."

"Then it's still in there," Lenny insisted. "I ain't touched that album, Blair. Or that Mexican box. I did not do this thing."

Resigned that she would not get an admission out of him, Blair changed tactics. She had decided on the drive to San Antonio that if she had to use threats as leverage, she would force Lenny Bond to turn over all pictures of Brandi. "Has Myles phoned you? Don't lie to me because I intend to ask him."

"No, I ain't heard from Myles. What would he be calling me about?"

"He believes you sold Rule the photos, too, and he's preparing to take legal action."

"Oh, man." Lenny whined in protest. "He can't do that. I'm on parole, Blair. And Mr. Worsham will fire me if I don't keep my nose clean." The book slipped from his bouncing leg. He caught it before it hit the floor. "You've got to believe me. You've got to make Myles believe me. I had nothing to do with them pictures."

Lenny's desperate tone told Blair she had him where she wanted him. "I have no control over Myles, but there might be a way you could head off a confrontation."

"Tell me. I'll do anything."

"Turn over every single picture you have of Brandi to me."

"I only got two." Lenny Bond twisted in the chair, pulled his wallet from his back pocket, and then tugged out a small stack of pictures. The one on top was a snapshot of Jewell, but not a duplicate of any in the book. He handed the two under it to Blair. "That's it. That's all I got. Brandi mailed them to me herself."

Blair instantly recognized the two school pictures. For no reason, she turned the more recent one over. *Lenny, follow the rules so you can be free soon. Brandi.*

A wave of sadness and regret washed over Blair, taking with it the sharp edge of determination she honed on the drive there. Without comment, she returned the two school pictures to Lenny. "If you didn't sell Rule the pictures, then who did? I don't know what Myles will do if another picture of Brandi turns up somewhere."

Lenny bit a piece of dry skin from his knuckle, and then picked it off the tip of his tongue with fidgety fingers. Blair could not ignore how pale the man's thin face had become or that both his hands had begun to shake.

By the time she arrived home, Blair felt hopeful. One way or the other, Lenny Bond would find his wife's treasure chest. Soon he would hand over more pictures of Brandi. Blair would hold the photographs in her hands, pretending that she had been the person aiming the camera and telling her daughter to smile.

♦　♦　♦

BRANDI SPRINKLED freshly grated cheese onto a pizza she was preparing from scratch. Alli's third of the pie was cheese only, the remainder liberally topped with mushrooms, black olives, and diced bell pepper. She slid the pizza into the oven, and then began her clean up. In the backyard, her mom and Alli were busily cleaning the picnic table, sponging away grimy film with Murphy's Oil Soap and warm water.

Heat from the oven warmed the kitchen. Brandi raised the window above the sink, letting the breeze cool her face. It was dusk, her favorite time of day. Even the fall day's colors seem crisper, the air fresher. It was at this time of day that deer wandered up from the woods near the creek, and then gathered in their quiet, gentle manner around a long wooden trough of feed-corn.

Her mom had gone to San Antonio that afternoon to confront Lenny about the pictures in Wilson Rule's book. Brandi had begged to go with her, but without success. She had wanted to be there when her mom blasted Lenny. How could he have done such a horrible thing? In all the years he claimed to be her adoptive father, Lenny had done more embarrassing, irresponsible, and stupid things than Brandi could count. He had been indifferent, sometimes oblivious, to how his foolish choices had affected his family. But Brandi had never seen Lenny be intentionally hurtful. She could only guess, despite how he sounded in his letters, that prison had hardened him.

Brandi was relieved that Lenny was out of prison. She had worried so much that his mouth would get him in trouble with a guard, or that he would offend another inmate and get beaten or worse. She had cautioned him about that in her letters. But now he was safe and working for a man who wanted to give people like Lenny a chance to start over.

Smiling to herself, Brandi remembered something her mom had said. "If Lenny doesn't give me every single picture he has of you, then he's going to start life over with great bodily injury." In a way, Brandi was glad she had not been allowed to go to San Antonio. Lenny needed to see that for the first time in her life, an adult was willing to stand up for her.

Filling the sink with hot water, Brandi added a generous squirt of Dawn. Through the open window, she listened to the conversation going on in the backyard. With their cleaning task complete, her mom and Alli sat side by side on the bench, facing the house. Alli was using the upturned plastic bucket as a footstool for her blue sneakers. "Aunt Blair, do you get scared being around dead people?"

"No. What do you think might scare me?"

"I don't know."

Brandi stopped scrubbing the cheese grater and watched. Her mom cupped her hand on Alli's head, swiveling her face toward her. "Your brother's been telling you stories again, hasn't he? What did Spencer say this time?"

"That sometimes dead people just pop right up—just sit up all on their own."

"Do you believe that?"

Alli shrugged her shoulders and pressed her lips together, her eyebrows raised in uncertainty.

"Tell me, Alli. What's your brother's favorite pastime?"

"Teasing me."

"Enough said?"

Allison nodded, and then turned to sit cross-legged on the bench. "One time my friend Lucy's grandmother died. And you know what? Lucy said you washed her grandmother's hair and curled it, and then put pink polish on her nails. Did you really do all that?"

"I might have. What is her grandmother's name?"

"Lucy just calls her Grammy."

Brandi continued to listen, conscious of a little twinge of envy. Alli was not even ten years old, and talking about the funeral home and the dead people in it did not bother her at all. Brandi wished she had the courage to talk to her mom about her job. After all, it was very important to her. But Dr. Westinghouse said that Brandi's reluctance had nothing to do with a lack of courage, but that overcoming her revulsion was a worthy goal.

"Aunt Blair," Allison continued, "how do you shampoo somebody's hair when they can't stand up in the shower?"

"Well, you see, the preparation room has a special table in it. We lay the person on it, and then shampoo their hair at the same time we bathe them."

"Bathe them?" Alli was wide-eyed. "You give dead people a bath. Why?"

Brandi plunged her hand to the bottom of the sink but stopped before pulling the stopper. A bath? The dead people were given baths? She raised her empty hand slowly, leaning toward the window.

"For one thing, honey, bathing a deceased person is a kind and respectful thing to do. But, also, the special soap we use washes away germs the person might be carrying."

"Like at the hospital? The soap that the nurses use?"

"Yes. A powerful disinfectant soap."

Brandi looked down at the sink and the dissipating suds. Soap, she thought. A powerful disinfecting soap. She turned her palms up and studied her glistening skin. If the soap her mom was talking about was powerful enough to kill germs on dead people, could there be anything stronger?

CHAPTER 12

SAN ANTONIO, TEXAS

Lucia DeLeon was as easy on the eyes as any girl Lenny had seen in far too long. He understood now why his friend Pete was always bragging about his niece. The girl had long black hair, thick and sleek as a horse's mane, and eyes the color of the coffee in her UTSA coffee mug. And if that wasn't enough, the girl was as sharp as Dub Black's knife collection. She was majoring in microbiology.

"What does a girl do with a degree in microbiology," Lenny inquired, "once she gets it?"

"I'm interested in research," Lucia answered simply, joining the two men at a painted wooden table in her uncle's kitchen. "I want to help find treatments and cures for diseases."

"We could sure use more of that." Lenny spooned sugar into his coffee, and then passed the bowl to Jamar. The last thing Lenny needed was caffeine. His nerves were shot, but he didn't want to be rude to Pete's niece. What he wanted was to head to the garage and start ripping open the boxes his sister Arlene had sent to him from Amarillo. "Too bad about Pete's mama falling sick. How long is he gonna be in Mexico?"

"Maybe a couple of weeks." Lucia poured a few drops of cream into her coffee and stirred, turning the liquid the color of her smooth complexion. "I'm house-sitting until he gets back. If your sister needs to send you more boxes, I'm happy to store them in the garage until you have time to come get them."

"That's real nice of you." Lenny gulped his hot coffee, almost choking, and then managed another minute of conversation. "Well, Jamar and me need to get out of your hair." He stood. "Is the garage that way?"

"Yes. I turned the light on for you." Lucia smiled. "I hope you find what you're looking for, Mr. Bond."

Lenny thanked the girl, and then followed Jamar through the kitchen and into the garage. Getting down to business, Jamar flicked out a blade from his pocketknife, and then zipped the sharp edge through strips of shipping tape securing the top on the first of three cartons.

Squatting beside the box, Lenny tore back the flaps, and then pawed through its contents. Underwear and T-shirts. Socks rolled into balls. Three pairs of faded Levis. Half a dozen shirts and his Budweiser gimmee cap. "Treasure chest ain't here, man."

Jamar ripped open the lid of the second carton. The contents were instantly familiar to Lenny. A pair of old sneakers. A zippered shaving kit. A box of CD's, their plastic cases cracked and yellowed. What Jewell had called Lenny's Elvis plate brought a smile to his face. He had bought the souvenir on a trip to Graceland years ago. For the longest time, he had used it to hold his change when he emptied his pockets at night. Before packing the keepsake, Pete had cushioned it in the folds of a ragged towel.

"Two down. One to go." Jamar cut the tape on the final box, and then tore back the flaps. "Dig in."

Lenny knelt beside the box. The blue sweater on top had been a gift from Jewell. Birthday. Christmas. He didn't remember which. He set it aside, and then reached into the box again. He fingered a copy of the *Laredo Morning Times* and lifted out the newspaper. Unfolding it, he held the paper in front of his face. "Wonder why Pete put this newspaper in here?"

With startling quickness, Jamar snatched the paper from Lenny's hands. "It's packing material, fool." He pressed Lenny's head toward the open carton until his nose was inches from the flaps. "To protect that carved wooden box you see there."

Lenny's head bobbed up when Jamar released it. Like a child at Christmas, he plucked wads of newspaper from around the wooden chest, tossing them to the garage floor. "Oh, man. Am I glad to see this thing?"

Wedging his fingers in the tight space, Lenny lifted the chest. When the carton came off the floor with it, Jamar gave the cardboard box a yank, freeing the heavy wooden chest. "So that's it, huh?"

Lenny's insides writhed. "I think I'm gonna be sick."

Jamar chuckled. "Let's take it inside. It's getting cold out here."

In the kitchen, Lenny set the wooden box on the table. It was a little smaller than he remembered, about sixteen by sixteen, and a good ten inches deep. It was just like hundreds of others stacked in Laredo's shops, darkly stained, heavily carved, held together with metal straps and hinges. Jewell had acted as if the box had been custom made just for her.

When he thumbed back the latch and lifted the lid, Lenny instantly detected a scent of perfume. Jamar's sniff said he noticed it, too, but neither man said a word. Instead, Lenny began quickly removing items from the chest, laying them on the table. A manila envelope marked *Report Cards*. A second one marked *Miscellaneous*. A pink box with a clear lid containing a little pair of shiny, black shoes. A plaster plaque with the imprint of a child's hand, the blue paint chipped in one corner. A small shoe box containing a baby-doll wearing a diaper and a single sock.

Lenny's anticipation surged when he picked up a thick binder. His hopes plummeted when he read the padded cover. "Baby Book."

Jamar took the book and paged through it. "No pictures in this thing."

Lenny groaned, and then continued to empty the chest. A baby blanket. A ruffled nightgown. And in a plain white box, a Christmas ornament and a nearly empty bottle of perfume.

"You gave her that?" Jamar asked.

Lenny shrugged. "I doubt it." Sighing, he returned the bottle to the white box. "Other than a hard time, I think this chest was about the only thing I ever gave Jewell." With that, Lenny dropped into the chair beside him. "What do I do now? The album ain't in here."

Jamar began returning items to the chest. "Why you asking me, man? You don't take my advice."

Jamar had told Lenny to be honest with Blair the day they met at Worsham Services, to admit that he was aware of the pictures in the book, and to swear that he had nothing to do with them getting there. "Point the finger at someone else." Jamar had said. "Defense attorneys do it all the time."

Instead of honesty, Lenny had chosen to act surprised when Blair showed him the book. He had opted for denial when she grilled him about the pictures. He didn't think Blair had bought a word that came out of his mouth.

Lenny slouched in the chair. "What good would the truth have did, man? Blair wasn't about to believe me. Anyway, who was I supposed to point the finger at?"

"We've been through this, Bond."

"Jamar, there ain't no way Pete stole that album while I was in prison and sold those pictures to Rule. The man is my friend," Lenny insisted. "And there ain't no way my sister or her banker husband ripped it off after Pete shipped the boxes to Amarillo."

"Then it was Pete's woman that lifted it. You said she moved in with Pete a few months after you got arrested." Jamar closed the lid on the chest and engaged the latch. "She sure as hell had access to your stuff."

Lenny nodded. "I know all that's true, but what was I supposed to say to Blair? That maybe Pete's girlfriend swiped the album. But I don't know the woman's name. I don't know where she lives either. And sure, Blair, I could ask Pete about her, but I don't know if he knows where she is."

Jamar twisted his full lips in exasperation. "Then just roll over and play dead, man. Let Blair draw her own conclusions. Let Lakeman's lawyer send a nice letter to your parole officer or to Worsham." He reached for the chest. "It's nothing to me."

Lenny popped out of the chair. "Wait. You can't bail on me, Jamar. You gotta tell me what to do next."

Jamar spoke to Lenny as if he were a troubled teen. "Get in touch with your friend Pete. Tell him you found the chest but that the album was not in it. Make him understand that you have to find that album. Then ask him if his ex could have swiped it." He picked up the chest. "If he says that's possible, find out the woman's name and where she lives. Then, if she's still around, you and I'll give her a nice little visit."

While Jamar loaded the cartons in his car, Lenny went in search of Lucia, calling her name as he moved about the immaculate house. She answered his call from a corner bedroom, and then stepped into the hall. She was dressed in jeans and a sweatshirt, her feet bare.

"Sorry to bother you, Lucia, but I need to talk to Pete in the world's worst way. But I don't have his number in my new phone." He tugged the Tracfone from his back pocket.

"Sure. No problem." Lucia removed her glasses, rubbed her tired eyes, and then put the glasses on again. "Let me enter it for you."

Lenny watched the girl's thumbs dance across the screen on his phone. She was as quick as Dub Black with a chef's knife. How did she know how to do that?

"There you are." Lucia returned the device. "Did you find what you were looking for in the cartons?"

Lenny shook his head, and then told Lucia about the mess he was in. "I just have to find Jewell's album. I'm gonna ask Pete if there's any chance that maybe his girlfriend could have took it." Lenny noticed that Lucia's smooth forehead tensed. "I ain't accusing her. I never met the woman. Don't even know her name."

"Her name is Sylvia Reyes. Unfortunately, I have met her." Lucia's pretty face became stern. "Believe me, Mr. Bond, Sylvia Reyes is exactly the type of woman who would steal from a man while he was in prison."

CHAPTER 13

HOUSTON, TEXAS

Taylor McFadden spotted Benjamin James Walters sitting alone on the stairs outside his apartment. The little boy needed a haircut and a warmer jacket. He was only six years old. Was it safe for him to be outside alone? Wood Shadows was in a seedy part of Houston, the kind of neighborhood where a good-for-nothing sociopath like Kyla Phelps would hide out.

At first glance, Taylor thought the little boy was talking to himself, but then he noticed an action figure balanced on Ben's knee. Taylor had phoned him once since their meeting last week, just to check in. There had been no sign of Kyla Phelps. Now, feeling the need for a face to face, Taylor pulled his truck alongside the sidewalk, and then asked Ben if he had a minute to talk.

"Sure, Mac. I'm just waiting for my dad to get home from Brake Check."

"Car trouble?"

"No, he works there."

"What time will he be home?"

"Six-thirty."

Taylor glanced at his watch, parked his truck, and then joined the little boy on the steps. They had twenty minutes to talk before Perry Walters returned home. "How's that strep infection, Ben?"

"I whipped it in five days." The boy raised an equal number of fingers, one wrapped with a gauze bandage.

"What happened to your finger?"

"I got wounded in battle." Ben picked up the action figure, a soldier dressed in combat gear, and then straightened his rigid, plastic legs. Positioning the soldier's arms, he prepared the fierce-faced fighting man for hand-to-hand combat. "I went back to school today."

Taylor sounded impressed. "You put up a good fight, huh?"

Ben tapped his shoe sole. "I took your number with me in my secret hiding place."

"Good job." Taylor rested his forearms on his thighs. "Still no sign of Kyla?"

"Not a peep."

"She must know the cops, I mean the police, are looking for her."

"The police and that other guy." Ben held the figure by the waist, manipulating him in an intense battle with an invisible enemy. "Boy was that guy mad at Kyla."

"What guy, Ben?"

Ben stilled the soldier, angled his legs, and then set him on the edge of the step. "The guy with the nasty ponytail."

Taylor's pulse quickened. He turned sideways on the narrow concrete step, studying Ben. "Some guy with a ponytail was here looking for Kyla. When was that?"

"Yesterday. And another day too."

Taylor's pulse continued to climb. Since hearing Rylie Thorp's name, he had combed the Internet to learn more about the man, even paying for multiple background checks. He had found Rylie Thorp's mug shot from a previous arrest. The side view showed a scraggly ponytail. Taylor had no doubt Thorp and Kyla had pulled off the carjacking together. How else could Dean Rennick's leather jacket have ended up in the man's closet?

Taylor knew now that the cops had been at Thorp's apartment to question him about a home invasion on Oakview. The intruder had stolen some jewelry, and then pistol whipped an elderly man when he awoke and resisted. Cameras in the neighborhood had captured pictures of Rylie Thorp's vehicle. There was no doubt that the thug had been on Oakview the night of the crime.

"Ben, are you sure the man with the ponytail wasn't a cop?"

"Police officers don't have ponytails, Mac."

"Did your dad talk to the guy?" Ben nodded, and then snatched up the action figure which had taken a tumble from the step. "Did he say why he was looking for Kyla?" Taylor pressed.

"He told my dad Kyla was a friend of his, but I don't think so." The boy scrunched up his face in disgust, and then poked his fingers in his ears. "He was cussing all the time he was banging on Kyla's door. He called her some really bad names."

"Doesn't sound very friendly, does it? Did you get a close look at him?"

"Yep. Then Dad told me to get back in the apartment, but I heard what they were saying." Ben bent forward and began tightening the bow in his right shoelace, tugging on the floppy loops until the knot was rock hard. "Mac, why do you want to get Kyla in trouble?"

"That girl got herself in trouble, Ben." Taylor shifted on the concrete step, and then rested his forearms on his thighs again. "I just want her to pay for what she did."

His laces tightened, Ben looked up with innocent curiosity. "What did Kyla do?"

Reluctantly, Taylor told the boy about the trip to the mall, the intentional collision, the carjacking, and Kyla Phelps pulling a gun on him. "My friend was trying to get out of the car, but that idiot Kyla floored the accelerator. Hannah fell out, and Kyla ran over her leg."

The startled look in Ben's eyes registered his shock. "She ran over your friend's leg? With a car?"

"Hannah was hurt really bad." Taylor couldn't make himself say that the surgeon had amputated Hannah's foot. "Kyla Phelps is going to prison for what she did, Ben. She's not getting away with this. I'll find her if it takes the rest of my life."

"We'll help you, Mac." Ben picked up the soldier from the concrete step, and then inched closer, touching his shoulder to Taylor's elbow. "But we won't help that creepy other guy, even if he begs us."

Hesitantly, Taylor pulled his phone from his pocket, and then tapped an image he had downloaded. Was he doing the right thing involving this little boy in his hunt for Kyla Phelps and Rylie Thorp? Maybe not, but he was desperate. "Ben, is this the guy that was pounding on Kyla's door?"

Ben studied the image, twisting his face and squinting. "I'm not sure, Mac."

"It's okay if you're not sure."

"Who is that guy?"

"His name is Rylie Thorp. I'm sure he was with Kyla the night of the carjacking." Taylor waited, not wanting to pressure the boy.

"He kinda looks like him, all right. That guy there's a little fatter. And there's more hair on his face." The boy nodded his head slowly. "But they both have a ponytail, and they're the same color."

Taylor smiled at the boy. "Do you mean the same color hair or the same color skin?"

"Both." Ben pointed at the image, raising his thin, blonde eyebrows. "This guy looks like he's kinda scared. The guy that was pounding on Kyla's door looked mad. Really mad."

With ten minutes to spare, Taylor cautioned Ben about sitting on the steps by himself. "It might be best if you waited for your dad inside the apartment. I know you're a smart, tough little guy, but you're just a kid, Ben. You have to be careful."

"Okay, Mac." The little boy stuffed the action figure in the pocket of his jeans. "I need to go to the bathroom anyway."

Taylor laughed. "You're a hoot, Ben. Know that? I'll wait here until you lock the apartment door, okay?" The little boy gave Taylor a thumbs up. "Keep in touch."

On the way home, Taylor pulled into the drive-thru at a neighborhood Chick-fil-A, his mom's favorite. "I'll have one chicken sandwich, one deluxe sandwich, and three orders of waffle fries." Ten minutes later, Taylor was placing the bags on the kitchen table at home. He sent his mom a text. *Picked up dinner. See you soon?* She replied with three hearts, and *You are the vest.* Taylor grinned. Someday Marta McFadden would proof her text messages before tapping send.

Taylor's mom arrived minutes later, looking tired. She smiled at Taylor, and then sighed loudly when she spotted the bags on the table. "Chick-fil-A. Oh, yum. You are so thoughtful."

"I know, Mom. I'm the vest."

"The what?"

Taylor chuckled. "Never mind." He took plates from the dish drainer and napkins from inside one of the bags. He set the table while his mom removed her jacket, and then hung it on a hook next to her purse by the back door. She called the spot a drop zone. After a really long day, she called it a drop-dead-tired zone.

"Oh, Taylor." Marta pecked her son's cheek, and then collapsed onto a dining chair. "I'm starved."

"Good. I got extra waffle fries." Taylor placed one order on his mom's plate, along with her sandwich. The food was still warm and smelled great. "Dang it. I forgot your sauce again. Sorry, Mom."

"No problem. I have a stash in the frig."

When his mom started to get up, Taylor said, "I'll get it. You want a Diet Coke?"

"Yes. Still in the can, please."

Taylor took two packets of Chick-fil-A sauce from a little bowl next to the ketchup bottle and two Diet Cokes from an open carton. Over dinner, they talked about his day and hers. His mom worked in the bakery at H-E-B. She liked her job and the people she worked with, but she came home tired at the end of her shift, often with a slice of cake for Taylor.

"Do you have plans tonight, son?" Marta asked, dipping the edge of her sandwich into the sauce.

"I need to finish up a couple of online job applications. I'm applying at Home Depot and Walmart."

"There's no rush, Taylor," Marta said, dumping more waffle fries onto her plate, and then sprinkling them with salt. "I know you don't like dipping into your savings, but it's okay. Given the circumstances, let me make your truck payment this month."

"Thanks, Mom. But I've got it covered." Taylor polished off the last of his fries, and then took a long swig of Diet Coke. His mom's words—*given the circumstances*—stuck in his mind. He would use the comment as an opening to update her on the investigation. She and Hannah spoke often. Taylor didn't want his mom to think that he was keeping things from her in case Hannah mentioned it. But no one could know that he was tracking down Kyla Phelps. "Mom, the police are finally making progress in the investigation."

"That's great news." Marta brought her sandwich to her mouth, and then set it back down. "Tell me about it."

"Crime Stoppers got a call from a two-bit used car dealer recently. The man said that the day after the carjacking, he bought the Taurus the police were looking for."

"That's fantastic, Taylor. Who sold the car to him?"

"A girl named Kyla Phelps, at least that's what she told the guy."

"Have they arrested her?"

"No," Taylor answered, knowing that his mom's questions would pick up speed. "The cops are still trying to track her down."

"Are they sure it's the same car? Does he still have it?"

"No, the guy sold it in a few days," Taylor explained. "But the police are sure it's the same Taurus. They asked the guy about the condition of the car. He described some minor body damage. It was a piece of information the police withheld when they asked for the public's help in locating the car. There's no doubt, Mom. The guy bought the Taurus from Kyla Phelps the day after the carjacking, and then sold it a few days later."

Taylor watched his mom's eyes. She was blinking slowly, like she always did when she was processing something he had said.

"So the guy called Crime Stoppers, huh? I guess he didn't ask to remain anonymous."

Taylor considered the question. "Apparently not."

"He probably wouldn't have come forward at all if Crime Stoppers wasn't offering a reward."

"I'm sure you're right." Taylor watched his mom wad wrappers and napkins, and then stuff them into a bag. "Ted Bellinger said the guy's a sleazy operator. "

"That's why he didn't come forward right away." Marta crushed the paper bag. "How could he not have known that the police were looking for a Taurus just like the one he had on his lot?" She was silent for a moment, and then said, "Kyla Phelps. Now we have a name for the lunatic that ran over Hannah."

"The cops won't say for sure, but they know she did it. And so do I." Taylor wiped salt and crumbs off the table with the edge of his hand. "And there's more, Mom. The cops found her accomplice, too, the man who was driving the Taurus when it bumped us from behind. His name is Rylie Thorp. Detectives were at the man's apartment investigating another crime. You won't believe what they found, Mom. Dean Rennick's birthday present."

"The jacket?" she repeated, incredulous.

"KDR monogram and all."

"Oh, Taylor. What a relief." Marta reached for her son's hand and squeezed it. "After all this time, they've identified those worthless crooks. Two of the three, at least. What about the driver of the truck?"

"Bellinger hasn't mentioned him." As he had done repeatedly, Taylor tried to picture the truck and the driver, but it was nothing but a blur. "I was no help at all. I don't even know what color the truck was."

"It doesn't matter, son. The other two will turn on him soon enough." Marta finished off her drink, and then leaned back in the dining chair. "Now what happens?"

"I don't know exactly," Taylor answered. "Thorp said he's never heard of Kyla Phelps, but he's lying. I know he is. The guy is a two-bit criminal. His arrest record is a mile long. The liar claims to have bought the jacket from some dude at a bar. Ridiculous."

"Is he in jail?"

"Not yet. Bellinger said they're still building their case." Pressure swelled inside Taylor's chest. "All they could charge Thorp with is possession of stolen property. Just a misdemeanor. I doubt he spent one night in jail." Taylor hurled a wadded paper napkin across the room. "But that's getting ready to change. Rylie Thorp and Kyla Phelps are going to pay for what they did to Hannah."

CHAPTER 14

LIVE OAK, TEXAS

Brandi dropped her backpack onto a bench by the front door, and then helped Hazel out of her quilted coat. "Thanks for picking me up at the bus stop." She righted the collar of the woman's neat blue blouse. "Usually, I like the quiet walk after riding that noisy bus, but today was just too cold and windy."

"Happy to do it." Hazel smoothed a lock of wind-tossed gray hair from her forehead and shivered. "It is nippy out there."

The two went to the kitchen where Hazel made hot tea. Over a plate of freshly baked oatmeal cookies, they chatted about Brandi's day. "Did you get your book report in on time?"

"I did. Just barely."

"Remind me again of what you read."

"I chose *Anne of Green Gables,*" Brandi answered. "The assignment was to read a book that was published in the 1900's, written for all ages, but considered a classic children's novel. Have you read the book, Hazel?"

"Oh, yes. More than once." Hazel sipped her tea, and then picked up a second cookie. "While we are on the subject of books." Reluctantly, Hazel said that she had seen a copy of Wilson Rule's book on Amazon. "I started not to mention it to you, Brandi, but that seemed a little strange."

"It's all right, Hazel. That's what Dr. Westinghouse would call ignoring the elephant in the living room." Brandi picked up a second cookie. "It's hard to do, and what's the point?"

The doorbell sounded. Hazel rose, walked heavily across the oak floor, and then inched back the front curtain. "Well, look who's here."

The young woman she invited in was a stranger to Brandi. She was hunched down inside her black, hooded coat, her cheeks rosy from the chill. She removed a key from her coat pocket, and then handed it to Hazel.

"I saw your car, so I thought I'd return this rather than leave the key under your mat. The house is absolutely perfect, Hazel. Are you sure that your neighbor Mr. Benson will lease it for just one month?"

"Positive," Hazel assured her. "Otherwise, the house will just be sitting there vacant until his grandson moves in."

"Great. Staying in a motel gets expensive in a hurry."

Hazel motioned toward the breakfast nook. "Come meet Brandi. We're having tea and cookies."

When the woman said that she did not want to intrude, Hazel insisted and took her coat, laying it atop hers on a bench by the front window.

The stranger's hair, short and sleek, was dyed jet-black. Black mascara, heavy eyeliner, and bronze lip gloss faded her fair complexion to an eerie pale. She wore black jeans, a black sweater, and a braided cord knotted around her thin neck. Hazel introduced the woman as Anna Mitchell, and then explained that Anna was looking at houses in the area. "Her mother wants to move to Live Oak. Anna is getting the lay of the land."

The weird-looking woman thanked Hazel for the tea she set before her, and then turned to Brandi. "I couldn't believe it when Hazel told me your mother is a mortician and that she owns the funeral home here."

"We have one in Austin too," Brandi volunteered, only to be polite. "My grandfather started them. He died several years ago."

"Oh, I'm sorry. You must really miss him."

"The whole family misses him."

The evasive answer was well practiced. Brandi had no memory of Millard Emerson and could not possibly miss him. Long ago, her mom had told Brandi that she was not obligated to respond to people's comments or questions with complete honesty.

Hazel passed the cookie plate around just as the doorbell rang again. "That must be Allison." She rose to answer the door, speaking as she left the room. "Your Aunt Charlotte phoned earlier, Brandi, and asked if Alli could stay here while she and Spencer go to Austin."

Alone at the table with Anna Mitchell, Brandi nibbled her cookie. She sensed that the woman was staring at her. Had she heard about Wilson Rule's hideous book? Had she read it? *A Stranger's Eyes.* Why had the man chosen such a scary title? It sounded like a murder mystery. He had probably made Jewell out to be a psycho. Who would buy a book about a normal woman who couldn't have a child and wanted one so badly she stole someone else's?

Allison bounced into the room. "Hi, Brandi." The girls hugged, and then Alli smiled at the stranger at the table. "Hello, I'm Brandi's cousin, Allison Harding. Who are you?"

"I'm Hazel's friend, Anna Mitchell."

"I'm pleased to meet you." Allison plucked two cookies from the plate. "My mom and my brother have to go to Austin to buy Spencer a sport coat. His choir is performing at church, and he just now told Mom that he has to have a black sport coat."

Brandi hid her grin. "I thought Spencer had a black sport coat."

"He does, but the sleeves come up to here." The child whacked a spot several inches above her wrist with a cookie. "My mom was thoroughly exasperated because Spencer always pro…cras…tunates."

The four sat around the table, Anna Mitchell peppering everyone with questions. Brandi didn't much like the woman. She watched too closely, and she smiled too much. She was creepy looking, too, with her pale skin and jet-black hair. Her contact lenses were as blue as a Barbie doll's eyes. A faded tattoo circled the ring finger of her left hand. The silver band she wore over it partially concealed the intricate design.

"Miss Anna, I like your ring." Allison stuffed half a cookie in her mouth and talked as she chewed. "Are those rubies?"

"They're garnets."

The woman looked down at her left hand, and then repositioned the band. Was she trying to hide the tattoo? Brandi wondered.

"Don't worry," Allison said absently. "My ring turns my finger black too."

Anna Mitchell chuckled, and then put her hands in her lap out of view. "Brandi, I'd like to meet your mom. What time will she be home?"

"I'm not sure," Brandi answered, wishing the woman would leave. "She might be a while."

"Some other time then." Anna Mitchell took a final drink of tea, and then stood. "Well, girls, it was cool meeting you. I look forward to being neighbors for a while."

♦ ♦ ♦

DINNER THAT NIGHT consisted of tomato soup and grilled cheese sandwiches prepared in an assembly line. Standing over a cast iron griddle, Brandi heated the sandwiches slowly, allowing the cheese to melt and the bread to brown uniformly.

She hoped Anna Mitchell didn't make a habit of visiting. The house she might rent for a month was in the mobile home park where Hazel lived, just across the street from her. Brandi worried that the creepy woman was a reporter, or maybe a researcher for another idiot author.

Just as the three sat to eat, Blair's cell phone rang. The ringtone signaled that it was the funeral home. "Excuse me, girls. I need to take this."

Brandi closed her ears to the conversation. Her mother was taking a death call. "Alli, do you feel okay? Your face is red."

The girl tugged at the neck of her sweater. "This thing's too hot."

"You can put on one of my t-shirts, if you want to."

Allison ignored the offer, instead turning her attention to her aunt when she returned to the table. "Why were you talking about Mr. Goode, Aunt Blair?"

"I'm afraid Mr. Goode died, honey." Blair cupped Allison's chin, and then sat. "He's worked at Lindquist's General Store for a long time, hasn't he?"

"How do you know he died? Mr. Goode lives all alone."

"His daughter phoned the funeral home," Blair explained, spooning soup to her mouth.

"Who'll take care of Mitzi now?"

"She can take care of herself, honey. Mitzi's a grown woman."

Allison screwed up her face. "No, she's not. Mitzi's a dog."

Brandi snickered, and then burst into laughter. Allison joined in, covering her mouth as she hunched her shoulders and giggled. "Aunt Blair thought Mitzi was a woman."

"No, I didn't." Blair chuckled, infected by the girls' contagious laughter. "I've known Martha Goode for years. I just got a little confused. I'd better get un-confused by the time I see Martha tomorrow."

After dinner, with dishes cleared and the washer loaded, Allison returned to the subject of the Shih Tzu. "Aunt Blair, I keep worrying about Mitzi. Where do you think she is?"

"I assume she's with Martha."

"Think you should call and be sure?"

Blair drew Allison to her. "You are so sweet to care about Mr. Goode's dog, honey, but I'm sure Mitzi is safe." She squeezed her in finality. "Go get the book you and Brandi are reading. You're almost finished with it."

In the family room, Allison opened the cabinet under the television, and then knelt before a shelf of books. Brandi spotted *A Stranger's Eyes* face down in the corner. Her mom had told her that the book was there. "Look at it if you want, Brandi, or put it out of sight in my bedroom, if you don't."

Brandi had no interest in reading the book, not now anyway, but she was curious about the pictures. There were four pages of them, according to her mom, five photos of Brandi herself.

Although Lenny would deny it until he was blue in the face, Brandi was certain he had sold the pictures to Wilson Rule. It was just the kind of stupid, thoughtless thing he would do. Lenny had never been able to think past his nose.

"Brandi, can I get a t-shirt now?" Allison asked, annoyed. "This sweater is too darn hot."

Brandi followed her cousin to the bedroom, Nixon at her heels. The girl shed her sweater, tossed it on the bed, and then reached for the t-shirt. Brandi flinched, and then frowned at an angry blue-black bruise on Alli's upper arm. "What happened there?"

Allison pulled the t-shirt over her camisole, moved to a trunk at the foot of the bed, and then sat. "I don't know what happened, but it doesn't hurt."

Brandi sat next to Alli on the trunk and lifted her arm. The dark oval was at least four inches long and two inches across. The bruise looked painful. "Did you bump your arm, Alli?"

"I don't think so."

Allison tensed when Brandi applied gentle pressure. "We need to show this to Mom." Ignoring her cousin's protests, she stepped into the hall. "Mom, come here a minute." Brandi could not remember the last time her mom had been in her bedroom, but this was an urgent situation.

Seconds later, she appeared at the door, and then paused. "What's up?"

Brandi stood by her cousin and lifted her arm, pulling back the sleeve of the t-shirt. "Look, Mom."

"Ouch." Frowning, her mom walked across the room, and then sat on the trunk next to Allison. Examining the injury, she said, "How did this happen, sweetie?"

"I don't know, but it doesn't hurt much."

Brandi noticed a cut on Allison's elbow. It was red and a little puffy. She retrieved a tube of Neosporin from the bathroom, and then handed it to her mom. Dabbing the medicine gently on the cut, she asked if Alli had shown the injury to her mom. The child shook her head. "Alli, I know you don't want to worry Mom, but this cut needed attention."

Allison pulled down the t-shirt sleeve and stood. Taking the tube of Neosporin, she stuck it in her backpack. "I'll put this stuff on my elbow every day. I promise. Just don't tell Mom."

"But your mom needs to know."

"Fine then." Allison snatched the tube out of her backpack, and then hurled it toward her aunt. It ricocheted off the wood trunk, hitting Nixon on the back. The dog yelped and hunkered next to Brandi's feet. Instantly, Allison collapsed to her knees, her defiant expression crumpling. "I'm sorry, Nixon. I'm sorry."

"He's okay, Alli." Brandi patted Nixon, startled but uninjured, and rubbed his back. "See, he's fine. Pet him. You didn't hurt him."

Allison extended her hand. The dog hesitated, and then welcomed the gesture with a swipe of his quick, pink tongue. Now his black eyes were round with pleasure, his playful posture reclaimed. Standing on his hind feet, the dog pawed Allison's chest, his tongue flicking. Forgiven, Allison let him lick her chin, her nose, and the tears from her cheeks, the incident ending as suddenly as it had erupted.

CHAPTER 15

LAREDO, TEXAS

The stucco house where Sylvia Reyes lived was painted beige, the trim a pale turquoise. The yard had been done in what Lenny Bond had learned since working for Worsham Services was called xeriscape—low maintenance, low water plants, more mulch or stone than thirsty sod. According to Pete, his ex-girlfriend drove a red Mazda, the down payment for which she had borrowed from Pete and had yet to repay. The spiffy little car was parked in the driveway at the side of the house.

In a phone call with Lenny, Pete had said that he knew nothing about a photo album. "But yes. Sylvia could have swiped it if she had a reason." When Lenny asked if Sylvia had known why he was in prison, Pete had said, "Everybody who read *The Times* knew, Lenny. The whole kidnapping and extortion story was on the front page for days." But had Sylvia known that Wilson Rule was working on a book? Pete couldn't say for sure. "She never mentioned it, but then there was a lot of stuff Sylvia forgot to mention."

Before leaving for Laredo, Jamar had phoned Sylvia at the number Pete had supplied. When the woman answered, Jamar had claimed to be with a task force the mayor's office had assembled. "We're doing a survey about city services. Will you be at home this evening to answer a few questions?" When Sylvia had happily agreed, Jamar and Lenny had headed south on Interstate 35. Two hours later, they were standing on the front porch of the woman's house.

Sylvia Reyes looked nothing like Lenny had expected. Her eyes were as green as a fertilized lawn, and her hair was the color of a new penny. Her skin was as tanned as a cowhide, and the veins in her face said she was a serious drinker. The way Lenny remembered it, Pete had been attracted to the slightly less haggard look.

Jamar flashed the woman a smile, and then extended his hand. "Glad we caught you at home, Sylvia. Pete told us we could find you here. I'm Jamar Warfield." He nodded over his shoulder. "This is Lenny Bond."

Sylvia's friendly smile melted. "You're friends of Pete?"

"Yeah," Jamar answered. "Mind if we come in a minute?"

Momentarily paralyzed by indecision, Sylvia suggested they talk on the porch instead, and then closed the front door. She seemed to make a point of speaking to her neighbor, who was lugging his garbage bin to the curb. Lenny didn't blame the woman for being cautious. She wasn't about to be shoved back inside the house by friends of an old boyfriend sent to collect a debt.

Was Sylvia's nervous state a good thing or a bad one? Lenny wondered. Was she likely to tell him the truth about Jewell's photo album if she was scared silly? Figuring she was more likely to lie, he leaned against the stucco wall, looking friendly and completely harmless.

Jamar took another tack, moving into the woman's space. "You haven't said hello to Lenny."

Shifting her gaze, Sylvia forced a tight, wrinkled smile. "I'm sorry. Do I know you?"

"Well, we've never met," Lenny answered, still leaning against the wall. "Me and Pete used to be roommates."

The woman's green eyes jittered. "Oh, of course. Lenny Bond. I'm sorry. Pete called you Lee."

"Oh, yeah." It had been so long since Lenny had used the alias, he had forgotten about it. "Lee Pickens."

When Sylia asked how Pete was getting along, Lenny told her that he was fine, but that his mother had fallen ill. "He's gone to Mexico to see her."

"I'm sorry, but I'm glad Pete's okay. I was afraid you were here with bad news of some kind."

To Lenny's ear, Sylvia sounded sincere, but his ear had been known to fail him. "You weren't worried that Pete was in some kind of trouble, though, were you?"

"No. Not Pete."

Jamar made a point of staring at the woman. "When trouble is rapping on a man's door, she stands in front of that guy's house."

"He's right about that." Lenny chuckled. "In fact, I've got a little problem now, and I'm hoping maybe you can help me with it."

"I can't imagine how."

"Well, I need to pick your brain." Lenny frowned. "You see, when I got arrested, Pete didn't just get stuck with the rent. He also got stuck with my belongings, everything from my boxer shorts to my Patsy Cline albums." Sylvia nodded but said nothing. "After the two of you split the sheets and Pete decided to move to San Antonio, he boxed up all my junk and shipped it to my sister. The problem is, I was searching through them boxes the other day and something turned up missing. When I asked Pete about it, he wasn't no help, but he said I should talk to you, since you were around back then."

"What are you looking for?" the woman asked, sounding legitimately puzzled.

"It wasn't a winning lottery ticket or anything like that. It was my dead wife's picture album. She kept it in a wooden box I gave her."

Something sparked in Sylvia's green eyes. "I remember the box, yes. It was on a shelf in your closet." She nodded with certainty. "I even asked Pete about it, and he said it had belonged to your wife."

"Did you open it?" Lenny asked. "No problem if you did," he added quickly. "None at all."

Jamar took a casual step toward the woman. "Frankly, we were hoping that you did open the box. Then Lenny would know whether or not the album was in there when Pete packed up Lenny's stuff."

Sylvia inched away from Jamar, creeping in the direction of the front steps. "No, I didn't open the box. I saw it on the closet shelf, asked Pete about it, but I never opened it."

"All right." Jamar paused, still staring at the woman. "Let's say I believe you. Do you remember seeing the album anywhere, at any point?"

Sylvia seemed to search her memory. "I don't. I'm sorry. I wish I could help."

"So do we." Jamar withdrew his wallet from his back pocket and produced a business card. "That's where Lenny and I work. Worsham Services in San Antonio. My cell phone number is on the back." He pressed the card into Sylvia's hand and held it. "Look around your house. Maybe you packed the album by *accident* in your rush to get out of Pete's life. How much money do you still owe the man?" He squeezed Sylvia's hand until she flinched. "Listen, lady. That album is important to my friend, and I'm gonna help him get it back even if I have to launch a little search of my own."

♦ ♦ ♦

IT WAS ALMOST midnight when Lenny climbed quietly into his upper bunk at Worsham Services, his hair still damp after a long, hot shower. He could tell by the rhythm of Jamar's breathing that his bunkmate was sound asleep. The image of the man nearly crushing Sylvia Reyes's hand lingered like the sting of a slap.

If she does have the album, Lenny worried, what will she do with it now? Toss it in her garbage bin and set it out by the curb?

Exhausted, Lenny closed his eyes, covering them with the crook of his elbow. It was a habit he had developed in prison to keep the corridor light from seeping through his eyelids. He wished he could block out his thoughts as easily. All he could hope for was that Blair would consider his second letter a demonstration of good faith.

In the letter, he had offered to meet Blair at the Hays County line and turn over Jewell's treasure chest. Would being handed some report cards, a baby book, and a chipped plaster plaque give Blair reason enough to keep her ex-husband from going on the attack? Lenny let out a moan of misery, and then rolled onto his side.

CHAPTER 16

HOUSTON, TEXAS

Taylor McFadden lifted Castaño's hind foot, and then rested the horse's ankle on his thigh. Using a hoof pick, he cleaned away debris and flaking horn, as he had done before. Cass seemed to have improved, but the horse was still reluctant to distribute his full weight evenly. Hannah had asked Taylor to make a bandage boot. Now she handed him a piece of thick, dense foam, custom fit for the horse's hoof. To hold the foam in place, he wrapped it with a self-adhesive bandage.

Hannah's dad was on his way to the stable with what he said was good news. Was it too much to hope that the police had arrested Kyla Phelps or Rylie Thorp? The lying scum claimed to have bought Dean Rennick's leather jacket from a guy at a bar and refused to even admit knowing Kyla. Taylor knew Thorp was lying, and so did Perry Walters and his little boy Ben.

For now, Taylor would keep quiet about what he knew. The cops would order him to stay out of the way, to let them handle things, but he wasn't about to do that. He had a score to settle with Kyla Phelps, and nothing was going to stop him.

Taylor smoothed the snug adhesive bandage with his palm, and then lowered the horse's foot to the ground. Castaño immediately tilted it, keeping his balance with the front of the hoof touching the ground. "That feel a little strange, big guy?" Taylor grasped the halter rope, and then handed the end to Hannah. "Lead him into the corral."

"You do it."

"He's your horse."

Taking the end of the rope, Hannah cut Taylor a sharp look. He pretended not to notice, and then began rolling her chair out of the barn. Cass walked next to her. A gentle breeze lifted her hair off her shoulders and fluttered the folded leg of her sweatpants. She was withdrawing from him. He could feel it, even see it in the lifeless look in her eyes. At least once, she had refused to take his phone call.

More than a month had passed since the carjacking, and it grew more unreal every day. How could this be? Taylor agonized. He and Hannah were supposed to be dreading finals at Sam Houston State. Taylor was supposed to be helping Hannah load Cass in the trailer and driving them on weekends to the next rodeo on the schedule. How could he have been so careless? Only an idiot would let scum like Kyla Phelps and Rylie Thorp sucker him into getting out of a car on a dark Houston street. Why didn't the cops get off their butts and find Kyla Phelps? She was the one who had pulled the gun. She was the one who had run over Hannah.

"Slow down," Hannah snapped. "You're jarring my teeth."

Taylor loosened his vice-tight grip on the wheelchair's handles and slowed his pace. He got so angry sometime that he thought he could actually kill those two lowlifes if he could get his hands on them.

In the corral, Cass walked next to Hannah's chair like a dog on a leash. When the horse stopped suddenly and kicked his hind foot, trying to throw off the bandage boot, Hannah giggled. The sound made Taylor simultaneously hopeful and sad. By the end of the first lap, Castaño had adapted and was left to roam.

When the wind picked up, stirring dirt and whipping Hannah's hair, Taylor took her back into the barn. Dean Rennick arrived minutes later, accompanied by a man Taylor did not recognize. His thick, salt-and-pepper hair was well cut and casually styled. Black brows arched over deep set eyes. His face was thin, lined, and expressive. The man wore sharply creased Wranglers, hand polished boots, and an expensive looking leather jacket over a dark blue shirt.

Dean Rennick introduced the man as Coy Becklund, owner of CB Western Wear. "Mr. Becklund needs to talk to Hannah about a business proposition."

Becklund sat on a hay bale and Dean Rennick joined him. Taylor rolled Hannah's chair in front of the men, and then remained behind her, his hands clenching the rubber grips.

Leaning forward in a sincere, relaxed fashion, Becklund rested his forearms on his thighs. He began by expressing how sorry he had been to hear about the injuries Hannah had suffered in the carjacking. "It's unfortunate that you're sidelined from the rodeo circuit, but your dad assures me you'll be back in the arena in good time. But in the meantime, I have a business proposition for you. My company is gearing up to introduce our own line of Western wear designed specifically for young men and women like yourself. What I need is a beautiful, successful cowgirl with name recognition to help launch the ad campaign, to be our signature model, if you know what I mean."

Standing behind Hannah, Taylor put a hand on her shoulder and squeezed. She stiffened and remained silent. Becklund leaned in closer, his black eyes intense and eager. "You are a remarkable young woman, Hannah. You're a skilled athlete and competitor. You have a beautiful, girl-next-door face. You're just what CB Western Wear is looking for."

Taylor's cell phone rang just as Dean Rennick spoke his daughter's name. *Chirp.* Taylor had assigned the ringtone to Ben because it sounded like a snare drum keeping soldiers marching in step. Taylor excused himself and walked outside into the corral. Watching Castaño trot away, comfortable now with the bandage boot, he tapped the screen. "Hi, Ben. What's up?"

"Kyla called my dad."

Taylor looked over his shoulder to be sure he would not be overheard. "Tell me what you know."

"Kyla asked my dad for a favor. I heard him say, 'What kind of favor?' Then Dad listened a little bit and told her he would meet her over there at six."

Taylor's pulse quickened. "Meet her where?"

"I don't know, but Dad just left a few minutes ago."

Taylor looked at his watch. It was five-thirty now. Kyla Phelps had to be in Houston somewhere. "Did you hear anything else, Ben?"

"No, but I got the number off caller ID."

"She called your digital phone?"

"Yeah. My dad's battery was dead."

"Good going, Ben." Taylor pulled a pen from his pocket and wrote the carefully recited number on his palm. "That's great work, Ben. I owe you."

"When my mom comes home, I'll tell her I helped you and the police track down that creepy Kyla Phelps."

Taylor thanked the boy again, feeling another stab of guilt. This nice little kid was keeping secrets from his parents, even spying on his father. The stab was fleeting, though. Benjamin James Walters and his family would be far better off with Kyla Phelps behind bars.

Taylor stared at the number on his palm. He didn't recognize the prefix, but there were so many in the Houston area now. Most likely Kyla Phelps had called from a cell phone anyway. He was still studying the number when Dean touched his shoulder and said that Hannah was ready to go home.

Taylor told the two men goodbye, and then whistled to Castaño. The horse trotted across the corral, kicking up dirt with his hind feet, and then followed Taylor back to his stall. Hannah rolled her chair to the stall door, and then stretched to stroke Castaño's velvety nose. "I'll see you tomorrow, Cass. Don't be trying to kick off your boot, okay?"

Taylor took up his spot behind Hannah's chair and rolled it forward. Her legs looked so frail. She went to physical therapy three times a week, and Taylor knew the exercises had to help. But Hannah was an athlete. If she didn't start a serious program, including riding again, her muscles would waste away.

"Aren't you going to ask what I told Mr. Becklund?" Hannah locked straight ahead, her hands resting on the armrests. "I told him I would think about it. But what I was really thinking is that

I don't have any intention of putting on a freak show in some western wear ads."

Taylor jerked Hannah's chair to a stop, jarring her. With startling quickness, he shot around the chair and flattened her hands against the armrests with his palms, his face inches from hers. "You are not a freak." He squeezed Hannah's hands against the padded rests. "Don't ever say that again."

Taylor spun away, tears burning his eyes. He stormed across the corral and threw back the gate, leaving Hannah to fight her way across the uneven soil. When she finally made her way through the opening, Taylor shoved the gate shut and locked it. Tears spilled over his lashes. He wiped his cheeks with angry swipes. The salty moisture smeared the phone number scribbled on his palm.

CHAPTER 17

LIVE OAK, TEXAS

At her desk, Blair opened a lengthy e-mail from Myles. He had seen the pictures of Brandi in Rule's book. At Blair's request, he agreed not to contact Lenny Bond. "I'll let you handle Bond for now." Then Myles brought Blair up to speed on the details for the weekend and the swearing-in ceremony in Washington. He would make all the arrangements for Brandi to attend. He ended with a word of caution. "My aide showed me your quote in the *Statesman*. I agree with everything you said to the reporter, Blair, but I think it would be best that in the future you refuse to speak to the press."

"Best for whom?" Blair snarled, clicking the delete button with a forceful finger.

Annoyed and frustrated, she gazed at the collection of family photos on the etagere. Had Lenny found Jewell's box and the album? Or had he known exactly where they were all along? Either way, she was certain he would hand over the pictures, alarmed as he was that she and Myles would cause him trouble.

Blair wanted desperately to hold pictures of Brandi in her hands, to arrange them in chronological order, to watch her child grow and change right before her eyes. With today's technology, a lab could remove Lenny and Jewell from snapshots that included Brandi. Blair would have some of the photos enlarged, framed, and placed throughout the house and her office. She would make copies for Myles, and he would be thrilled. He had said, after seeing the pictures in Rule's book, that he would have recognized Brandi anywhere. Blair would not have, and it hurt to admit it.

The Goode family arrived at two o'clock. Blair joined them in the arrangement office, careful to greet the daughter as Martha and not Mitzi, remembering Allison's concern about the Shih Tzu. Martha Goode, nearing fifty, never married, and known for her unchecked frankness, said affectionately, "Your father was one of my father's best friends."

It was a characterization Blair heard often from clients, as well as other people who had known her father. Millard Emerson had been a marvelous conversationalist — not idle chitchat, but warm, earnest, getting-to-know-you talk. The warm, embracing quality of his personality had been passed on to Allison. Would it have been the same for Brandi, but for the abduction?

At the conclusion of the arrangement conference, Blair reviewed notes she had prepared for Martha and her brother, who had been silent for the most part during the conference. She provided the list to Martha, and then offered to answer questions. When there were none, she escorted the family to the front door. "Take care of each other. I'm a phone call away when you need something or have questions."

The weather report had warned that a cold front would hit the hill country by late afternoon, bringing with it sleet and freezing rain. A mild wind had already found its way from northeast Texas. Brittle leaves on live oaks appeared to shiver in the falling temperatures. Despite the chill, Blair returned to her office, buttoned up her long, wool coat, and walked the few blocks to Al's Diner for an afternoon snack.

Unthinkable a year ago, Manny Taggert and Paul Dillard were sharing a table for four. The deputy sheriff, a longtime friend of Blair's, waved her over. Manny stood to pull back her chair. She thanked him, raising an eyebrow at Paul who rose only from the waist up while ripping open a packet of saltines.

Manny signaled the waitress with a nod towards Blair, and then pierced a potato chunk with a fork. "Enjoying your new bathroom?"

"It's terrific, Manny. Wouldn't change a thing. Looks like you're making good progress on Miss Linquist's roof."

"Doing my best. I think she's satisfied."

Paul blew on a spoonful of steaming chili. "Believe me, Manny, you'd know if Ethel wasn't satisfied. She'd wait until you were on the roof, and then ram your ladder with her walker."

Blair ordered peach cobbler and hot tea. The conversation moved to Myles's swearing-in ceremony, Waylon Goode's funeral arrangements, and a newcomer to town named Anna Mitchell. Manny had met her at the Stagger Inn. "Looks like she's gonna be your neighbor for a while, Blair."

The Stagger Inn was a local beer joint and Manny's second home. Based on Brandi's description of Anna Mitchell, Blair had a hard time picturing the woman dancing the two-step with the locals.

Manny continued his update. "Anna's gonna rent Jack Benson's mobile home for a month while she's looking for property for her mother. She's interested in the Minor house over there by you, but she said it would need a few repairs." When Paul asked if that would then qualify them as minor repairs, Manny looked puzzled, and then moved on. "I was wondering, Blair, since you know the Minors, if you might, you know—"

"I'd be glad to give them a call, Manny. I believe I owe you one."

Manny was relating to Paul his face-to-face with this "punk reporter," when Blair's cell phone rang. Even at Al's Diner, she resisted sitting at a table and taking a phone call, opting instead for a short corridor outside the restrooms. It was Charlotte. She sounded upset. "Can you meet me at your house? I need my sister."

"I'm on my way." Blair returned to the table and retrieved her purse. "Something's come up. I have to go." She asked Paul to pay her check, and then headed for the door.

On the sidewalk, she looked up and down the street for her car, and then remembered she had walked from the funeral home. Paul emerged from the diner carrying her coat, and then opened the door to the patrol car. "Get in." He tossed Blair's coat onto her lap when she slid onto the seat, her left knee inches from a secured shotgun. Sleet pecked at the windshield as Paul drove down Main Street. The racket set her nerves on edge.

"Are you all right, Blair?"

"Charlotte took Alli to the doctor this morning. She has a cut and a big bruise on her arm. Now Char needs to talk to me."

Paul pulled to a stop under the porte-cochere at the funeral home and gave her a quick hug. "I hope it's not bad news."

Charlotte was using her key when Blair got home. A sharp, damp wind parted her sister's hair in the back, shoving it forward, concealing her face. Not hearing the crunch of gravel, she went inside and shut the door. She flinched when Blair opened it seconds later and quickly turned off the alarm.

"Sorry, Char. I didn't mean to startle you." Blair closed the door against the cold air trailing in behind her. She hung their coats, and then sat next to her sister on the sofa.

Charlotte looked achingly tired. Her face was pale and strained. Fine, red lines threaded her eyes. She sounded defeated when she spoke, saying that the cut on Allison's elbow was infected, as well as the surrounding tissue. The doctor had recommended a couple of days in the hospital. "He wants to give her antibiotics intravenously." Charlotte's tone changed from defeated to uncertain. "He assured me it's a precaution, but I can't help worrying."

"Where is Alli now?"

"At home with Butler. She was begging us not to take her to the hospital. I had to get out of the house." Charlotte's body sagged. "More needles. More blood draws. But we have to be sure the infection doesn't spread." She rested her head against the sofa back. "I feel like such a traitor. Alli's just a little girl, so powerless. All I do is side with the doctors."

"Oh, Char. You're always on Alli's side." Blair wished she could take back the empty reassurance. It was the kind of platitude she had resented after Brandi disappeared. *Mothers everywhere leave their children in the backyard to play.*

"Before I left the house, Alli begged me to call her doctor. *Please, Mommy. Just tell him to call in a prescription.* Are those the words of a little girl, Blair?" Charlotte's voice gave way, snapping like an ice-layered twig. "All I could do was say no. It's what I always say."

Blair suspected that her sister, as concerned as she was about the infection and another hospital stay, was deeply worried that Alli was feeling abandoned by her own mother. "She needs to be in the hospital, Char. There's nothing you can do about that. But maybe we can do something to let Alli know that you're on her side." Finally, Blair saw a spark in her sister's eyes. "We have to get Alli to ask for something that you can say yes to. You could even say that you overruled the doctor."

"Yes. Something that would let me be the good guy for a change." Charlotte was silent, focusing on the pictures on the mantel. "What she would want more than anything would be for Brandi to spend the night in the hospital with her."

Without question, Charlotte was right, but the solution came with complications, not the least of which was getting Brandi from Austin to Live Oak in time for school. And, Blair worried, what if a night in a hospital caused Brandi's washing ritual to resurface?

CHAPTER 18

SAN ANTONIO, TEXAS

The waitress set a bowl of chunky salsa and a red plastic basket of tortilla chips on the table. Lenny salted the golden chips liberally, and then slid the basket closer to his sister. Arlene picked up a broken chip, and then dipped a corner into the spicy mixture. Lenny, using a large chip as a scoop, piled the salsa high before popping it into his mouth. Instantly, his tongue was on fire. "Whew!" He gulped tea. "That's hot."

Arlene chuckled, and then told Lenny he had gotten soft. "When we were kids, you practically drank this stuff."

Lenny laughed, and then sucked air to cool his tongue. His sister was right. Mexican food had always been his favorite. "Maybe that pig swill at the prison altered my taste buds, Arlene, that and all those years of choking down Jewell's home cooking."

Arlene's pleasant expression hardened a little at the mention of Jewell's name. Lenny didn't blame her. Arlene was a proud woman, and everybody in Amarillo had to know that her sister-in-law had kidnapped a baby a decade ago, and that her brother served time in the pen. Lenny figured that had to be a double dose of shame for the wife of a Baptist deacon.

Lenny was glad to see his sister. Arlene had lost a few pounds and looked good in her black wool pantsuit. She had always been hefty, so even a little extra weight made her face rounder and her neck thicker. As children and teenagers, the two of them had gotten along fairly well. Arlene had walked the straight and narrow. Lenny had staggered down life's road, dodging potholes, stumbling into a bunch of them.

When Arlene had learned the truth about April, she had written Lenny off like a bad debt. "Stealing that couple's child wasn't a mistake," she had insisted angrily. "So quit calling it that. What you and Jewell did was a sinful, evil thing. And you, Lenny, trying to sell Blair Emerson's own child back to her. I'm ashamed to be your sister." The words had pained Lenny, but all that misery was behind them now.

"Sure was nice of you to fly all the way down here to see me, Arlene." Lenny ripped open two packets of sugar, and then emptied them into his tea. He wished the glass had a thick stem and a salted rim. "What did your husband have to say about you flying from one end of the state to the other?"

"Oh, Herb didn't mind. Despite everything, Lenny, he understands that you're my only brother, and that I care about you." Arlene dipped another chip into the salsa. "Herb would have come with me, but he needed to prepare for a deacon's retreat that's coming up soon."

"I see." Lenny didn't have a clue what went on at a deacon's retreat, but he would bet a Worsham paycheck that the men from First Baptist Church of Amarillo didn't tap a keg when they got where they were going. "So, how's my niece doing these days?"

Arlene sighed, and then dabbed at her lips with a napkin. "As well as can be expected, I guess. But, Lenny, Eden has never been the same since her husband died. Kyle was such a fine young man."

"Sorry to hear that," Lenny responded, his tongue still stinging.

"We've begged Eden to move back home, even offered to buy her a house. But she says there are too many memories there. I'm sure she's barely making ends meet."

Conversation moved to Lenny's job. "I'm working over on San Pedro at a medical complex. It's a landscape enhancement project. My crew is building a retaining wall. It's five-foot high and a block long. Talk about hard work. And, Arlene, thanks to my friend Jamar Warfield, I haven't broken a single one of Mr. Worsham's rules." He tapped his tea glass with his index finger. "You notice that's not a margarita."

"Mr. Worsham doesn't allow alcohol consumption?"

"Nope. Not in the dorm. Not on the job."

"But you're not drinking now. Why is that?"

Lenny popped bare chips into his mouth. "My friend Jamar says drinking alcohol lowers a man's inhibitions. He said I already have a serious problem with impulse control."

Arlene chuckled, nodding repeatedly. "I'm glad things are working out for you, Lenny." Her smile slowly dissolved. "I'm sorry you didn't find Jewell's picture album in the cartons I sent you."

"Yep. Me too." Jamar was convinced that the unnamed thief was Pete's girlfriend. Lenny was inching in that direction, but he hadn't admitted that to Jamar. The look on Sylvia Reyes's face when Jamar had nearly crushed her hand still weighed on Lenny's mind.

The waitress set an order of crispy beef tacos in front of Arlene, and then served Lenny a plate of enchiladas. "Hot plate, sir." When the woman walked away, Lenny picked up his fork. He stopped it in midair when his sister covered his free hand with hers and bowed her head.

"Thank you for this food, Lord, and for this time together. I ask that you bless my brother as he starts his new life. In Jesus name I pray. Amen." Arlene raised her head, squeezed Lenny's hand, and then picked up her fork without making eye contact. Lenny had seen people pray in restaurants a time or two, but he sure hadn't been sitting at the table when it happened.

Half an hour later, when their plates were cleared, Arlene scanned the check, and then laid twenty-five dollars on the black tray. She returned her wallet to her purse, and then withdrew an envelope, thick with its contents. Lenny recognized the fancy blue paper as being his sister's personal stationery, but he couldn't imagine what was inside it.

"Before I take you back to … home, Lenny, I want to say a couple of things."

Lenny instantly tensed. "Sure, Arlene." The cloth napkin slid from his lap to the floor. Lenny banged his forehead on the table when he reached down to pick it up. "Ouch. Okay, Arlene. Fire away."

"I believe you when you say that you didn't sell those pictures to Wilson Rule. I'm praying that, in time, Blair and Brandi will come to believe you too." She leaned toward Lenny, her expression earnest. "I know how worried you are that Myles Lakeman will cause trouble for you with Mr. Worsham or with your parole officer. It's critical that you not give him any ammunition. Just tell Blair the truth when you talk to her again. Tell her that you honestly don't know where Jewell's album is, but that if it turns up, you will give it to her, just like you're going to give her the treasure chest. I have a feeling that the items in the chest will be of great comfort to Blair."

"I sure hope so." Lenny nervously picked at a scab on his knuckle, waiting for the next shoe to fall.

"I want you to give Blair this too." Arlene handed Lenny the thick, blue envelope. "I went through all my family photographs, looking for any that had Brandi in them. I only found a few. They are in this envelope, along with a letter to Blair. I didn't seal the envelope. You can open it if you want."

Later that night, sitting at a table in the sleeping quarters at Worsham Services, Lenny opened the envelope. He studied the pictures first, gazing at one of them for a particularly long time. It had been taken in a cemetery in Texarkana. The long, black hearse that had carried his mama's body to her grave was parked in the background. People dressed in dark clothes stood in clusters, under and around a sagging tent. April stood off to the side, away from the others. She was holding a single flower to her nose. Lenny had a clear recollection of April laying the flower on his mother's coffin before it was lowered into the ground.

He was sliding the pictures back into the envelope when his Tracfone rang. "Hell. How do I answer this thing?" Somehow, he tapped the correct button, repeatedly saying, "Hello. Hello."

"Lenny, it's Lucia."

Lenny stilled his index finger, not wanting to accidentally hang up on the girl. "How are things going, Lucia? You studying hard?"

"Definitely. I have a microbial genetics quiz tomorrow." The girl groaned. "I'm calling to pass on a message from Uncle Pete." Lenny thought the girl sounded hopeful. "He's on his way home. He said to tell you that he's been racking his brain, trying to remember if he ever saw your wife's photo album. It finally came to him."

Lenny tensed. His over-filled stomach began to churn.

"Not long after you moved in with him in Laredo, you told Uncle Pete that you had a daughter living in Austin." She paused for emphasis. "Then you showed him pictures of her. They were all in a photo album."

Lenny gripped the phone hard. "Pete remembers that?"

"For sure. So unless you later threw away your wife's album, then it had to have disappeared *after* you were arrested, probably from the apartment."

Lenny slowly digested the information, his stomach still churning. "Well, I sure don't remember throwing it away."

"I doubt that you did," Lucia said confidently. "Why would you? That album belonged to your deceased wife. It must have meant a lot to you."

Knowing that he had never been the sentimental type, Lenny agreed with the girl anyway. "So Pete saw the album while we were living in Laredo, but it was gone when I unpacked the boxes he sent to my sister."

"Exactly. That means someone took your album while you were in prison. And it wasn't Uncle Pete."

Lenny knew exactly what Lucia was thinking, and the girl was probably right. Sylvia Reyes had lived in that apartment with Pete. She had known about the kidnapping. The conniving woman had probably heard that Wilson Rule was writing a book and had seen her chance to make some quick money with the pictures. The problem Lenny faced now was how to convince the woman to own up to what she did. Something told him that if Sylvia had another face-to-face with Jamar, she would be a lot easier to convince.

CHAPTER 19

Houston, Texas

Taylor McFadden stepped out of the shower, and then wrapped a towel around his lower body. The room was like a steam bath. He wiped moisture from the mirror with a hand towel, and then started the mindless process of shaving. He had overslept that morning and had dashed to a job interview. In a week, he would begin stocking shelves on the graveyard shift at Walmart. College was out of the question. He couldn't possibly concentrate on his classes, not until the police arrested Kyla Phelps and Rylie Thorp.

The phone number Ben had given Taylor had turned out to be a bar called The Dive, not far from Wood Shadows, the apartment complex where Ben lived. Perry Walters had left home in plenty of time to meet Kyla Phelps and take care of the favor she had asked of him. The bartender, when Taylor went to The Dive, had remembered a woman fitting Taylor's sketchy description of Kyla Phelps. "She asked to use the phone," he recalled. "Said she couldn't get a cell signal inside the building. We hear that a lot. Seems like her hair was black, though, not red. But, yeah, this woman was as skinny as a mop handle." The man added that she kept her sunglasses on, and that she chain-smoked on the patio. "The man who joined her was an average Joe in his early thirties. He seemed more than a little glad to see the woman, if you know what I mean."

Taylor held his razor under the flow of water. Clumps of shaving cream peppered with stubble dissolved and disappeared down the drain. Kyla Phelps had been in that bar. Taylor was certain. She had phoned Perry Walters from there, and he had left his little boy alone to go meet her. The woman was still in Houston, or somewhere nearby, and she still had her claws in Perry Walters.

Taylor put on jeans and a blue and white striped shirt. He and Hannah were going to a movie tonight. It would be the first time they had gone anywhere together, except to the stable, since the night of the carjacking. Hannah had been quick to explain the reason for her sudden change of heart. "I have to get out of this house. Dad keeps pressing me about that ridiculous modeling offer."

Before the carjacking, Hannah would have jumped at the chance to model western wear. She was a beautiful girl. As Coy Becklund had said, she had a wholesome, girl-next-door face. In her humble way, Hannah loved the limelight. Whether she was singing a solo in the church choir, telling a joke to her family or friends, racing around barrels in a crowded arena and then posing with Cass for the winner's photo, Hannah was energized by attention.

Now, except for her physical therapy or to check on Cass, she rarely left the house. She continued to lose weight and muscle tone, but it was more than that. Her personality. Her confidence.

Her eagerness. They were shrinking too. Hannah was vanishing, Taylor thought, and it was all his fault.

Whatever Hannah's reason for going out tonight, Taylor would capitalize on it. Maybe if she started living again, she would stop disappearing. A movie was as good a place as any to start.

Marta McFadden was stirring soup in a saucepan when Taylor entered the kitchen. She smiled approvingly at her son. "You look mighty handsome."

"Better than this morning?" Taylor checked his watch. He needed to leave soon, but there was one more thing he had to do, something he did not want his mom to see. "What are you doing tonight?" he asked, pulling back a chair at the round, maple table, and then sitting.

"My fingernails," she answered, chuckling. "How's that for an exciting evening?"

"Typical. When are you going to change that?"

Taylor's mom poured soup into a thick ceramic bowl, and then took it to the table. "When my boy is all grown up and doesn't need me anymore. That'll be any day now, right?" she teased.

Taylor nudged the salt and pepper shakers toward his mom. His parents had divorced when he was thirteen. His dad had remarried in less than a year. As far as Taylor knew, his mom had never brought a man into their house. She was not a pretty woman. Her hair was too frizzy, and she was slightly overweight, but everyone who knew his mom liked her. She had a great sense of humor and never complained, even when she was holding down two jobs to make ends meet. Taylor felt guilty that his mother was alone because of him. Maybe he would have liked having a stepfather, but he doubted it. One thing was certain, though, he would have hated having a mother who brought men home like stray dogs.

"Taylor, I saw Adam today." Marta unfolded a paper napkin in her lap. "He really wants you to rope with him in Sonora, son. He said you can ride Blanco again, and that he would pay the entry fee."

"I've already told him no, Mom. I haven't roped in two months. I don't want Adam to depend on me. I don't want *anybody* depending on me." He pushed back from the table and stood. "I've gotta go."

"Can you give me a minute?"

"I'm in a hurry, Mom."

"Just one minute." Taylor sat. "I'm worried about you, son. I've mentioned to you before about seeing a counselor. You're carrying so much on your shoulders, and from the outside, it looks like you're dealing with what happened as well as any man could. But, Taylor, I'm seeing some things that concern me."

"Mom, I—"

She raised a cautionary hand. "Listen, please. You're not sleeping well. You're irritable. Not with me, son, but things really get under your skin now. In the past, you would have just shaken them off. And the nightmares, Taylor. They're getting more frequent, which is one of the reasons that you're not sleeping well."

Taylor knew his mom was right, but nothing would change until Kyla Phelps and Rylie Thorp were in jail. Nothing. And he could not leave it up to the police to make that happen.

"It's the guilt, son, that's torturing you." His mom's voice was gentle with compassion. "You may need to talk to someone about the guilt. And, Taylor, I know a thing or two about guilt."

Taylor nodded slowly, a painful memory gathering. When he was a boy, about Ben's age, his mom got pregnant. His parents were crazy excited when the sonogram showed that the baby in the picture was a girl. They even made a copy of the picture for Taylor and hung it in his room next to a calendar. Every day, he marked an X through the date, counting off the days until he would have a baby sister. He vowed to be the best big brother in the world, to love his sister, to teach her things, and to always protect her.

In the sixth month of her pregnancy, Taylor's mom had made a terrible choice. Determined to clear space in an upstairs closet, she had loaded a cardboard box with items for Goodwill. Despite her husband's repeated warnings, she began lugging the box down a flight of stairs. She was almost at the bottom when she lost her balance and tumbled forward. At the bottom of the stairs, her abdomen smashed against the hard, unforgiving cardboard. Years later, Taylor could still hear his mom's ear-piercing scream.

"Carrying around guilt is a soul-crushing burden, son." Taylor's mom fished an index card from the pocket of her uniform, and then placed it on the table. "When you're ready, look at this website. It may be too soon to start chiseling away at your guilt, but this might help when the time comes."

Taylor rose and went to stand beside his mom. When she stood, he held her tight. "I love you."

"Love you, too."

When Taylor released his mom, she pointed to a tin box on the counter. "That's for Hannah. I baked her some brownies. Have a good time."

"Thanks, Mom." Wiping moisture from his eyes, Taylor turned on the television sitting on the kitchen counter. He had one more thing to do before leaving to pick up Hannah. Watching the evening news would keep his mother distracted while he got what he needed from her bedroom. Picking up the tin of brownies, he gave her a peck on the cheek, glancing at the index card. "I'll be home early."

"Okay, son. Be careful."

Taylor couldn't count the times his mother had told him to be careful before he left the house. Dean Rennick always gave him a similar warning. Would he say that tonight?

Taylor had never considered himself to be thin skinned, but since the carjacking even well-meant comments rubbed him wrong. When Adam had said that he was so sorry about the accident, Taylor had wanted to say, "It wasn't an accident, fool. It was a carjacking." His uncle had said that he was so sorry about what happened to Hannah, as if a force of nature had caused the whole horrible ordeal. Why hadn't anybody said, "I'd like to get my hands on those low-lifes."

Tucking the tin of brownies under his arm, Taylor slipped down the hall to his mother's bedroom. Opening a top dresser drawer, he ran his hand under a stack of scarves, and then gripped the butt of a snub nose revolver.

CHAPTER 20

AUSTIN, TEXAS

The air in the hospital room was stifling and thick. The lingering smell of the meal Alli had hardly touched mingled with a chemical scent wafting in from the restroom. But for her empty stomach, Brandi would be struggling to keep from being sick. It was after nine o'clock, and she had not eaten since lunch at school. By morning, she would be starving. She had known better, though, than to eat the spaghetti with tomato sauce Hazel had prepared before leaving for the day.

Brandi looked around the room. She loathed hospitals and would rather be anywhere than lying on the portable bed her Aunt Charlotte had requested. Nurses and aides spread germs from patient to patient on their hands, on their clothes, even in their hair. Every single person tracked all sorts of disease-carrying microorganisms on the soles of their silent shoes. But as much as she hated hospitals, Brandi loved Allison. How could she have refused to spend the night in the hospital with her?

The door opened and a nurse stepped in, thermometer in hand. It was a forehead thermometer. Brandi cringed at the thought of an old-fashioned thermometer. How many hundreds, thousands, of other patients had held the same thermometer in their mouths?

"It's me again, Allison. Just need to check your temperature." The nurse placed the sensor head at the center of Alli's forehead. Touching the skin, she slowly slid the device across her forehead, toward the top of Alli's ear. With the reading secured, she thanked Alli, and then recorded the data on the computer.

Before leaving the room, she smoothed the stiff, white bed linens, and then turned out the light. "Try to get some sleep now, girls. Both of you. I'll check on you before I leave for the night."

As soon as the door clicked shut, Allison yawned. When she raised her hand to her mouth, the IV tubing caught on the bedrail. "Ouch. Stupid thing."

"Are you all right?"

"I just want to go home," Alli insisted, her tone angry, not whining. "Will you be here when I wake up?"

"I'm not sure. Uncle Butler is taking me to school. We'll have to leave early." She did not mention that Alli's dad was spending the night in a waiting room down the hall. "Aunt Charlotte said that if you're feeling okay, you can go to my dad's party with me this weekend. It's at a fancy place here in Austin called The Headliners Club. We'll get to meet the governor."

"Cool. What's his name?"

Brandi giggled, identified the woman, and then rolled onto her side. "Let's get some sleep. Wake me if you need something. Love you."

"Love you too."

In the dimness, Brandi could see Alli's profile. She looked so tiny, almost disappearing under the sheets. Brandi's thoughts took her back to the weeks at MD Anderson. Endless tests. Chemotherapy. Vomiting. Sores on Alli's lips and in her mouth. How hard she had cried at times. The bravery she had mustered.

Brandi pushed the images away, thinking instead about the reception and the trip to Washington, D.C. It would all be very exciting, and she knew how much her dad wanted her there. Still, she was nervous about it all. Charmaine was so beautiful, so poised. But she had forgotten what it was like to be thirteen, and she had never known what it was like to be raised by Lenny and Jewell Bond.

Brandi had expected Lenny to deny selling pictures to Wilson Rule, but was it possible that he was telling the truth? Probably not. He lied as easily as he breathed. But one thing was certain. Lenny did not want Senator Myles Lakeman breathing down his neck. If it took calling in a psychic, he would remember what he did with Jewell's album and her treasure chest. Brandi hoped he found it, but she wished she didn't care. Why would a kid want to hold on to something that had belonged to her kidnapper?

Closing her eyes, Brandi tried to quiet her mind, but it was impossible. Alli was in the hospital again. The reception at The Headliners Club meant shaking hands with maybe a hundred people. The flight to Washington meant breathing re-circulated microorganisms for hours. And then there was the hotel room. Yes, she would have her own bathroom, and the sheets and towels would be clean, but what about the blanket and the comforter?

She had seen an undercover investigation online about hotel housekeeping practices. Maids thought nothing about using the same blanket repeatedly. Held under a special blue light, blankets were disgustingly soiled and contaminated. And there was no way hotel owners paid to have comforters cleaned every time a guest checked out.

Brandi ordered herself to stop fretting, but her mind continued its ceaseless churning. Certain that Alli was asleep, she eased her legs off the side of the bed, and then wiggled her feet into slippers. Quietly, she opened the closet, retrieved a bottle of Mr. Clean from her backpack, plucked a pair of disposable gloves from a dispenser, and then slipped into the bathroom. Leaving the door ajar so she could hear if anyone entered the room, she soaked paper towels with cleanser, and then hid the bottle behind the toilet.

Alli was sleeping soundly when Brandi stepped quietly into the room again. Careful not to bump the bed, she ran the damp paper towels across the headboard, back and forth over the side rails and the call-button. The presence of the IV pole was oddly reassuring. Powerful antibiotics were coursing through the tubing and into Alli's vein.

She returned to the restroom twice to moisten more paper towels. Disinfecting the portable bed frame last, she removed her gloves, and then doused her hands with Mr. Clean. Still, she thought, not even Mr. Clean was as potent as the soap used to bathe dead people at the funeral home.

♦ ♦ ♦

LIVE OAK

THE SPECIAL AT Al's Diner was chicken pot pie. Blair placed an order to go, and then waited in a booth by the window. She had received another letter from Lenny Bond today. She retrieved it from her purse, and then stared at the name scrawled in the corner. Had he found Jewell's treasure chest? Was the album inside it? If he didn't admit to having it, she would tell him that Myles had threatened to contact his boss and his parole officer, if Lenny failed to turn over the album.

Blair tore off the end of the envelope, and then slid out a carelessly folded piece of paper. The handwritten lines were scrunched and sloping. They could have been written by a third grader.

Dear Blair. How are you and Brandi? I'm doing ok. I'm glad to tell you that I found Jewell's treasure chest. I can't explane why but the album wasn't in it. I don't have any idea where it could be right at this time, but me and my friend Jamar are not giving up on finding it. If you or Brandi want the treasure chest you can sure have it. I'm gonna leave everything inside it just like I found it. There is things in there that you might want too. Course that's up to you. I sware if I had that album or if I knew where it was I'd do whatever it took to hand it over to you. My friend Jamar said he would drive me over to the Hays County line any time after work so I can give you the treasure chest. If you want it. Just tell me when and where. I hope you will pass it on to Senator Lakeman that I'm coperating to the fullest. Sincirly Lenny Bond.

Blair folded the letter, and then slid it back into the envelope. Was it possible that she was wrong? Lenny's denial seemed genuine. But if not Lenny, then who? "Stop," she muttered. "He did it. You know he did it." She jammed the letter into her purse. How many other pictures did he have of Brandi? Given the chance, that lying criminal would sell those too.

A bell above the door jingled when it opened. Blair looked up and smiled as Hazel entered. The dear woman began smoothing her unruly silver hair, tossed by the wind, and then turned down the collar of her overcoat. Blair's smile froze when a woman entered behind her. She was dressed all in black, including tall leather boots with impossibly high heels. Her cropped hair was raven black and her cosmetics absurdly overdone. Even her silver hoop earrings were trimmed in black. Based on Brandi's description, the woman had to be Anna Mitchell.

"Hi, Blair." Hazel unknotted her scarf as she neared, and then tugged it from around her neck. "Can we join you?"

"Of course." Blair stood to let her friend slide into the booth. "I'm waiting for a take-out order."

"Chicken pot pie, I'm guessing." Hazel shrugged off her coat, and then squeezed into the narrow space. "I don't think you've met Anna."

"I haven't," Blair answered, sitting next to Hazel, noticing right away the intense blue of Anna Mitchell's eyes. Brandi was right. Her contact lenses made them look like a Barbie doll's eyes. "I hear we're neighbors."

"For a month at least." The young woman slid into the booth and unbuttoned her jacket, making herself comfortable. "I met your daughter recently, and your niece. I'm so sorry to hear that Allison is in the hospital. Hazel told me she had leukemia. It hasn't returned, has it?"

"No," Blair answered curtly, instantly resisting the woman's intrusive question. "Your mother is considering a move to Live Oak, I understand. Where does she live now?"

"Big Spring."

"Why Live Oak?" Blair pressed, remembering what Brandi had said about Anna Mitchell asking too many questions. Blair would turn the tables.

"She likes the hill country."

"Has she lived here before?"

"No, but she's visited friends."

"In Live Oak?"

"Uh, no," Anna stammered. "In Austin."

Blair was about to ask her mother's name when Al shouted to her from the cash register. "Got your order ready, Madame Mortician. Get it while it's hot." Shaking her head, Blair smiled indulgently. "Be right there, Al." When she stood and said goodbye, Blair intentionally did not toss a pleasantry to Anna Mitchell. The woman was her neighbor, but that didn't mean that Blair had to be neighborly.

On the way home, she passed by the Stagger Inn. Manny Taggert was walking toward his truck. Impulsively, Blair made a U-turn, and then pulled onto the gravel lot. Parking behind Manny's truck, she lowered her window and called his name. The man couldn't have been more shocked if she had turned on lights and a siren.

"What in the world are you doing here, Blair?"

"I need a favor."

"Name it."

"I need you to make friends with Anna Mitchell."

Manny placed his elbow on the side view mirror and leaned. "I can do that. Any particular reason?"

"Paranoia?"

Manny's chuckle was warm with compassion. "You got a right to be suspicious, Blair, considering all you've been through. And now that damn book."

Blair patted Manny's forearm. "I just want to be sure Anna Mitchell is who she says she is. Do you know where she's from? She said her mother lives in Big Spring."

"Yeah, I think that's what she told me." Manny ran his palm over his stubble-darkened jaw, tugging at the flesh. "You could ask Wanda. She might know. She carded Anna the other night."

"Wanda saw her ID?"

Manny nodded and leaned away from the door. "Let's go ask her what she remembers. I'll buy you a beer." Laughing, the man opened the door of the Range Rover. "You ever been inside a beer joint?"

"It's been a while," Blair joked. "I'm buying, though. I owe you. Again."

Side by side, they walked across the parking lot. Gravel crunched noisily under Manny's boots. On the narrow front porch, he held open the door and the two entered. Blair paused just inside the place, allowing her eyes to adjust to the dim light. *Should Have Been a Cowboy* played on the jukebox, but the small, sawdust-covered dance floor in the rear was vacant. Most of the mismatched wooden tables were empty, too, but all heads turned when Blair and Manny entered. She smiled pleasantly, as if she were a regular at the Stagger Inn making her way toward the bar.

Wanda Lamb was standing behind it, drying a beer mug with a white cloth. The buttons of her bright red shirt tugged at the fabric. Her blonde hair was board straight, a sharp departure from her previous pile of curls. Her bartender, Del, was filling a wooden bowl with peanuts in the shell. Their shocked expressions were nothing short of comical.

"What are you doing here, Blair?" Wanda nodded toward Manny. "And what are you doing with that guy?"

"I owe the man a beer." Blair slid onto a stool, and then dragged a bowl of peanuts between her and Manny. "I placed a losing bet on the Cowboys."

"So he made you come here?"

Blair laughed. "Not at all."

"I'm just teasing you." The good-natured woman set aside the towel. "What can I get you?"

"Club soda with lime for me. I'm on call."

Wanda turned to Del. "Get the man another Budweiser."

As soon as Del stepped away, Blair said, "Actually, Wanda. I need to ask you something. It's about Anna Mitchell."

Wanda grimaced, her bright red lips dipping dramatically in the corners. "Stranger than fiction, isn't she? She looks as out of place here as you do, Blair. No offense."

"None taken. You saw Anna's ID. Did you happen to notice where she's from?"

"Houston." Wanda cocked her hip, and then leaned against the bar. "But to be honest, I'm not sure it was her ID. Sure couldn't tell it by her picture."

"Mine either, I hope." Blair picked up a peanut, crushed the shell, and then popped the nuts into her mouth. She couldn't make herself drop the shell on the floor, as was clearly the tradition at the Stagger Inn. "Do you ever card a customer twice? I sure would like to know the address on that ID."

"Not a problem. I'll tell Del and my waitress to card her again."

"I'd really appreciate it, Wanda." Blair crushed another peanut. "As I confessed to my friend here, I'm probably being paranoid."

"I heard about the book." Wanda set a glass of fizzing club soda on the bar, and then swept the crushed peanut shells onto the floor. "That man Rule better be glad he didn't show his face in here."

Blair grinned, squeezed lime into her drink, and then nodded at Manny. "I rather wish he had."

CHAPTER 21

NEW BRAUNFELS, TEXAS

Lenny had gone weak with relief when Blair agreed to meet him and Jamar in New Braunfels, a town on Interstate 35, between Live Oak and San Antonio. He had apologized to Blair for not being able to deliver the treasure chest to her in Live Oak. "But if I set foot in Hays County, I would be violating my parole." They were meeting in the parking lot of a German restaurant called Alpine Haus. Blair would be driving a black Range Rover, license number EFH-5. Jamar had made sure he and Lenny were right on time. He spotted the vehicle first. "There she is, man. Just like she said. So that's Blair Emerson, huh?"

Lenny opened his door and got out of the car, waving to Blair in a friendly way. She did not wave back. She drove toward him stone-faced, and then pulled the spotless vehicle to a stop several spaces away from Jamar's car. Lenny smiled as she got out, and then approached her. She was dressed in gun-metal gray jeans, a blue shirt as dark as midnight, and a black leather jacket. Her expensive-looking ankle boots were black leather, too, with a silver zipper up the side.

Blair Emerson was one classy looking woman, Lenny thought, as he approached her. "Howdy, Blair. Thanks for driving down here. I would have been glad to bring the stuff to you, but like I mentioned, that'd be a violation of my parole."

"So you said."

Lenny motioned over his shoulder with his thumb. "I've got Jewell's treasure chest over there in my friend Jamar's car. I'll get it for you in a minute, but first I want to bring you up to date. Jamar and me are not done trying to find Jewell's album. In fact, we might just have a lead on it." Lenny thought he detected a flash of interest in Blair's dark, brown eyes. "When I got arrested in Live Oak, I was living in Laredo with my friend Pete. He remembers me showing him some pictures of Jewell and April—I mean Brandi. Sorry.—and he says the pictures was in a album." Blair stepped closer, straining to hear over the sound of cars coming and going. "After I went to prison, Pete's girlfriend moved in with him. From what I hear, she's the type of woman who would steal from a man when he was down and out."

"Have you confronted her?"

"Dang straight. Me and Jamar tracked her down in Laredo. She denied ever seeing the album, but Jamar don't much believe her."

"I want that album, Lenny."

"I know that. Believe you me, I ain't give up on getting it. In fact, while we was down there in Laredo, Jamar kinda put the squeeze on Sylvia, if you know what I mean. I think she got the message." He noticed a slight nod of Blair's head and figured the conversation was going well. "Me and Pete and Jamar have came up with a plan that'll let Sylvia return the album, no questions asked, if she's still got it. If she turns it over, I'll get the thing to you as quick as I possibly can. I know how much them pictures mean to you."

"You can't possibly know."

Lenny cleared his throat nervously. "No, I can't. That was a stupid thing to say." He motioned toward Jamar's car again. "In the meantime, you can have the treasure chest and all the stuff inside it. Oh, and this." He produced the thick, blue envelope Arlene had given him. "I told my sister I was meeting you today. She flew all the way to San Antonio from Amarillo so I could give you this." He handed the envelope to Blair. "It's a letter from Arlene and some pictures. Arlene said I could read it, but I didn't. She sent every single, family picture she could find that has Brandi in it."

Blair looked down at the envelope but didn't open it. "That was very kind of her."

"You betcha. Arlene is a good person." Lenny rubbed his palms together in a task-accomplished fashion. "I'll get that treasure chest for you." He walked briskly to Jamar's car, and then opened the back door. Leaning in, he told Jamar he thought things were going just fine. "I told Blair we have a lead on the album, just like you told me to say. She asked me if I'd confronted Sylvia yet, and I told her yes." Lenny picked up the wooden chest, but then sat on the edge of the seat, holding the box in his lap. "I'm so damn nervous I can't remember what else I was supposed to tell her."

Groaning, Jamar swiveled in the seat to face Lenny. "Four things, idiot." He held up his fist and popped up his index finger. "One. Give her the envelope from your sister. You did that." He extended a second finger. "Tell her you've got a lead on the album. You did that." He extended his ring finger. "Give her that damn box. You're getting ready to do that, if you don't forget by the time you walk twenty feet. And four, ask her if—"

"Oh, yeah. I remember." Lenny popped off the seat, and then closed the door with his hip. He had to hurry and be done with this meeting. Jamar was getting impatient with him, and Lenny needed a beer in the worst way. Jamar had agreed to buy him a beer since he would be around to be sure Lenny stopped at one.

The glare on Blair's face made Lenny even more nervous. He did not want to be at war with Blair Emerson, knowing she was the take-no-prisoners type. Hopefully, she would consider Jewell's treasure chest as a kind of peace offering.

"Well, here it is, Blair." Lenny held the carved box on his forearms. "The only thing I took out was a bottle of Jewell's perfume. Everything else is just like I found it. Want me to put it in your car for you? Nice Range Rover, by the way."

Blair opened the rear door on the driver's side and stepped back. "Set it on the seat."

Lenny did as he was told, and then closed the door. "All safe and sound." He rubbed his hands together again, this time in finality. "Sure hope you'll tell Senator Lakeman that I'm playing it straight. I swear on my mama's grave that I didn't have nothing to do with them pictures turning up in Wilson Rule's book."

"If I find out you lied, there'll be hell to pay."

"I didn't lie," Lenny repeated, wiping beads of sweat from his lip. "And I'm not lying now."

Blair stepped toward the driver's door, her expression a warning. Lenny grasped the handle, preparing to open the door for her, but stopped. There was one other thing he needed to say to her. *Number four.* What was number four? he puzzled.

"Is there a problem?" Blair asked, annoyed.

Lenny continued to grip the handle, not opening the door. "Not a problem exactly."

"If you're keeping something from me, Lenny Bond, you'll regret it."

"No. It's not that. I'm trying to think." Lenny's pulse raced. He could actually feel his heart thudding in his chest. What was number four? He could not let Blair drive away thinking he was withholding something from her. "Oh, I remember." Lenny released the door handle, and then popped himself on the forehead with his fist. "E-mail. I just found out that the computer in our dorm at Worsham Services is connected to the Internet. My friend Jamar set up this mailbox deal for the two of us. It's way faster than regular mail, and—"

"I know how it works," Blair interrupted.

"Good. I was thinking that if I get any news about that album, it'd be a lot quicker if I could e-mail you. I know you don't want me calling you on your phone."

"I suppose you could e-mail me."

Lenny snatched a scrap of paper from his shirt pocket. "Here you go. That's my address. Can you read that okay? It says Warbond at Worsham dot com." He chuckled nervously. "Jamar's last name is Warfield. Get it? Warbond?"

Blair smiled—a small, reluctant tilt of her lips—and then opened her purse. From it, she removed a business card, and then wrote on the back. "That's my address."

Lenny took the card. "BEmerson at Emerson dot com." He tucked the card in his shirt pocket, and then opened the door of the Range Rover. "I guess that's about it. Don't forget now. Me and Jamar are hot on the trail of that picture album."

Blair climbed into the vehicle. "Brandi's furious that you sold pictures to that man, but she said to say hello."

"She did?" Lenny grinned. "That's nice. Would you say hi to her for me?"

Blair nodded, and then started the engine. "She said to remind you to follow the rules at work."

Lenny gave himself a thumbs-up. "You tell her I'm battin' a thousand, okay?"

Blair pulled the door shut, looked straight ahead, and then drove away. Lenny sucked in an urgent breath. "Whew. I think that went real good."

Exhaling loudly, Lenny trotted back to Jamar's car, plopped onto the passenger seat, and then drummed the dash. "All right, my man. Let's go pick up Pete and head to Laredo."

CHAPTER 22

Houston, Texas

Taylor McFadden parked his truck in a darkened corner in the parking lot at Wood Shadows. Rain streamed down the windshield. When the downpour let up, he would have a clear view of the front windows of Kyla Phelps's apartment. He was probably wasting his time watching the place, but he had to do something. He had to find that sorry excuse for a woman.

Popping the top of a Red Bull can, Taylor took a swig, and then let his mind drift back to the night of the carjacking. Rylie Thorp and Kyla Phelps had been watching him and Hannah walking across the mall parking lot to her Camry. They had seen him put the garment bag into the trunk. Security cameras showed the Taurus following them off the parking lot.

"Why did I not notice?" Taylor agonized. "How could I have been such an idiot?"

Even when the truck and the Taurus were boxing in the Camry, Taylor had suspected nothing. He and Hannah had been talking and listening to music. Within minutes, Hannah was sprawled on the pavement, screaming, as the rear tire of her Camry ground into her leg.

Rylie Thorp had been driving the Taurus that night. Taylor was sure of it. The man was a thug and a criminal. The cops suspected that Thorp committed the home invasion on Oakview, pistol whipping the elderly homeowner. They had been at Thorp's apartment to question him about the break-in when they found Dean Rennick's leather jacket in Thorp's closet. There was no doubt in Taylor's mind. Rylie Thorp and Kyla Phelps had nearly killed Hannah. That was why Kyla sold her Taurus the next day. That was why she was hiding from the cops.

"Damn you both," Taylor muttered, bringing the Red Bull can to his mouth again, picturing the revolver under the seat of his truck. "You'll pay. I'll make sure of that."

Taylor's phone pinged. He fished it from his pocket and tapped the screen. It was Adam. *Headed to Whataburger. You hungry?* With little thought, Taylor replied. *In the middle of something. Another time.* Adam's one-word response was immediate. *Later.* Taylor scrolled up on the screen. How much longer would his friend keep reaching out?

Taylor had bookmarked the website his mom had written on the index card. The site offered a range of mental health resources. His mom had directed Taylor to information about survivor's guilt. His initial reaction had been confusion and resentment. What was his mom thinking? He didn't have survivor's guilt. No one died in the carjacking. How could he possibly have survivor's guilt? Furthermore, survivor's guilt was some kind of mental disorder, which did not apply to Taylor at all.

According to the website, though, there were multiple kinds of survivor's guilt. One definition had snagged Taylor's attention. *Survivor's guilt is remorse or regret for having not suffered injury or trauma that others endured during a catastrophic event.*

With rain still streaming down the windshield of his truck, Taylor returned to the website. He scrolled down to a section entitled *Common Indicators.* There were seven listed. All but one applied to Taylor. He was not having suicidal thoughts.

The other six held a mirror before him. His mom was right. He was irritable, even with Hannah sometime, and emotionally volatile. Nightmares kept him awake at night. Sometimes they were so bad, he didn't want to go to sleep again. He was withdrawing socially, even from Adam.

What his mom could not know, though, was how powerless Taylor felt, particularly when a flashback struck like a lightning bolt. And no one could understand the mental torture of the never-ending cycle of rethinking his actions during the carjacking.

Taylor's pulse began to race as he scrolled down the page. When he reached a section about coping mechanisms, he closed the page, and then tossed his phone onto the passenger seat.

The rain at last let up, allowing a watery view through the windshield. It was nearly midnight. How much longer should he stay? Perry Walters's vehicle was still gone. He and Kyla Phelps could be somewhere together at this very minute. Was Ben inside the apartment alone? Probably. Taylor hated thinking that

Perry Walters was sleeping with Kyla Phelps while his wife was sleeping in a barracks in Germany.

Taylor was preparing to leave for the night when he noticed a white Toyota truck pulling slowly onto the parking lot. The driver circled the lot, and then pulled to a stop near building 2A, opposite the stairs leading to the Walters's apartment and to Kyla's.

The door to the truck swung open. The man who climbed out was dressed in jeans, a dark t-shirt, a camouflage jacket, and work boots. He climbed the stairs, and then went directly to Kyla's door. Without knocking, the man grasped the knob, but the door remained closed.

Taylor felt an onslaught of nerves, watching as the man withdrew something from his pocket, and then squatted by the door. The balcony rail and the semi-darkness obscured Taylor's view. He could not see what the man was doing, but he got a clear look at his face when he walked back toward the stairs.

"It's him." Taylor snatched up his phone. "It's Rylie Thorp." Stunned, he tapped the screen, creating a video. The camera captured the man descending the stairs, returning to his truck, and then speeding off the parking lot.

His mind racing, Taylor saved the video. Should he follow him? No, he knew where Thorp lived. What he wanted to know now was what Thorp had left at Kyla's door.

Taylor scanned the quiet lot and the darkened apartment windows. Then he left his truck, raced across the parking lot, and up the stairs to Kyla Phelps's door. For a moment, he stood there staring, puzzled. Then he saw it. A thin strip of folded cardboard tucked between the weather stripping and the edge of the door. Rylie Thorp was determined to know if Kyla Phelps was still around or if the woman had skipped town.

"What an idiot," Taylor mumbled. "Does he think Kyla is the only person coming and going from her apartment?"

CHAPTER 23

LIVE OAK, TEXAS

With pallbearers walking alongside, Blair and Jay Lytton rolled a draped bier bearing the casket of Waylon Goode out the side door of the chapel. Family and close friends walked behind, Manny Taggert and Paul Dillard among them. The silent procession halted at the rear of the funeral coach. Under Blair's guidance, the pallbearers lifted the casket, placed the foot on a system of rollers in the floor of the coach, and then eased it forward until the far end rested against what was commonly referred to as a casket stop. Inserted into a notched chrome strip in the center of the floor, the rubber-padded device worked in concert with an identical piece on the near end. The pair of stops prevented the casket from shifting during turns and stops of the funeral coach.

Minutes later, with the immediate family seated in a limousine, other family members and friends in their vehicles, Blair eased the lead car off the parking lot. The pallbearer limousine and the funeral coach pulled in behind her. On the short drive to the church, she reviewed the procedure she and her staff would follow, each man's duties having been assigned earlier in a brief meeting. "The term funeral director in charge means exactly what it says," her father had instructed her years ago. "And remember, you never gain enough experience to become incapable of making a mistake."

The service lasted just under an hour. After the committal service at the cemetery, Blair went straight home. She was chilled to the bone. Her feet were like blocks of ice when she kicked off her black pumps, undressed, and then took a long, hot shower in her spacious new bathroom. Blair wondered sometime if the accommodations she had made since learning about Brandi's battle with OCD were actually perpetuating the disorder. Maybe she should steal a few minutes of Brandi's hour with Dr. Westinghouse this afternoon and seek a bit of reassurance.

No, she told herself, knowing exactly what the psychiatrist would say. "Blair, trust yourself. You are Brandi's mother. You instinctively know what's best for your child."

Warmed by the shower and dressed in wool slacks and a turtleneck, Blair glanced at the clock on her nightstand, and then sank into a chair by the window. With Nixon curled beside her, she placed a call to her sister.

Charlotte's voice was little more than a whisper. "Hold on a minute. I need to step into the hall." Seconds later, she explained that Allison was napping. "I was just going to call you." Charlotte sniffed, as if she had been crying. "Her oncologist came by after I talked to you earlier. He said it was just a precaution, but he did a bone marrow biopsy this afternoon."

Blair groaned. The test involved needle aspiration of bone marrow from Alli's hip. She had endured the procedure so many times. "When will we know the results?"

"I'm not sure."

Blair told her sister that she would stay with Alli while Brandi was in session with Dr. Westinghouse. "I'll be there as soon as I can."

An oppressive silence settled over the cabin. Blair closed her eyes. Oh, Alli. You brave little angel. You've been through so much. Please, God. Not again."

When Blair opened her eyes, her gaze fell on Jewell's treasure chest, well within reaching distance. She had not opened it after returning from New Braunfels. But she had read the letter from Lenny's sister, eager to see pictures of Brandi. Picking it up from atop the wooden box, she read the handwritten note again.

Dear Blair:

Words cannot express how deeply I regret the pain my brother and his wife caused you, your daughter, and all the other people who love Brandi. Jewell's actions were heartless, selfish, and cruel. Lenny's were cowardly and unscrupulous.

I have only one child, my daughter Eden, who is twenty-one now. I cannot imagine the agony of losing her at any point in my life. My heart aches for you.

Lenny told me how desperately you want pictures of Brandi. He is earnestly trying to locate Jewell's album. Until then, I want you to have the enclosed pictures.

I so seldom saw Lenny and Jewell that Brandi appeared in only three family photos. Now I understand why. I regret the somber setting in two of them, and the fact that each includes Lenny and Jewell. Perhaps you can have the snapshots professionally altered. The images of Brandi, I am sure, will be precious to you.

Sincerely,

Arlene Stegall

The letter touched Blair, but nothing compared to the snapshots. One had been taken at a graveside funeral service. Lenny looked forlorn in his dark suit, and Jewell quite thin in her loose-fitting black dress. Brandi stood in front of them. Jewell's hand rested on her shoulder. It was summer and Brandi's bangs were stuck to her forehead. One strap of her sun dress had slipped off the shoulder. Lenny, at the instant the photo had been snapped, was reaching down to right it. Years ago, Arlene had written in ink on the back of the snapshot: *Lenny, Jewell, and April at Mama's funeral.* The date indicated that Brandi had been eight years old.

The second snapshot had been taken on the same day outside a church fellowship hall. According to the description, the women of the church had served the family lunch after the burial. In the photo, the group formed a semi-circle. Jewell stood with her shoulders slumped and, again, her thin hand resting on Brandi's shoulder. Brandi was looking down at a flower in her hand. Eden, according to the notation, stood between and slightly in front of her parents. Arlene's letter indicated that Eden was twenty-one now. Based on the picture's date, she would have been about fifteen. The girl's hair was as straight as broom straw and similar in color. She wore black, and far too much makeup for a teen. The expression in her heavily made-up eyes was decidedly defiant.

The third picture had been taken in front of Lenny and Jewell's tiny house in Virginia Beach. Arlene had written: *Lenny and Jewell, Arlene and Herb, Eden and April.* The date indicated that Brandi would have been eleven. The two girls were sitting on the front porch steps with the four adults standing behind them. Eden—head cocked, small provocative smile, thin legs extended, ankles neatly crossed—could have been a hooker propositioning the photographer. Brandi, dressed in shorts and a knit top, her feet bare, seemed to have studied the girl's pose and attempted to duplicate it.

"Dear, God," Blair whispered, studying Eden Stegall's face. What influence would this girl have had on Brandi had Jewell Bond not died when she did? Where would Brandi be now had Lenny not wanted to be rid of her?

Blair set the letter and the photos on the chairside table, and then removed the lid from an empty cardboard box. She would transfer the contents of Jewell's treasure chest into the box. When the time was right, she would offer the empty chest to Brandi. She had referred to the chest as the only nice gift Lenny had ever given Jewell. In truth, Blair hoped Brandi would not want the chest, that she would tell Blair to give it back to Lenny or throw it in the trash.

Reluctantly, Blair lifted Jewell Bond's treasure chest onto her lap. The wooden box was darkly stained and heavily carved, its Mexican origin obvious. The strap-hinges were hammered metal and painted black. What had Jewell Bond seen fit to keep?

Blair drew in a shaky breath, and then lifted the lid. Instantly, one hand flew to her lips. She pressed her fingers to them to stop their quivering, as she gazed down at a plaster plaque atop the chest's contents.

"It's Brandi's handprint." Instinctively, Blair aligned her hand with the imprint, heel to heel. The tips of Brandi's fingers reached only to Blair's second knuckle. She cupped her hand, worked her fingertips into the mold, and left it there. Pressure built in her eyes. "Brandi made this," she whispered. "This is her little handprint."

With her index finger, Blair traced the outline of Brandi's hand, trying to picture her child pressing her little hand into firm white plaster, holding it steady while her teacher, not Jewell, pressed each finger, assuring an even imprint. Probably with a toothpick, the teacher had helped her student scratch her name in the plaster. *April. Age 6.* Had the blue painted plaque been a Mother's Day gift? Blair wondered. Or maybe a Christmas present?

"It doesn't matter." She held the cold, stiff object to her chest. "This gift was meant for Brandi's mother. This was meant for me."

Carefully, Blair laid the plaque next to the photos and the letter from Arlene Stegall. Balancing the open chest on her lap, she removed a manila envelope marked *Report Cards*. She stared at Jewell Bond's handwriting, aware of a vague scent of perfume. The letters slanted left. Some were cursive, some block. The words angled upward on the envelope front. This was the handwriting of a sociopath, a child abductor, a kidnapper who saved report cards.

Blair removed the stack from the envelope. The cards were bound with a thick, red rubber band. "April Bond," she read aloud. "Kindergarten. Teacher: Francis Gee.'" She opened the card, scanning in seconds the skills assessment. E's and a smattering of S's. The teacher's remarks were of supreme interest. "April is adjusting well to kindergarten. She gets along well with others but prefers solitary play. She follows directions well, keeps her workspace tidy, and is eager to please." Similar comments appeared for other reporting periods. The final one contained the teacher's conclusion. "April has enjoyed a successful year. She excels in all skills areas and reads at the second-grade level. She continues to be quiet and shy. Academically and socially, April is ready for first grade."

The next two report cards reflected continued academic progress, but a comment made by her second-grade teacher caught Blair's eye. "Despite her excessive tardiness and high rate of absenteeism, April continues to be an above average student." Blair closed the card, images instantly taking shape in her mind. Her sick child, home alone, Jewell at work. Brandi arriving late for school, scolded in front of the class by her teacher. Brandi presenting a letter from Jewell, a feeble excuse for yet another missed day.

Blair felt herself getting upset. She could not read anymore, not tonight. Resolved, she returned the report cards to the envelope, and then dropped them in the cardboard box. She was lowering the lid of the chest when she noticed a small box wedged in the corner. The clear plastic lid protected a pair of black leather shoes. Unable to resist, Blair tugged the box free and removed the dented lid. The tops of the shoes, size three, were scuffed and nicked. The soles were worn, but in acceptable condition. One strap was buckled, the other dangled free.

Instinctively, Blair set the shoe on the chair arm, and then attempted to work the frayed end of the strap through the buckle. Her fingers trembled so badly that she gave up and thrust the shoes back into the box.

"Damn you, Jewell Bond." Putting the shoebox in the carton with the report cards, she wiped her stinging eyes. "Eleven years. Damn you."

Again, Blair started to close the chest. She would finish this process tomorrow. But this time, words on a worn envelope caught her eye. *Birth Certificate.* Stunned, she removed the document and read it.

"Lies," she said through gritted teeth. "Every word on it." She folded the fake document and forced it back into the envelope. How many times had Jewell Bond presented that birth certificate, and to how many people? Had no one been suspicious? Someone somewhere must have wondered how people like Lenny and Jewell Bond could have adopted a child.

Blair dropped the envelope into the cardboard box with the report cards and the shoes, and then slammed the lid of the chest. Trembling, she bent forward, set the chest on the floor, and shoved it away with her foot. She never should have opened the thing, not when she was here alone.

Crying angry, bitter tears, Blair picked up the plaster plaque, feeling a paper clip hook protruding from the back. Brandi had made it for Jewell. Would she remember giving it to her? What had Jewell said? *Oh, April, thank you so much. I will treasure this forever.* What would Brandi think now when she saw it?

Blair pushed away the thoughts, and then turned out the lamp. Sitting in the darkened room, she nestled her fingertips into the impression on the plaque and left them there.

♦ ♦ ♦

BRANDI NEVER HAD to worry about Dr. Westinghouse running behind schedule like Alli's doctors did. The door marked *Private* always opened precisely on the hour. The same crooked smile said he was glad to see her. But Brandi thought the way the short, wiry man routinely raised his dark eyebrows made him look surprised to find her sitting where she always sat—in the comfortable, blue chair by the window overlooking Lady Bird Lake.

Like the therapist she and her mom had seen, Dr. Westinghouse referred to a session as an hour. His session, too, only lasted fifty minutes. Brandi figured the ten-minute window was meant to let one patient get out the door before the next one arrived. That way, the patients wouldn't each be wondering what kind of mental problem the other was being treated for.

As Brandi had expected when Dr. Westinghouse sat opposite her, he asked how things were going at home. "Terrific," she answered.

"And at school?"

"Couldn't be better." She told him about the caricature and the school assembly. She could tell by his crooked smile that he thought the gift was as awesome as she did. "Of course, keeping my chin up got a little harder when Wilson Rule's book hit the stores." Suddenly curious, Brandi said, "Have you read it?"

"I bought a copy, but, no, I haven't read it. Would you mind?"

"It's okay. There are pictures of me in it. That rotten man refused to tell my dad where he got them, even when Dad threatened to sue him. Mom thinks Wilson Rule bought them from Lenny. She even went to San Antonio to let Lenny have it. I asked to go with her, but Mom wouldn't let me."

"Did she give you a reason?"

Brandi nodded. "She said that Lenny would love to see me, but she wasn't going to give him the pleasure."

Sitting as he always did with his right ankle resting on his left leg, the doctor wrote something on the notepad propped against his knee. Then he dipped his chin and simultaneously raised a single index finger. "One-word answer, Brandi. How did that cause you to feel when your mom said she wouldn't give Lenny the pleasure of seeing you?"

Brandi gazed out the window. Giving Dr. Westinghouse a one-word answer always required extra thought, but she had gotten much better at it. The trick was to recreate the event in her mind, and then to focus on the way she had felt inside, more so than on the words anyone had said.

Deliberately, she pictured sitting on the couch with her mom, eating popcorn and drinking a Diet Coke. She pictured her own face and remembered smiling. *Lenny Bond would no doubt love to see you, and I'm not going to give him the pleasure.*

"Treasured," Brandi answered. "I felt treasured." Knowing she would be asked to expand on the thought, she did so without prodding. "It's weird, Dr. Westinghouse. Knowing everything Mom knows about Lenny—what a dope and a jerk he can be—

my mom still believes that he cares about me. It's like Mom decided that the worst punishment she could dish out was not letting Lenny see me. *Me.*"

"I can see why that would cause you to feel treasured."

"Of course, there was another reason she wouldn't let me go. Mom said she didn't want a witness if she had to shoot Lenny on the spot." Dr. Westinghouse burst into laughter. "But as far as I know, she left him standing."

Still chuckling, Westinghouse jotted words on his notepad. "Talk to me about Allison."

"She's in the hospital again. I spent the night with her."

"Tell me what that was like for you."

"Not horrible. I only disinfected the room once." She didn't tell the doctor that she had swiped a little stack of masks from a supply closet and had worn one to bed. She had taken it off, though, when she started getting sleepy. She would have died of embarrassment if a nurse had caught her sleeping in a mask, or worse yet, her Uncle Butler.

While Dr. Westinghouse jotted notes, Brandi checked her watch. Her hour was half over. She had planned to tell him that she was going to Washington this weekend, but she was running out of time to bring up the most important matter of all. "Dr. Westinghouse, I think I might be ready to try that torture therapy."

The doctor laughed again. "I prefer exposure therapy, but then I'm not the one with OCD. Tell me what you have in mind."

"The funeral home. I think I'm ready to go inside."

"The funeral home. Any particular reason?"

"Definitely," Brandi answered truthfully, a half-truth close behind. "The funeral home is important to my mom, but I've never set foot inside the door."

The complete truth was that she had to find the powerful soap her mom used to bathe the dead people. Alli might need her to spend another night in the hospital.

CHAPTER 24

HOUSTON, TEXAS

Taylor set the brakes on Hannah's wheelchair, and then helped her out of his truck. She grasped his hand when he reached to steady her. The gesture was welcomed. Sometimes Hannah pushed his hand away when he tried to help. Whether or not she meant it to be, Taylor always took the gesture as a rejection.

Ivan waited in the corral, holding Castaño's reins in hand. Hannah had phoned ahead and asked the man to saddle her horse. Taylor had been shocked to hear Hannah say that she wanted to ride today. "Why today?" All she had said was, "Why not?"

Next week, Hannah would consult with a specialist about a prosthesis. "In case you don't know, Taylor," Hannah had joked with only a hint of sarcasm, "a prosthesis is a fake foot." The amputation wound was still healing, but her parents were encouraging Hannah to begin the learning process.

Taylor had done his best to encourage Hannah. He was guardedly confident that he had succeeded. Hannah seemed to be coming out of her withdrawal, despite having learned that the police still had not arrested Kyla Phelps or Rylie Thorp. Taylor's mom had said that Hannah's extreme moods were to be expected, that she was going through stages of grief. "That precious girl lost more than her foot that night, son. She lost her sense of security."

His mom had not mentioned the website again or asked if he had a minute to talk. Taylor liked that about her. Adam's mom was just the opposite. Taylor guessed that she was attempting to be an involved parent, but sometimes she crossed the line.

That morning, Taylor had found another index card on the table. His mom had left it there before heading off to her shift at H-E-B. *Jesus said, Come to me, all you who are weary and burdened, and I will give you rest.* His mom had been leaving Bible verses for him for years. She didn't do it every day, so Taylor was always surprised when he found one. All the cards, every single one, were in a shoe box in his closet.

I will give you rest. Taylor reflected on the Bible verse. I don't deserve rest, he decided. Not until Kyla Phelps and Rylie Thorp are behind bars.

Castaño's ears pricked when Hannah called his name. Taylor positioned her chair inside the corral gate, but he was at a loss as to what to do next. For the first time in weeks, Hannah was going to ride Cass. Taylor's apprehension ticked up. The best course, he decided, was to let Hannah take the lead. She soon did just that.

"Ivan, lead Cass over here, please." She looked up at Taylor with exaggerated impatience. "Are you going to help me out of this thing or not?"

Grinning apprehensively, Taylor stood to Hannah's right. As was their routine, he leaned forward as she moved to the front edge of the seat, and then looped her right arm around his neck. Rising easily, she balanced on her left foot, letting her arm slip to Taylor's waist. With her free hand, she nudged the dangling left stirrup and said, "Talk about luck. At least the car tires crushed my right foot. It could have been my left."

Taylor tried to force a chuckle, but he couldn't. There was nothing funny about what happened that night. That maniac, Kyla Phelps, could have killed Hannah.

Yesterday, Taylor had sent Ted Bellinger the video of the man in the camo jacket leaving Kyla's apartment. The detective had agreed that the man was Rylie Thorp, but then he had given Taylor a warning. "You need to step back, son. Rylie Thorp is a thug, and he is dangerous. You have to let us handle this." Taylor had held back saying, "Kyla Phelps is dangerous too. She pulled a gun on me. She ran over Hannah. But nothing will stop me from tracking her down."

For weeks, Rylie Thorp and Kyla Phelps had been walking around completely free. "But not for long," Taylor muttered. "Not for long."

"Not for long?" Hannah repeated, teasingly. "If I manage to get on this horse's back, I may never get off again."

Taylor scrambled to gather himself. He hadn't realized that he'd spoken out loud. How could that happen? His mom had said he hadn't been himself lately, and she was right. All he could think about was finding Kyla Phelps. Focusing on anything else was impossible.

Hannah took the reins from Ivan, and then crisscrossed them on the horse's neck, just in front of the saddle horn. "Okay, Taylor. I think I'm ready. Stand behind me. Put your hands on my waist. Give me a big boost when I tell you."

Taylor did as Hannah asked, grasping her narrow waist with both hands. She extended her left arm, reaching for the saddle horn. Losing her balance momentarily, she fell back against him. Taylor leaned into her. "I've got you. You're okay."

"Don't let me fall," she pleaded, her voice a whisper.

"I won't," he whispered back, tightening his grip on her waist. "Just say when."

"Count of three." Hannah stroked Castaño's thick neck, reached up, and grasped the saddle horn. She took three preparatory hops and another anxious breath. "One. Two. Three."

Timing their movements perfectly, Taylor lifted as Hannah pushed off the ground. Instinctively, she flung her right leg up and over, the bottom of her jeans leg bending when it grazed the cantle. Grasping her left ankle, Taylor guided the toe of her boot into the left stirrup.

With breathless ease and grace, Hannah settled into the saddle seat. "We did it." Smiling for the first time in weeks, she patted Castaño's neck loudly and lovingly. "You're a good man, Cass. Good job."

Hannah picked up the reins in one hand, and then distributed her weight evenly in the saddle seat. Responding to a barely discernable flick of the leather rein, Castaño turned sharply away from the fence, and then pranced toward the center of the corral. The empty right stirrup flapped freely against his side.

With tears stinging his eyes, Taylor watched nervously at first, but then began to relax. Hannah was an amazing athlete. She was a champion barrel racer. "You can do this, babe."

Taylor flinched when his cell phone rang. *Chirp.* The ringtone he had assigned to Ben. He checked the ID and answered eagerly. "Hi, Ben. It's Taylor. How are you doing, big guy?"

"Taylor? Umm … I'm calling Mac."

Realizing his mistake, Taylor recovered quickly. "Oh, it's me, Ben. My good friends call me Mac. Do you have some news for me?"

"She called again," the boy said excitedly. "Kyla. She called my dad just now."

Taylor's pulse quickened. "What did you hear, Ben? What were they talking about?"

"Kyla wants some stuff out of her apartment. Dad said it was no problem, and then he asked if his key still works."

Taylor processed the information, watching uneasily when Hannah nudged Cass to a trot. "Doesn't sound like Kyla plans to come home anytime soon, does it, Ben?"

"I hope not. I hate Kyla."

"I do too."

"I hope she goes to jail."

Taylor felt a twinge of guilt. "Listen, Ben. You've done so much to help me, but maybe you've done enough. I feel bad asking you to keep secrets from your dad. If you want to call off the operation, I'll understand."

"No," the boy said forcefully. "We have to complete our mission."

"The police and I can do that, Ben. You don't have to."

"Yes, I do. I want Kyla gone before my mom gets home."

Taylor watched Hannah nudge Cass with her foot, signaling the horse to gallop. Their bodies fell into a graceful rhythm. "Okay, Ben, let's complete our mission." The sight of the empty right stirrup infuriated Taylor. Rylie Thorp and Kyla Phelps deserved to burn in hell.

CHAPTER 25

Live Oak, Texas

Brandi followed her mom down a carpeted hall. She had already taken a quick tour of Lillie's office, and then said hello to Harley Fox. The nice man understood Brandi's reluctance to visit the funeral home. "My sister is sixty years old, and she won't set foot in this place. Says it gives her the creeps."

The two offices across from Lillie's were called arrangement offices. "That's where a funeral director meets with the family to make arrangements," her mom explained. Brandi did not ask, but she figured the families were making arrangements for what to do with the dead person.

At the end of the hall, her mom unlocked a door, stepped inside, and turned on the light. "This is my office," she explained. "It used to be my dad's."

"It's pretty, Mom."

"I haven't changed much of anything. I can't count the hours I sat on the sofa over there talking to Dad or listening to him as he spoke with families on the phone. See the painting over the credenza? Aren't the bluebonnets amazing?" She sat behind her desk, and then ran her fingers along the mahogany surface. "But this is my treasure. Sometimes I still have trouble calling it my desk."

"That was my grandfather's too? That's so special." Brandi touched the wood with her fingertips, gazing about the room. Her stomach churned with nerves. Spotting an open-shelf bookcase full of knickknacks and photographs, she walked across the room and stood in front of it. "I've never seen this picture, Mom. It's really nice."

The family portrait had been taken under a live oak tree. A field of Indian blankets and paintbrushes served as a backdrop. Her grandfather, Millard Emerson, leaned against the tree trunk. His smile was relaxed, crinkling the corners of his eyes. Wisps of salt-and-pepper hair framed his round, kind face. One arm was slipped around his wife's narrow waist. Maryruth Emerson's neatly coiffed hair was ash-blond, her face oval, her features delicate. At the feet of their grandparents, Spencer and Allison sat on a blanket the color of the sky peeking through the oak leaves. Their parents knelt next to them. Brandi's mom stood behind them, wearing jeans and a crisp white shirt.

"I look happy there," she explained, standing elbow to elbow with Brandi. "But even now I remember the empty feeling in the pit of my stomach. I missed you so much."

Brandi wished she could say, "I missed you, too, Mom." Sometimes she thought that she actually *had* missed her parents. Maybe that was why she had felt confused so much of the time living with Lenny and Jewell. Dr. Westinghouse believed that the trauma of her abduction might have caused her to start washing her hands when she felt anxious.

When the tour of the office suite was complete, Brandi followed her mom through the visitation parlor. It was a spacious room in peach and blue, its fireplace a welcoming focal point. The furniture arrangement provided two sitting areas. In one, wing chairs and a sofa were drawn near a raised rock hearth. In the other, a loveseat and chairs were positioned around a polished cherry coffee table. Brandi's mom referred to the rooms on both sides of the parlor as staterooms. "Some people call them reposing rooms. That's where the family and friends pay their respects to the deceased."

"Which room was Mr. Goode in?" Brandi asked.

"Actually, he lay in state in the chapel. That's where the rosary service was held. Come. I'll show you."

In the chapel, her mom turned on a bank of lights. Brandi's eyes widened. "This is beautiful, Mom. It's so big."

"People in Live Oak are so thoughtful about attending funerals. We have a full chapel quite often." She chuckled. "I remember the first time Spencer followed me in here. He was maybe four or five. We were walking up the center aisle and he said, 'Aunt Blair, I didn't know your office had a theater in it.'"

Brandi giggled. "Long aisle. Lots of seating. How was he to know there wasn't a movie screen behind the curtain up there?"

When they returned to the foyer, her mom suggested that they go home. "Eighteen minutes seems quite long enough for your first exposure."

"What's back there?" Brandi pointed to a door on the far side of the visitation parlor. "Why does the sign on the door say *Private.*"

"It's not a public area."

Brandi started in the direction of the door. "But what's back there?"

"Sweetie, I think maybe you've done enough for tonight."

"No, I'm okay. Really, Mom."

The door marked *Private* opened onto a wide hallway. Brandi noticed how her mom remained in the opening, and then pointed to the right. "The room over there has a dual purpose. By day, it's the employee lounge. By night, it's a bedroom for Harley or Max."

Brandi nodded but cringed inside. Surely people didn't eat in that room. She rejected the disgusting possibility and redirected her thoughts. "So what's the other way?"

"Those doors lead to the preparation and dressing rooms. At the end of the hallway, beyond the double doors, is the garage and lots of storage space."

"Do you park there?" What Brandi really wanted to ask was if the special soap was in the preparation or dressing room.

"I park where we did when we got here."

Her mom was turning to leave when Brandi said, "What does that sign say? The yellow and black one on the wide door."

"It's a hazardous chemicals warning sign."

"What kind of hazardous chemicals?"

"As far as the federal government is concerned, everything from WD-40 to embalming supplies."

"Do I smell Clorox?"

"Yes. We do laundry there. Plus, we use Clorox as a disinfectant." Her mom let the door close. "Let's go say goodnight to Harley."

Following her mom to the front of the building, Brandi sharpened her plan. The powerful soap was in the preparation room. It had to be.

Harley Fox was seated at a small desk when they returned to the reception area. "Brandi, what do you think?"

"It's very pretty. Nothing like I thought it would be."

"I think you're very brave to come in and take a look around."

Brandi thanked the nice man, and then looked at her watch. "Mom, I'd like to wander around by myself for a few minutes. Would that be okay?"

"Are you sure?"

"I'm sure. Promise me, though," she added jokingly, "if I'm not back in ten minutes, you'll come looking for me."

In the chapel lobby, Brandi pretended to admire a painting hanging over a credenza, while she kept an eye on her mom and Harley Fox. When they turned their backs, she slipped across the lobby, and then made her way quickly through the empty visitation parlor. She pushed open the door marked *Private,* and then hurried down the hallway to the left. Her pulse quickened when she paused outside the wide door with the yellow and black sign. She was oddly reassured by its warning. Surely, she thought, the chemicals it warned of were as deadly to germs as they were hazardous to people. Nevertheless, she tugged a pair of latex gloves from her back pocket, wiggled her hands into them, and then pulled open the door.

Holding her breath, Brandi stepped inside the shadowy, windowless room, and then tugged a hospital mask from under her sweater. Putting the mask on brought back miserable memories of the COVID outbreak. Even through the barrier, she smelled the strong scent of Clorox bleach. The light switch was next to the door, and she flipped it on. The room, now bright with florescent light, was larger than she had expected. Its walls were pastel blue. The floor was blue and white checked vinyl.

Across the room, upper and lower cabinets ran from wall to wall. So many, she thought. She approached them quickly, eager to begin her search. On the far end of the countertop was a small sink, but where was the special soap?

Brandi's sneakers squeaked on the shiny floor as she walked past a long narrow table on wheels. Another identical table had been pushed against the wall. On the end of the one nearest the counter sat a peculiar rubber block. Brandi stared at it over her snug fitting mask. The block was flat on the ends and concave on the top and bottom. She had no idea what its use might be.

A blow dryer sat on the countertop next to a can of Aqua-Net and a basket with combs, brushes, and clips. Was this where her mom or someone else fixed dead people's hair? Yes, it had to be. And that, she decided, was what the rubber block was used for. If a dead woman was lying on the table, then the block kept her head from wobbling side to side.

Pushing away the image, Brandi opened the top cupboard on the left. She had to hurry. Seconds were ticking by. She scanned the contents of the shelves. Boxes of panties, all white. Men's boxer shorts. Socks, all black. The next cupboard held rolls of cotton and other packages labeled *prep towels*. There were neatly folded sheets and pillowcases, and three baby blankets in pink, blue, yellow.

Growing more and more nervous, Brandi closed the cupboard door and moved quickly to the next. In it she found tweezers, emery boards, clippers, polish remover, cotton balls, and bottle after bottle of nail polish. Hurriedly, she opened the adjacent cupboard. It held all sorts of cosmetics. Brushes, from tiny to large and fluffy, were stored in a plastic tray, along with lip pencils and at least a dozen tubes of lipstick.

Her anxiety increasing with each second, Brandi closed the cupboard door, and then opened the final upper cabinet. The shelves were full—hairspray, curling irons, electric rollers—but no soap. None. Where could it be? She was preparing to search the lower cabinets when she noticed a door across the room. A thought struck. "There must be another sink in there."

Brandi slid the door aside, wincing when it squeaked on the overhead track. Before her loomed another windowless room, dark and silent. She groped for a light switch, found it, and then squinted in the glare. Straight ahead were two long white tables. Each had a trough on all four sides and a single drain hole in the end. A rubber tube extended from the hole and hung over what looked like a urinal. What, she wondered, could the urinals possibly be used for?

Again, Brandi pushed away the thought, almost despairing when she saw all the cupboards on the far wall. There wasn't enough time to search them all, but she had to try. She had to find the powerful soap. She was leaving for Washington this weekend.

Then she saw it. A plastic bottle of pale green liquid next to the sink. Her heart began to pound, and she rushed across the room. The label on the bottle read Safe-T Soap. Trembling, she pulled a plastic bag from under her sweater, and then laid it on the counter. Then with gloved hands, she rinsed the bottle of soap under hot water, dried it with a paper towel, and then stuck it in the plastic bag. The bottle wasn't quite full, but that was all right. Somehow, she would make the powerful soap last through the long weekend facing her at the Willard Hotel.

CHAPTER 26

Austin, Texas

Blair stepped inside an elevator at Children's Hospital and pressed the appropriate button. Minutes later, she was making her way down the hall to her niece's room. She tapped the door gently, and then eased it open. Butler and Charlotte were leaning against one another at the window, their backs to the door. Allison was sleeping, free at last from her IV. Her cheeks looked flushed, and her hair was pressed flat against her head on one side. The index and middle finger of her left hand had found their way into her sagging mouth. It was a habit that surfaced when the precious child was under stress.

Blair whispered hello. Butler and Charlotte turned toward her. Her sister's strained face was damp with tears, her eyes red-rimmed. Butler looked exhausted. His thin face seemed to have aged since yesterday. Without speaking, he left his wife by the window, and then led Blair to the hall.

"The doctor just left. We got some bad news." Butler's lips were tight when he spoke, his voice flat and defeated. "Alli's come out of remission. The leukemia is back."

"No, Butler." Blair moaned in protest. "That can't be. She was taking chemotherapy."

"We've always known it was a possibility, so we're headed back to MD Anderson. We want a second opinion on where to go from here."

The door to Allison's room opened. Charlotte walked into her husband's open arms, and then buried her face in his chest. "My baby. After all she's been through." Butler Harding drew Blair into his embrace. The three huddled in the hall outside Allison's room, releasing silent tears.

Before leaving, Blair slipped back into Alli's room and kissed her warm, moist forehead. How could this be? she agonized, resisting the urge to say, "Why, God?"

Half an hour later, Blair was sitting in her car outside the bank tower where The Headliners Club was located. She was vaguely aware of the muffled voices of pedestrians and the whir of passing cars. The reception for Myles had been underway for more than an hour. Fortunately, Blair had had the presence of mind to tell Brandi to meet her outside. Most of her cosmetics were smeared on the tissue wadded in her pocket.

"Oh, Alli. You precious, helpless little angel." When would Butler and Charlotte tell her that the leukemia was back again? Tonight? Tomorrow? They hadn't decided when Blair left them, but they would leave for Houston as soon as possible. Blair had volunteered to keep Spencer, but Butler had suggested that his son might like to stay with Eldon Sumner. The man was like a grandfather to Spencer. Seventeen-year-old Kenny, Eldon's grandson who lived with him, was like a big brother. Blair would contact Eldon and take care of the details for Spencer's stay.

She would not tell Brandi that Allison had come out of remission until after she returned from Washington. Charlotte had agreed. "Why ruin what's going to be a wonderful trip?" Blair hoped the trip would be a wonderful adventure, but she had her doubts. Neither Myles nor Charmaine understood how unsure of herself Brandi was in unfamiliar settings. They did not know that she needed to be told ahead of time what to expect, even what to say and do in some circumstances. Worst of all, because they had no knowledge of her OCD, they had no idea that stressful situations could plunge Brandi deep into her obsession with germs.

Pressure gathered inside Blair's head and chest. Leukemia with its aggressive cells had crept into Allison's little body again. What treatment would the doctors at MD Anderson recommend now? Why hadn't the chemotherapy kept the disease in check? A brief period of remission was surely a bad sign.

Unable to resist the swelling pressure behind her eyes, Blair crossed her arms on the arc of the steering wheel and hid her face. Tears spilled down her cheeks, dripping onto her pants legs. Quietly, she sobbed over the sound of passing cars and the tap, tap, tap of shoes on the busy city sidewalk.

Her cell phone sounded. The caller was Wanda Lamb. Gathering herself, Blair took the call. "Hi, Wanda. It's Blair."

"I'm glad I caught you, Blair. I got the info you wanted off Anna Mitchell's ID, including her date of birth. I don't believe for a minute it was her driver's license. The girl was nervous as hell when Del was looking at it."

"That's great, Wanda." Blair wiped tears from her face with her fingertips. "Could you text me the information?"

"You bet. And my daughter did a little research on the Internet. I've got a phone number associated with the address too."

"Thank you so much, Wanda, and Georgia too."

"You're welcome, hon. Give my love to Butler and Charlotte. I hear little Allison is in the hospital."

◆　◆　◆

WITH HER EXHAUSTED daughter at last in bed, Blair retrieved Wanda's text message. Anna Mitchell's license indicated that she lived in Houston. Blair measured the risk of calling the number Wanda's daughter had located. It was possible that Wanda was wrong about Anna Mitchell using someone else's ID. If the woman was on the up and up, then Blair needed a cover story in case she answered.

With little effort, she quickly manufactured one. Hazel's birthday was a couple of weeks from now, and Blair was planning a small get-together. If you're in town, she would say to Anna Mitchell, you're welcome to join us.

Where would Alli be two weeks from now? Blair worried. Please, God. Not at the cancer hospital. Please.

Gazing at the text message, Blair considered letting the whole matter drop. What did it matter if Anna Mitchell was using someone else's ID? Maybe she had a perfectly good reason. "Like what?" she muttered. Unable to think of one, she tapped the screen, and then waited anxiously as the call went through. A woman answered right away.

"This is Anna."

"Hi, Anna. It's Blair." Pausing, she waited for a reaction. When none came, she continued. "I'm sorry to intrude on your evening."

"Did you say Blair?"

"Yes. Blair Emerson."

"Do I know you?"

"It would appear not." Blair's stomach knotted. Wanda was right. There was no doubt now. "I don't mean to alarm you, but I suspect that someone is using your identification."

"Oh, no. Who? Where?"

"I live near Austin," Blair explained, "in a small town called Live Oak."

"Never heard of it."

"I'm not surprised. There's a stranger here in town who says her name is Anna Mitchell. Her license indicates that she lives at 1300 Three Oaks Court."

The woman cursed under her breath. "I was afraid of this. A few weeks ago, I left my purse in a restaurant. When I went back to get it, it was gone. I cancelled my credit cards and took other precautions. But now you're telling me someone is using my ID."

"Unfortunately, yes. The woman used it at a local bar."

"Is that the only place?"

"I wouldn't know."

"Of course not. Do you know anything else about her?" Anna Mitchell pressed.

"I don't," Blair answered. "But I would like to. Can you give me a few days before filing a police report? I don't want to scare the woman off before I find out who she is and what she's doing here in Live Oak."

♦ ♦ ♦

WASHINGTON, D.C.

THE POURING RAIN made sightseeing in the nation's capital a trial. The driver Myles Lakeman hired did his best to park the sedan as close as possible to the sights. Finally, Brandi's dad declared the effort a losing battle. "Let's go back to the hotel. You will be back here for another visit before we know it."

At dinner in the hotel that evening, Charmaine attracted approving glances in her elegant black suit, her black and bronze silk blouse. Brandi thought her dad looked handsome too. She had seen him before in the dark blue suit, but the red and blue striped tie was new. "His politician's tie," Charmaine teased when Brandi complimented it.

Thanks to her mom, Brandi felt well-dressed too. Her long wool skirt was Hershey brown, its matching sweater trimmed in brick red. At Dillard's, her mom had said, "This will be perfect with your boots." But when Brandi had tried on the outfit, her mom had teasingly ordered her to put it back. "You look like a high school girl."

Brandi didn't feel like a high school girl, though. She felt like a kid. Every introduction that day had ignited her face. Every question had left her tongue-tied as she struggled to frame just the right response. Every word of encouragement from her dad had piled on layers of expectation. Still, her dad had beamed with each introduction. He had looked happy, almost proud, each time he said, "This is my daughter Brandi."

Now, standing at the door to her hotel room, eager to be alone, Brandi kissed her dad's cheek and hugged Charmaine. "See you in the morning. It's been a great day, despite the rain."

Her cell phone rang minutes after Brandi closed the door. She tugged it from her purse, hoping it was her mom, glad when it was. "Hi, Mom. I've missed you."

Brandi stood next to the bed while they chatted. She was afraid to sit on a comforter that previous guests had sat on and slept under. "It rained like mad here today, Mom, so we didn't get as much sightseeing done as we had hoped. I really wanted to visit the Vietnam Memorial so I could find Frank's cousin's name. I was going to take a close-up picture of it."

"Oh, that would have been wonderful. We texted today. Frank still plans to stay in Montana until his dad's illness … resolves itself."

"I'll get the picture next time." Brandi quickly changed the subject from the prospect of another trip to Washington. "Mom, is Alli out of the hospital?"

"Uh … no, sweetie. The doctors want to keep an eye on her."

"But why?" Brandi pressed. "I thought the infection was going away. Maybe I should call her."

"I don't think so. You never know when Alli might be sleeping. Are you ready for the big day tomorrow?"

"I guess," Brandi answered, noticing how quickly her mom had changed the subject. "Did you know I have to stand in front of everybody, right next to Charmaine during the swearing-in deal?"

"Your dad wants to share the spotlight. He's proud of you."

Brandi already felt the weight of staring eyes, heard the clatter of cameras. "You'd think I was just a normal kid," she muttered.

"What, honey? I didn't understand you."

"Never mind," Brandi answered, oddly resentful that her mom always explained her dad's thinking. "So does Nixon miss me?" she asked, taking her turn at changing the subject.

"More than you can imagine. Poor little guy can't decide whether to look for you out the front window or wait for you in your bedroom. I'll take him with me to the airport tomorrow evening. Speaking of dogs, Brandi, remember how worried Alli was about Waylon Goode's little dog?"

"Yes," Brandi answered. "The Shih Tzu."

"I asked Charlotte if I could speak to Mr. Goode's daughter about a new home for Mitzi."

"Oh, Mom, that's great. Does Alli know?"

"No, I didn't want to get her hopes up, just in case Mitzi already has a new home."

"If Miss Goode says it's okay, when will you give the dog to Alli? I just have to be there to see her face."

"I'll wait until you're home, honey. I promise."

After saying goodbye to her mom, Brandi suddenly felt lonely and anxious. She dreaded the ceremony tomorrow, but more than that, she was worried about Alli. Why was she still in the hospital? Why hadn't the antibiotic worked? She wished she could phone Alli, but her mom was right. Alli slept a lot when she was sick, and she was a bear when she woke up before she was ready.

Again, her thoughts returned to the ceremony. It was supposed to have been held outside, but because of the rain, her dad would be sworn in inside the Senate Chamber. Brandi wished for her mom. She would tell her exactly what to expect, where to stand, what to do.

Brandi knew exactly what to wear, though. A black skirt, a short, red and black plaid jacket, and a red turtleneck sweater. She would wear black tights, her new black boots, and carry the little red leather purse Alli had given her for Christmas. She would wear her silver cross outside the sweater. It was an Easter gift from her mom. Brandi wanted her to see it when she looked at the pictures later.

Her dad had warned her that lots of photographs would be taken. Some would end up in newspapers and online. What he hadn't speculated about, though, was what the articles might say about her—about the long-lost child her kidnappers had named April because that was the month they had snatched her. Adults often said that children of public figures should be off limits, but she held out no hope that reporters would pay attention—not when the kid had been missing for eleven years and hadn't been able to tell the difference between adoptive parents and her very own kidnappers.

Standing at the hotel window, Brandi wondered about Wilson Rule's book. Thousands of people, maybe millions, would read it. *A Stranger's Eyes*. Brandi had read some of the book. The way the man pretended to know what her life had been like made her furious. He even wrote that friends of Lenny and Jewell described how the kidnapped toddler had quickly bonded to the couple and had been raised, by all accounts, in a loving environment, although at times a somewhat unstable one.

"How could anyone know what it was like to live with Lenny Bond?" Brandi grumbled.

Remembering her promise to Dr. Westinghouse, Brandi took out her journal and sat at the desk. The room was quiet. The steady drizzle outside blurred streetlamps and headlights of passing cars and limousines. She recorded bits and pieces about the day's events, and then closed the entry by writing that she was eager to get back home.

With her obligation met, Brandi pulled on latex gloves, and then folded back the bulky duvet. She tugged it off the bed onto a bench at the foot. How long, she wondered, has it been since this thing was washed or dry-cleaned? Weeks, maybe longer?

After setting the security lock on the door, she undressed, hung her clothing carefully, and then stuffed her underwear in a plastic bag she had found in the closet. Finally, she retrieved her suitcase from a closet shelf, and then removed a travel size bottle of Safe-T Soap. The large bottle she had taken from the funeral home preparation room was hidden in her bedroom at home.

In the shower, with the water uncomfortably hot, Brandi stepped into the pulsing stream. Using her thumbnail, she flipped up the spout and squeezed. As the green liquid puddled in her palm, she pictured her mom using this same kind of soap to give dead people baths, or to disinfect her hands after she finished touching them. Bubbles formed and burst, blasting away germs that then slid lifelessly down the sparkling chrome drain.

Tired and sleepy after her shower, Brandi dried off quickly, and then tugged panties up her splotchy red legs and over her narrow hips. When her face appeared through the neck opening in her sleepshirt, she caught her reflection in the steamy mirror. Her wet hair was flat against her head, and her cheeks were beet-red from the hot shower, but Brandi was unconcerned. The redness would be gone by morning. Now, she could get a good night's sleep, knowing that the germs she had picked up in the sedan were dead and gone.

Housekeeping had replenished the supply of bath towels. Eight of them, clean smelling and enormous, were stacked neatly on the metal rack above the toilet. Brandi carried three bath towels and a hand towel into the bedroom. She laid the hand towel on the pillow to protect it from her damp hair, and then unfolded the bath towels atop the crisp white sheets.

With the deadbolt set and her cell phone charging, Brandi folded back the corners of the top two towels, and then turned out the lights. Exhausted and yawning, she slid into bed. Drawing her towel-blanket over her shoulders, she was grateful for its size and thickness. Soon her eyelids grew heavy. Each weary sigh, each shallow breath, brought reassurance. The scent of Safe-T Soap and the laundry's chlorine bleach reminded Brandi that two powerful allies would be standing guard as she slept.

CHAPTER 27

SAN ANTONIO, TEXAS

Lenny Bond was not sure that a railroad tie had a heavy end, but if it did, Jamar always saw to it that Lenny wounded up lifting it. When Dub Black, the crew foreman, had said Lenny would be building a retaining wall, he had pictured himself laying brick, not hoisting and stacking railroad ties from daylight to dark.

"Hey, Bond." Dub Black yelled from midway of the block-long wall. "Have you learned how to use that level yet?"

Lenny bit his tongue. The man had been barking like a junkyard dog all morning. He wished Jamar would put a muzzle on the guy. "Yeah, Dub. I know how to use a level. Somebody need a lesson?"

"Then use it," Dub Black ordered. "Your end of that wall is starting to lean out."

"Yes, sir," Lenny answered with a military snap. He picked up the five-foot-long level, and then placed it horizontally on the top tie.

"Dammit, Lenny." Jamar yanked the tool from his hand, and then pressed it against the front side of the wall. "That's the third time you've done that," he complained, studying the floating bubble. Easing the top of the level away from the wall, he held it steady. "Black's full of crap. This wall is close to perfect." He set the level aside, and then ordered Lenny to grab the end of another tie. "As soon as we get this short piece in place, we'll go get some lunch. Skin Head ought to be here with the forklift by the time we get back."

Lenny adjusted his leather gloves, soiled with sticky black creosote. He leaned over the tie, and then stood upright again. "Did you say forklift?"

"Yep."

"Are you telling me that Dub Black's got a forklift on the way to this job?"

"That's what he said."

"Then why the hell have we been breaking our backs stacking these suckers?"

Jamar took two quick steps toward Lenny, and then grabbed him by the back of the neck. Squeezing, he propelled Lenny toward a cluster of trees next to the newly constructed wall. "How wide is that gap there, huh?"

Grimacing, Lenny pried Jamar's vice-like fingers from his neck. "About four foot, looks like."

Jamar shoved him into the narrow space. "Then tell me how Skin Head is supposed to get a forklift in there, you idiot."

"All right. All right." Lenny slapped brittle leaves out of his hair, backing out of the space. "I wasn't thinking."

"Then keep your mouth shut until you do." Jamar yanked on his leather gloves, and then pointed to the five-foot piece of tie. "Now grab that sucker, and let's get it up on the wall."

Lenny squatted next to the tie, and then worked his gloved fingers under it. Grunting, he lifted the end from the ground, adjusting his grip quickly to avoid dropping it. Jamar grasped the opposite end as if the heavy piece were made of foam. Walking sideways, they shuffled to the wall. On the count of three, the men hoisted the final piece onto the chest-high stack. Lenny bent forward at the waist, rubbing his lower back, and moaning.

Jamar pulled off his leather gloves, and then slapped Lenny on the head with them. "Come on, Atlas. Let's go get some lunch."

The convenience store was a block away. To Lenny, the walk seemed like a mile. He was dead tired. He hadn't been sleeping more than a few hours a night. Without fail, he went to bed worrying that pictures of Brandi would turn up somewhere, and that he would get the blame.

Early that morning, he had had the worst nightmare of his life. He dreamed that he had been coerced into signing a false confession, admitting to selling pictures of Brandi, and then lying to a United States senator. In the courtroom, Lenny had noticed right away that the black-robed judge had an alarming resemblance to Hortense Holder, the director of human resources at Worsham Services. Glaring down at Lenny from her bench, the green-eyed woman had imposed the death penalty. Dreaming that he was being gassed to death, Lenny had waked himself, coughing and choking. The hissing sound he heard in his sleep had been Jamar spraying deodorant under his arms.

In the convenience store, Lenny and Jamar bought ham and cheese sandwiches, a large bag of Fritos, and a liter of Pepsi to share. For the third day in a row, Lenny complained to the clerk about having to pay for two cups of ice. They ate their lunch on a bus stop bench. Lenny brought up the subject of Sylvia Reyes. She hadn't been at home when Lenny, Pete, and Jamar had shown up at her house. "I wonder why she ain't answering the phone now."

Jamar answered over the crunch of Fritos. "She knows we're on to her."

"So you don't think she's hiding from Pete?" Lenny asked, knowing he risked irritating Jamar, but needing reassurance. "I mean, the woman owes him fifteen hundred dollars."

"We've been over this a dozen times." Jamar refilled his paper cup with Pepsi. "You think she's avoiding Pete. I think she's avoiding me. You saw the look on her face when I told her that if that album didn't turn up, that I was gonna launch a little search of my own."

Jamar was right. If the woman had decided to disappear, she had done it to avoid Jamar, not Pete. "Well, I guess the most I can hope for is that Arlene's letter scored some points with Blair. She stuck some pictures in there too. Of course, they had me and Jewell in them. I guess Blair can always take some scissors and whack us out."

Lenny had upset his sister the last time they spoke. He had been explaining to her that the album had disappeared while he was in prison. Arlene had snapped at him. "Surely you don't think Herb or I went through your things. Or Eden." Lenny had apologized, assuring her that he thought no such thing. But at this point, Lenny didn't know what to think, and he was running low on options.

After lunch, Lenny and Jamar returned to the store for a Snickers and an Almond Joy. Lenny laid both candy bars on the counter, paid for his, and then waited for Jamar to do the same. When Jamar picked up a tabloid newspaper, rather than coming to the counter, Lenny paid for his friend's Almond Joy, and then headed for the door. "You ready, man? I got your candy right here."

Jamar did not look up but continued to read the front page of the tabloid. "Hey, Bond. Come here. Take a look at this."

Joining Jamar at a makeshift newsstand, Lenny stuck the Almond Joy in his friend's pocket. "What you got there?"

While Jamar thumbed through the tabloid, Lenny peeled back the wrapper of the Snickers bar, and then bit off the end. When Jamar found the page he was looking for, he stopped dead still, and said, "What the hell is this?"

Lenny felt the color drain from his face. *A picture. Another damn picture.* He tried to swallow, but the sticky clump of candy was lodged in his throat.

CHAPTER 28

LIVE OAK, TEXAS

Blair sat on the edge of Allison's bed, and then drew her niece between her knees. Charlotte was packing some last-minute items. Butler was delivering Spencer to Eldon Sumner's home. Blair was grateful to have a few minutes alone with Allison before the three of them left for Houston. The child looked pale, and her eyes had lost their mischievous spark. Even her ponytail seemed to have lost its bounce . The sight of her caused Blair's stomach to tense, trapping inside it a flutter of sadness and dread.

She spoke over what felt like a rock-hard pill lodged in her throat. "Brandi will be so sad that she didn't get to say goodbye to you, sweetie. If the doctor wants you to stay in Houston a while, I promise we'll come for a visit. And you know Brandi. She'll phone you every day."

"Maybe I won't be there long."

Blair drew the child closer. "I'm so sorry you have to leave, precious. Your Aunt Blair loves you so much."

Allison's quivering lower lip was chapped from days of high fever. Her solemn face contorted when she burst into tears. "Promise that Brandi can come see me."

"I promise, Alli." Blair hugged the child tightly. "We love you so much. I'm so sorry that you're having to go through this again."

"I tried not to."

"I know you did." Blair's eyes burned with persistent tears. She released Allison from her embrace, and then cupped the child's face in her hands. "This is not your fault, sweetie. You did everything right, everything you could, everything your doctor told you to do."

"I didn't tell Mommy about the bruise," she cried.

The impact of the simple statement stabbed Blair's heart. "Alli, the leukemia came back before the bruise, not *because of* the bruise. Do you understand that?" The child nodded uncertainly. "The bruise was actually a good thing. That was your body's way of warning you that the leukemia cells were acting up again."

"Maybe the bruise would have gone away."

Blair was not sure where Alli's logic was taking her, but she did not get the chance to ask. Butler had returned from Eldon's. He and Charlotte were standing at the bedroom door, leaning against each other. Their patient expressions told Blair to take her time, but delaying would only make the parting harder on Allison.

Foregoing a tempting pep talk, Blair kissed Allison's feverish cheeks, and then locked the child's arms around her neck. "You're not too big for Aunt Blair to carry you, are you?" Lifting Alli as she stood, Blair said, "Hold on tight."

Alli clamped her legs around Blair's waist, legs that were far too long for the child who in Blair's mind should still be in kindergarten. Looping one arm under Alli's bottom, she wrapped the other around her waist, and held her tight. "The bruise wouldn't have gone away if you had kept it a secret. You know that, don't you?"

"Uh-huh." The child nodded weakly. "That's why I let Brandi see it. I knew she would tell you."

In the driveway, Blair forced herself to let go of Alli, to help her into the back seat where pillows awaited her. It was all so unfair, so sudden, and so uncertain. "We'll see you soon, angel." She closed the door, hugged Butler and Charlotte, and then waved a kiss to Allison. The precious child caught it through the closed window, and then pressed it to her cheek.

Blair fought tears as she watched the car roll down the driveway. The struggle continued as she locked the house where she and Charlotte had grown up, and then headed to the cabin. She had just passed the entrance to Seven Oaks, the mobile home park where Hazel lived, when she spotted a woman walking toward her on Southworth Road. As she neared, Blair realized it was Anna Mitchell — or the woman claiming to be Anna. Who was she really? A legitimate reporter, if such a thing still existed? Someone wanting to amplify her social media presence with a few posts? A pathetic young woman trying to claim her ten minutes of fame at Brandi's expense?

Blair pulled the Range Rover to a stop, and then lowered the window. The woman smiled as she approached the vehicle. "Hi, Anna. Enjoying your walk?"

"It's a little nippy, but yes. I was getting a bit of cabin fever."

With the woman standing close, Blair got a clear look at her eyes. She was without doubt wearing contact lenses. Her eyes were an unnatural color of blue, and her hair was definitely dyed. Why would the woman disguise her appearance unless she thought someone in Live Oak might recognize her? Blair certainly didn't recognize her.

"Hazel told me that Alli and her family are on their way to MD Anderson."

"They just left." When the woman placed her left hand on the edge of the car window, the loose band on her ring finger slipped toward her knuckle, revealing a tattoo of some kind. Realizing Blair was looking at it, she lowered her hand, and then tucked it in her coat pocket. Why was she hiding a finger tattoo? Blair wondered. That was odd.

"I understand that Brandi returns from her trip to D. C. today," she commented. "I hope she had a wonderful time. I watched the swearing-in ceremony online. Brandi's outfit was adorable. How exciting for her."

Hoping to catch the woman in a lie, Blair changed the subject. "What's the status with the Minor home? Do you think it would be a good fit for your mother?"

"Oh, yes. She would love it. I've told the realtor that Mom will be making an offer soon." The woman stepped away from the car. "I'll let you get on home, Blair. Say hi to Brandi for me."

At the cabin, Hazel's VW was parked in the driveway. Blair had expected that she would be gone by now. Entering through the back door, she immediately disarmed the security system. Nixon was finishing his afternoon meal. Hazel was digging around in her oversized purse.

"Hi, Blair. I can't seem to find my keys." She released a long, frustrated sigh. "I'm so worried about Alli, and I don't like Brandi being so far from home."

"I understand." Blair hugged the dear woman firmly. "I don't say this often enough, Hazel, but you are a blessing. In all our lives. Knowing that I can rely on you and trust you is such a comfort."

"Oh, thank you, Blair." Hazel returned the hug. "I was just saying to Anna that you and Brandi are my family. I love you both."

Blair patted the woman's shoulder, and then stepped back. "Anna was here?"

"A little while ago, yes."

"I just saw her on Southworth Road. We spoke a minute, but she didn't mention being here at the house. Did she come inside?"

"Yes," Hazel answered, still flustered. "She was out taking a walk, and she saw my car."

Blair asked Hazel to sit for a minute. "I need to tell you something in confidence. It's about Anna Mitchell. That's not her real name, Hazel."

"Not her real name? What do you mean?"

"She's using someone else's ID." Blair told Hazel about her conversation with the real Anna Mitchell living in Houston. "And I think the imposter Anna is trying to change her appearance, although I have no idea why. She obviously colors her hair, and she wears blue contacts. I'm concerned that she might be spying on Brandi."

"Oh, no, Blair. Surely not. But Wilson Rule's book has put the spotlight on Brandi, that's for sure." Hazel pursed her lips, looking angry and resentful.

"I'm worried that this woman, whoever she is, might be trying to capitalize on it somehow."

Hazel groused. "Well, damn that girl."

Blair chuckled. "My thoughts exactly."

"Well, she won't be getting any more information out of me. I'm not saying another word to her."

"Actually, Hazel, I'd like for you to continue your relationship as usual," Blair confessed. "I want to find out who the girl is, so let's not do anything that might cause her to put her guard up."

"I can do that, if that's what you want."

"But don't let her come in the cabin again."

"Of course not. I apologize for that."

"None needed." Blair patted Hazel's arm, and then stood. "I'll let you head on home."

Hazel located her car keys in the pocket of her coat, and then asked if Brandi knew that Anna Mitchell was an imposter. Blair grinned. "She's been suspicious of the woman since the day she was here eating your oatmeal cookies."

With Hazel gone and Nixon finished with his meal, Blair picked up the dog and cuddled him on the sofa. The comforting act triggered a trickle of relentless tears. Alli wanted a dog so badly, but Blair had told her that her mom had too much on her plate. "But I've been in remission for months," Alli had argued. "Surely Mom's had time to scrape some things off her plate in all that time."

Blair could not imagine a home without a dog or a pet of some kind. She had mentioned Waylon Goode's Shih Tzu to Charlotte, telling her how concerned Alli had been for the dog's well-being. Tomorrow, with Charlotte's reluctant permission, Blair would stop by to see Martha Goode and ask about her plans for Mitzi. The little dog might just give Allison one more reason to face the dreadful days ahead of her.

♦　♦　♦

BRANDI HAD GOTTEN good, she thought, at detecting when something was bothering her mom. She acted a little too cheerful or a little spacey. But on the drive from the Austin airport to Live Oak, she handled the Range Rover as if she had just gotten her license and had to concentrate on what she was doing.

Holding Nixon in her lap, Brandi asked about Alli and was relieved to find out that she had been released from the hospital. When her mom said she would fill her in on the details later, Brandi let the subject drop, and then asked if she had heard anything more from Lenny. "Has he found Jewell's album?"

"Not yet, so he says."

Stroking Nixon's back, she mimicked Lenny's voice. "I can't find that album to save my life, Blair, but you gotta believe me when I tell you, I didn't sell them pictures to Wilson Rule."

Her mom chuckled. "You sound just like him."

"Have you looked at the things in her treasure chest?"

"I did. They're treasures, all right. Would you have any interest in looking at all that?"

"Maybe," Brandi answered, watching her mom's face for a reaction. She seemed to have relaxed a little, so Brandi broached another subject she had on her mind. "Did you know that Wilson Rule will be on CNN tonight?"

"I hadn't heard that, honey." Her mom tightened her grip on the wheel, changing lanes with excessive caution. "Rule is doing exactly what we knew he would do. He's getting his mug on TV every chance he gets."

At home, Brandi unpacked her suitcase, and then went to the kitchen for a snack. She was cleaning the top of a Diet Coke can when her mom asked her to walk to the mailbox with her. "Okay. But let me call Alli first."

"She's not home, sweetie."

Brandi took a sip of Diet Coke. "Oh, okay. I'll call her later."

"She'll love to hear from you."

Brandi thought it was odd when, instead of putting on her jacket, her mom pulled back a bar stool and sat. "What about the mail?" Brandi asked.

"That can wait."

Brandi leaned against the counter. "Mom, did something happen while I was gone? Is something wrong?"

"We need to talk about Alli."

Brandi listened without speaking as her mom told her that Alli was at MD Anderson. That explained why her mom had seemed upset and distracted. What didn't make sense was why Alli had gone back to MD Anderson because of an infection in her elbow. "I don't understand, Mom. Can't the doctors in Austin cure an infection?"

"It's not just an infection, Brandi. I hate to tell you this, but Alli has come out of remission."

"What do you mean?" Brandi asked, her mind leaping to an impossible conclusion. "Are you saying that Alli has leukemia again?"

Her mom's answer was a weary nod of her head. She had no answers to the litany of questions that followed. How could Alli have leukemia, Brandi agonized, when she was taking her pills? Can the doctors give her a different kind of pill to make her well? What are they going to do? When will we know?

A hard fist of anxiety gripped Brandi's stomach and tightened as the evening crept past. Worry and fear kept her awake well into the night. Alli had leukemia again. Soon, she and her mom would drive to Houston to see her in the hospital. *MD Anderson Cancer Center.* The very thought of being inside that hospital again ignited a hot flame of apprehension. *Germs on every surface. Airborne microorganisms in every breath.* She could down a whole handful of Dr. Westinghouse's pills, and it wouldn't be enough to make her walk through the door of that hospital again.

But I have to, Brandi conceded. Alli needs me.

She had but one hope—that she could sneak into the preparation room at the funeral home again and smuggle out another bottle of Safe-T Soap, maybe even two. Then she would volunteer to spend the night in Alli's room. Just as she had done at Children's Hospital, she would wait until Alli was asleep, and then disinfect the contaminated place from top to bottom.

Despite her troubled thoughts, Brandi was enormously grateful to be in her own germ-free bed and to have Nixon warming her feet under the covers. She used the quiet time to devise her plan.

It was really quite simple. She would phone Dr. Westinghouse to tell him that she was ready to go in the funeral home again. She would sound proud of herself, and he would agree that she should be. Then she would tell her mom that Dr. Westinghouse had given her the go-ahead. Once inside the funeral home, she would joke with Harley Fox again. Her mom seemed to like that. She would tell him she had brought a slice of bread, so that she could leave a crumb trail behind as she explored the funeral home alone. Then she would sneak into the preparation room again.

Brandi's eyelids grew heavy, and then closed. She lay perfectly still, listening to Nixon's soft snoring. As if by gravitational pull, her troubled thoughts returned to her plan. She pictured the pale blue walls and floor, the two sparkling white tables pushed close to the urinals, and on the far wall, a stainless-steel sink with closed cupboards above and below—cupboards stocked with bottle after bottle of powerful, germ-killing chemicals.

CHAPTER 29

HOUSTON, TEXAS

The sun was rising. Taylor McFadden had been parked by the laundry room at Wood Shadows Apartments for half an hour. When he first arrived, he had slipped up the stairs to look for the thin scrap of folded cardboard Rylie Thorp had wedged between the weather stripping and the edge of Kyla's door. It had still been there. No one had entered her apartment, including Ben's dad. A few days ago, Perry Walters had promised his lover to retrieve something from her apartment. Late last night, Ben had found out what Kyla Phelps needed and when she needed it.

The determined little boy had found a voicemail from Kyla on his dad's cell. "She needs some clothes from her apartment," Ben had said, his tone victorious. "And some money she hides in a cereal box." Taylor's first thought was to ask Ben if he knew when and where Kyla and his dad were meeting, but he hated to put more pressure on the little boy. It seemed so wrong. But it had turned out to be unnecessary.

"Kyla said to meet her at the … the … drive, something like that."

"The Dive?"

"Yeah. Maybe. I think so."

"Did she say when?"

"Tomorrow night. Nine o'clock. Then she made a kissy sound." Ben's triumphant tone had changed to disgust. "I hate Kyla."

"I hate her too." Taylor had thanked the little boy again. "Your part of the mission is over now. Okay, Ben? I've got it from here."

Weighing his options, Taylor had considered calling Ted Bellinger, telling him when and where they could arrest Kyla Phelps. But Taylor had shot down that option. He would confront Kyla Phelps himself. He would point a gun at her, and then watch fear paralyze her face. He would slam her to the ground, and then listen to her scream in panic like Hannah had.

The hunger to confront Kyla, to get it all over with, gnawed in Taylor's gut. He hoped to catch her alone somewhere, but if he had to deal with her in public, then he would. All the pain Kyla had caused Hannah would be worth the price, whatever it was.

Taylor checked his watch again. Seven o'clock. He took another drink of Red Bull, and then a deep, ragged breath. Taut with tension, he clenched the can so hard that it bent when the door to the Walters's apartment opened. Perry Walters, empty handed, crossed the second-floor landing. Without pause, the man unlocked the door to Kyla's apartment and went inside.

"This is it," Taylor murmured, his heart pounding. "Tonight's the night." Tossing aside the crumpled can, he picked up his cell and tapped a ready number. "It's me, Ben."

"My dad just left, Mac. Just this minute."

"I saw him. He's in Kyla's apartment." A wave of guilt washed over Taylor. "Listen to me, Ben. You can stand down now, okay? I've got this."

"Okay, Mac. But promise me. You'll make sure that sneaky, lying Kyla goes to jail."

"You have my word."

"Mac, is my dad going to be in trouble?"

The question caught Taylor off guard. He was trying to decide what to say when the door to Kyla's apartment opened. Perry Walters emerged, carrying a canvas tote. Taylor flinched. The man was headed back to his apartment. "Hang up, Ben. Quick."

♦ ♦ ♦

PARKED OUTSIDE Brake Check, Taylor cat napped inside his truck while Perry Walters put in his eight-hour shift. He and Kyla had not met at The Dive last night as planned. Ben's intelligence gathering had momentarily failed him. He had phoned the boy earlier. "It's okay, Ben. We're a great team. I couldn't have done without you."

Kyla's canvas tote was still in the Walters's apartment. Taylor had considered asking Ben to look inside it, but he couldn't risk it. What if Kyla's gun was in the bag? No. The little boy had done enough. More than enough. Now, Taylor would not let Perry Walters out of his sight until he met up with Kyla Phelps again.

At six o'clock, Walters left Brake Check, got into his coupe, and returned home, unaware that he was being followed. Twenty minutes later, he reappeared from his apartment, this time carrying the tote.

"This is it. The man's going to lead me right to her." Taylor pulled in behind the coupe when Perry Walters left Wood Shadows, keeping a safe but reliable distance. "I've got you, Kyla Phelps."

Ten minutes later, Perry Walters parked his car at The Dive and went inside. Was Kyla there already? Was Kyla Phelps in that bar? Taylor scanned the parking lot, wondering which car was hers. Ben didn't know what kind of car she drove. If she was not there yet, Taylor would see her drive up. Should he confront her then?

Taylor considered going inside the bar to look around but decided against it. Perry Walters had never seen him, but the bartender had. He couldn't take the risk.

Each time the door to the bar opened, Taylor's pulse spiked. It soared when Perry Walters and a woman with short black hair emerged. Was she Kyla? Of course, she was. She had to be.

The couple walked to the side of the building where the coupe was parked. Perry Walters opened the car door, removed the bag, and then closed the door again. The woman had to be Kyla, Taylor decided. To change her appearance, she had cut off her hair and dyed it black. She knew the cops were after her.

Perry Walters and Kyla Phelps walked within ten yards of Taylor's truck. He snapped a few pictures, and then quickly lowered his phone. Taylor watched Kyla unlock the door to a Nissan Altima, charcoal gray or black. Had she stolen that car too? He snapped a few more pictures.

Perry Walters put the bag in the back seat, and then closed the door. With his back against the car, he pulled Kyla to him. Looping her arms around his neck, she said something, and then touched his lips with her fingertips. As they kissed, Walters tugged at the back of Kyla's shirt, pulling it out of her jeans, stroking a wide strip of pale skin. Kyla locked her arms around the man's neck, pressing hard against him.

I promised my dad I wouldn't tell my mom that Kyla wants to keep her bed warm while she's gone.

I hate Kyla.

Be sure she goes to jail.

"I won't let you down, Ben," Taylor whispered. "Or you, Hannah. Not again."

Two men dressed in work clothes emerged from the bar. The loud one told his friend that he would see him in the morning, and then strode across the small parking lot. When the patron climbed into his car, Walters grabbed Kyla around the waist again, crushing her to him. Kyla pulled away, and then began tucking her shirt into her jeans. Words were exchanged, and then Kyla kissed the man goodbye. Walters helped her into the Altima, patted the window, and waited as the car pulled away.

On the street, Taylor eased in behind the Altima. He had no idea where Kyla was heading, but twenty minutes later, it was clear that she was on her way out of Houston. Miles and minutes passed at glacier pace. Taylor drank another Red Bull, noticing when he checked his rear-view mirror that the white Toyota truck he had noticed earlier was still there. "Forget about it," Taylor ordered himself. "Kyla Phelps is in the car in front of you. You've finally got her in your crosshairs."

CHAPTER 30

AUSTIN, TEXAS

Barton Creek Club was located off Bee Cave Road. The private club boasted four golf courses, a conference center and hotel, and a frequent lunch spot for Blair and her friend Liz Elrod. The restaurant overlooked distant hills, a spacious open-air pavilion, and the eighteenth hole of the Fazio Foothills course. Liz, a beginner, had parred two holes the day before on the less difficult Crenshaw Course.

"Bill cautioned me that improving my lie by toeing the ball two feet out of the rough is not within the rules, even for beginners."

"So what did you make on the hole?" Blair asked, chuckling.

"Let's just say cheating doesn't pay."

Blair's report on Brandi's trip to Washington was overshadowed by an emotional discussion of Allison. "Butler phoned last night. No test results. He's so worried. We all are."

"I didn't realize a child could come out of remission during chemo."

"From what Butler said, it's not a good sign."

Lunch was served—grilled chicken salads with spicy southwestern dressing. When the server stepped away, Liz asked if Blair had heard anything more from Lenny Bond since meeting him in the restaurant parking lot in New Braunfels. When Blair said that she had not, Liz screwed up her face and shook her head. "I still cannot believe you and Lenny Bond exchanged e-mail addresses. Bizarre."

Blair snickered. "You should have seen him, Liz. He practically groveled. If I didn't like wielding the hammer so much, I'd almost feel sorry for the guy. But after the hell he and Jewell put us through, I get a sadistic pleasure out of seeing him duck and dodge." Blair retrieved her purse from the chair back, and then handed Liz the letter she had received from Lenny's sister. "Take a look at that."

While Liz read, Blair studied the three snapshots Arlene Stegall had included. Had Brandi been fond of Eden Stegall? How well had the girls known each other? Blair had looked at the snapshots so many that Eden had begun to remind her of someone.

Blair's cell phone pinged. She glanced down at a text message from Hazel. *Misplaced key to cabin. Will meet B at bus stop. Drive her home.* Frowning, Blair tapped *OK.*

Before giving Hazel a key to the cabin, Blair had placed it on a unique key ring, identical to hers and Brandi's. Dangling from each of the rings was an ornament shaped like a cozy home or cabin. Blair had found the key rings on Amazon. She had ordered them in different finishes to avoid confusion. Now Hazel's key was missing. If she didn't find it immediately, Blair would have to have the locks changed.

Tamping down her concerns, Blair turned her focus to Liz who was folding the letter from Arlene Stegall. Blair exchanged it for the snapshots.

Liz characterized Arlene Stegall as a decent sounding woman, and Lenny Bond as a man running scared. "He wouldn't know what the word meant if he heard it, but Lenny Bond's life goal right now is to avoid becoming a recidivist." Liz studied the snapshots with intense interest. "Jewell Bond is such an ordinary looking woman. How could she do such a thing? How can a woman become that desperate?" Liz looked up at Blair, and then down again. "She looks sad in these pictures." Instinctively, she turned one over. Silently reading Arlene's description, she shook her slowly. "Unbelievable. Two kidnappers, probably standing outside a church fellowship hall, after having a meal prepared by the women of the church."

Liz was studying the third picture, when Blair's cell phone rang. It was Myles. Apologizing to Liz, she stepped onto the balcony. "Hi, Myles."

"Can you talk a minute?" His tone was curt.

"I'm at the club with Liz. Is something wrong?"

"What did you and Bond do?" Myles demanded. "Team up together to make me look like a complete fool?"

"What are you talking about?" Blair snapped. "And why are you so angry?"

"Humiliation, Blair. It has that effect on me. *The Public Eye*. Have a look at their website."

The call went dead. *The Public Eye*? Why would she look at that ridiculous tabloid? Stunned, Blair returned to the table. "That was Myles. He was livid. Something about *The Public Eye*."

They both tapped furiously on their phones. Liz was the first to gasp. "Oh my gosh! It's Myles. It's a picture of Myles."

Blair stared in stunned disbelief at the headline. **Texas Senator Abandons Long-lost Daughter. Shocking Story. Exclusive Photos.** She read the article in a whisper, racing through the content, skipping some. "Myles Lakeman .... ambitious new senator from Texas ... hungry for political power ... grab it at any cost— even if it means abandoning his child who was missing for eleven years." Blair continued to speed read, skipping the predictable hyperbole. "Lakeman's daughter Brandi ... abducted at age two ... kidnappers raised the child as their own for eleven years. When Jewell Bond died suddenly, Lenny Bond initiated an elaborate scheme ... large sum of money from the child's mother ... owner of the Emerson Funeral Homes in the Austin area. The desperate mother cooperated, turning over thousands of dollars and recovering her child. Lakeman, who divorced his wife during their child's long absence and married Austin socialite ... was appointed ... unexpired seat in the United States Senate. At a recent gala reception, Lakeman was honored by the Lone Star State's rich and powerful, an event attended by his daughter Brandi, now thirteen. Blair Emerson was barred from the event, forced to wait in her car outside the posh Headliners Club." Blair scrolled down the screen. "That is such garbage." Her denial was shrill. "I wasn't barred from that silly gathering."

"That's not what it looks like in that picture." Liz pinched the screen, enlarging the photo. "Look at that thing." She read the caption aloud. "Lakeman's ex-wife weeps—barred from farewell reception."

Seconds passed before Blair understood what she was looking at. The picture had been taken through the windshield of her car. Her hair fell forward, shadowing her face. Her lips were separated, as if she were sobbing. Her expression could only be described as distressed.

"Oh, Liz," she groaned. "Look at that hideous thing. I was crying because I had just heard about Alli."

Liz continued to scroll, and then pinched the screen again. "Good grief, Blair. Is that you too? That *is* you." She read the caption aloud. "Desperate mother meets secretly with kidnapper." Wide eyed, she looked up from her phone. "Oh, Blair. That's you and Lenny Bond."

Blair gaped at the crystal-clear snapshot of Lenny standing in front of her, holding Jewell's treasure chest on his forearms. He appeared to be presenting it to Blair as if it were a gift.

Liz skimmed more of the scandalous article. "Lakeman's ex-wife, Austin mortician Blair Emerson, met secretly with her child's kidnapper. Lenny Bond, on parole from a Texas prison, presented Emerson a gift for her daughter, Brandi." Liz groaned. "Sources say that Bond remains devoted to the girl he considered his daughter for eleven years."

Blair's face felt hot, and her breathing shallow. "I don't believe this. It's such garbage. Who took those pictures, Lizzie?"

"If I had my guess, I'd say your new e-mail buddy saw another opportunity to make some easy cash." Again, Liz studied the picture, shaking her head. "What is it with that guy? Does Lenny Bond have a death wish or what?"

◆ ◆ ◆

BLAIR SAT ON THE sofa next to her daughter. On the coffee table was the cardboard carton containing the transferred contents of Jewell's treasure chest. The empty chest itself sat next to it, the envelope from Arlene Stegall lying on the lid. "Are you sure you want to see this?" Blair asked. Without answering, Brandi picked up the empty treasure chest. "It's been a long time since you've seen that, huh. You can keep it in your room if you want to."

"You don't mind?" Brandi asked, opening the lid.

"No, I don't mind," Blair lied. What she really wanted was to bust the thing to pieces and use it for kindling wood. "Jewell saved all sorts of things in it. Your report cards. A pair of little leather shoes. Do you remember making a handprint in plaster?"

"Yes. In kindergarten, or maybe first grade." Brandi closed the empty chest, and then ran her fingertips over the carved lid. "Was it in here?"

"Yes. Would you like to see it?" Blair removed the lid to the carton. The plaque rested atop the other items. She gave it to Brandi, and then watched as the child imposed her hand on the imprint, exactly as Blair had done. "Such a tiny hand," Blair commented, failing to control a quiver in her voice.

Brandi returned the plaque to the carton without comment, and then picked up the envelope. "Why did Aunt Arlene—" As if she had been pricked with a pin, Brandi flinched. "What did she write to you?"

"Read it if you like," Blair encouraged patiently.

Brandi read the letter, and then studied the pictures Arlene Stegall had included. Blair sighed inside, awash with a sad realization. In fewer than fourteen years, the child had lived two distinct lives. Did two girls exist in her mind, in her psyche? In a way, it was the same for Blair, only her nearly forty years were divided into thirds. The blissful years before the abduction, the agonizing eleven that had followed, and the fleeting months since her child's recovery.

Brandi examined the picture taken in Virginia Beach with intense interest. "I remember this day." Her tone suggested something significant had happened. "Eden's parents were furious with her."

"Why?" Blair asked, genuinely curious.

Brandi picked up a pair of reading glasses from the coffee table, and then handed them to Blair. "Look at Eden's hand."

Blair put on the glasses, her curiosity growing. "At her ring?"

"It's not a ring. It's a tattoo."

"That's a tattoo?" She took the picture from her daughter, and then scrutinized it closely. "No wonder they were mad. She's just a high school kid here, right?"

"Yes. Look how Eden's kind of showing it off in the picture."

Brandi was right. Eden Stegall had posed for the picture with her legs outstretched and her hands conspicuous on her knee. "Why did she do that? I mean, what is the tattoo?"

"It's her boyfriend's initials … all connected together."

"Ooh," Blair groaned, and then smacked her daughter with the picture. "If you ever do …"

Brandi chuckled. "I'd better be prepared to lose a finger."

Grateful for the lightened mood, Blair studied the pictures while Brandi read the letter from Arlene again. Soon Blair would take the snapshots to a professional for editing. In time, she would forget where the pictures had been taken and whose hands had rested on Brandi's shoulders. She would pretend her child had never known a girl named Eden Stegall who had a boy's initials tattooed on her finger.

♦ ♦ ♦

AFTER BRANDI WENT to bed, Blair fired off an e-mail to Lenny Bond, demanding to know who had taken the picture of them in New Braunfels. The man's response came right away.

"I seen that awful picture. But I sware to God I had nothing to do with it. The only people that knew I was meeting you in New Braunfels was Jamar and Arlene and her husband. No way would they get involved with such a thing. Neither would I. I'd have to be crazy to pull a stunt like that. I sware I had nothing to do with this mess. Please believe me. Lenny."

CHAPTER 31

SAN ANTONIO, TEXAS

Rain pounded the metal roof of the dorm at Worsham Services. The racket was music to Lenny's ears as he finished chopping the last of the green chiles. The retaining wall crew had gotten rained out midafternoon. Lost time meant lost pay, but Lenny could not care less. Standing within striking distance of Dub Black's cleaver sure beat arm-wrestling railroad ties from daylight to dark.

"Bond," Dub Black barked, "is that cheese not aged enough for you?"

"Say what?"

"What are you waiting on? Get busy grating that cheese. And use the side of the grater that I told you to. I better not find any chunks either."

"You bet, Dub. I was just fixing to get started on that." Lenny pushed the plastic bowl of chopped green chiles toward Dub. "Is that the way you wanted them?"

Ignoring the question, Dub pressed a lid on the bowl, and then put it in the refrigerator. He slid a larger bowl across the island, and then told Lenny to fill it to the top with grated cheese.

"Stick it in the refrigerator when you're done. I grilled the chicken yesterday. You be here at six sharp to help me cook the quesadillas. Got that?"

"Loud and clear," Lenny answered, picking up what Dub had called a box grater. He stood the contraption on a piece of wax paper, studied the four sides, and then began raking the wedge of cheddar over what looked like medium size holes. "This is the size you told me to use, right?" When Dub gave him a wordless nod, Lenny continued. He didn't have the foggiest notion what a quesadilla was, much less how to cook one, but Dub would take care of that a few hours from now. At breakfast, the bossy man had told Lenny how to butter a skillet for the scrambled eggs.

When Dub was out the door, Lenny turned the four-sided grater around, and then dragged the cheese over the largest holes. If he used the holes Dub told him to, he could forget about taking a nap. He was dog-tired. He hadn't slept more than a few hours since getting an e-mail from Blair. She was convinced that Lenny was behind the picture taken of them in New Braunfels, even suggesting that his friend Jamar could have taken it. But she blamed Lenny entirely for the fact that the picture ended up in *The Public Eye*.

There was no convincing Blair that she was wrong, that the last thing in the world he would do was cause trouble for her and Brandi, or for a United States senator. In her follow up e-mail, she had called him a liar and a con man.

"No matter who took that picture and sold it," Lenny grumbled, fumbling with the grater, "I'll be the one that has to pay."

Lenny looked up when Jamar wandered into the kitchen. He poured himself a cup of coffee, and then offered the rest of the pot to Lenny. He declined. "I'm swearing off for a while."

"It's not caffeine keeping you awake at night." Jamar pinched grated cheese from the pile, and then dropped it in his open mouth. "It's Blair Emerson and her threats. Why do you let her get away with all that?"

Lenny didn't answer, and he would never tell Jamar that Blair suspected he might have taken the picture in the restaurant parking lot. Jamar knew good and well why Lenny didn't give Blair any lip. She and Myles Lakeman could cause Lenny more trouble than he could get out of. It didn't matter that this time he had done *nothing* wrong.

"Have you called your sister yet?" Jamar leaned against the island, swigging his coffee. "Maybe she's tracked down that daughter of hers by now."

"I'll call her when I'm done grating." Lenny set the grater aside, and then slid pyramids of cheese from the wax paper into the bowl. "Two inches short," he mumbled, and then resumed his assignment.

He dreaded calling Arlene again. She had taken offense when Lenny asked if she had mentioned to Eden that he was meeting Blair in New Braunfels. "Herb might have told her," Arlene had snapped, "but I didn't. How dare you point your finger at my daughter? Do you actually think Eden is capable of such a thing?"

Lenny had pleaded with his sister. "Don't get mad, Arlene. I wasn't suggesting Eden took the picture herself. I was just wondering if she knew I was meeting Blair. She could have mentioned it to somebody else. I wasn't accusing Eden of anything malicious."

The truth was, Lenny didn't know what Eden Stegall was capable of doing. He wasn't sure he would recognize the girl if she was standing three foot away from him. Although Arlene had never said as much, Lenny knew that Eden had caused her parents some heartache over the years, starting when she was a teenager. In high school, when the girl had gotten a tattoo, Arlene's head had nearly exploded. Lenny didn't blame his sister. Girls had no business with tattoos.

Lenny's apology for upsetting Arlene had been genuine. She was the only family he had. He wanted her in his life. Before ending the call, Arlene had said she would ask her husband if he told Eden that Lenny was meeting Blair to give her the treasure chest. "If he did, then I'll find out where Eden was that day, without letting on why I'm asking. But I assure you, Lenny, Eden was nowhere near New Braunfels." The thought occurred to Lenny that his sister was less sure about her daughter's whereabouts than she let on.

Lenny set the grater on the wax paper again, raked the cheese back and forth on the coarse side a few times, and then stopped. Dub was sure to notice that some of the cheese was medium-large, so Lenny rotated the grater. When the wedge was knuckle-scraping small, he gave the chunk to Jamar, and then dumped the piles in the bowl. With his fingers, he spread the cheese neatly, hiding the thicker pieces with a two-inch layer of medium size shreds.

Lenny snapped the lid on the bowl, and then put it in the refrigerator. Jamar poured the rest of his coffee down the sink, as Lenny crumpled the sheet of wax paper, dropped it in the trash, and then started scrubbing the grater.

"Look, man, if you don't want to call your sister, that's fine with me." Jamar set the cup in the sink. "But why are you stalling?"

"I'm not stalling. I'm just trying to keep Dub from crawling up my back." Lenny washed the cup, and then placed it in the dish drainer. He was squeezing water from a sponge when the new guy—Lenny had forgotten his name.—stuck his bald head in the kitchen door.

"One of you guys named Lenny?"

"That'd be me."

"You left your phone on the coffee table." He waved it in the air. "I answered it for you. The woman says she's your sister."

Jamar stomped across the room, and then yanked the phone from the man's hand. "Next time, let it go to voicemail. What the hell is wrong with you? Don't ever touch a man's phone."

Lenny dried his hands hastily, and then rescued his phone. Jamar had a short fuse these days. "Arlene? Hey. Everything okay?"

"No, Lenny. I'm afraid not."

Lenny plopped onto a bar stool, his legs suddenly weak. What now? What the hell was wrong now?

"Lenny, I had to leave multiple messages, but I finally spoke with Eden." Arlene seemed to be forcing out the words. "She said she was calling from her apartment in Houston, but she … wasn't telling the truth."

Lenny filled the sudden silence. "No big deal, Arlene. So Eden fibbed to you. Kids do that."

"There's more, Lenny. Herbert and I bought Eden a new car recently. She has no idea, but we are able to track her whereabouts."

As so often happened, Lenny was unable to follow his sister's train of thought. He said the first thing that came to his mind. "I'm sorry you had to do that, Sis. But I'm sure you and Herb had a good reason."

"We do." Arlene sighed. When she tried to speak again, her voice broke. "Eden has disappeared a few times over the years. We were so scared, Lenny. Afraid she might be dead. We couldn't go through that again."

"Of course not," Lenny agreed, sorry for his sister's pain. "And now you don't have to. You can always track her down if you need to."

"That's what we did." Arlene struggled to control her quivering voice. "And now we need your help. I am so sorry, Lenny. Eden's car is in Live Oak."

The words whipped in so quickly that Lenny flinched. As Arlene continued to talk, he thought he heard her say something about Jewell's album and *A Stranger's Eyes*, but he couldn't be certain. The train wreck happening inside his head was deafening.

Arlene was sobbing now. "Lenny, please find Eden before she does more damage."

Speechless, Lenny looked wide-eyed at Jamar, and then mouthed the words, "My niece is in Live Oak."

Arlene could barely speak when she said. "I'll text you a picture of Eden, and I'll send you her license plate number."

"Are you sure Eden's in Live Oak?"

"I'm sure her car is there." Arlene cleared her throat, and then sighed in despair. "I have to believe she's there too."

Lenny's heartbeat was pounding in his ears, making it hard to hear. Arlene said something about grief, and Eden's deceased husband Kyle, and desperately needing Lenny's help.

"Will you go get her, Lenny?" Arlene pleaded. "Herb and I are nine hours away."

The question hammered in Lenny's head. Had Arlene forgotten that entering Hays County was a violation of his parole? But what the hell was he supposed to do? He couldn't turn his back on his sister after all she had done for him in the past three years. He had to stop Eden from causing him even more trouble.

"I'll text you right away, Lenny," Arlene said, her composure regained. "And one other thing. Sometimes Eden goes by the name of Kyla Phelps."

CHAPTER 32

LIVE OAK, TEXAS

Seven Oaks Mobile Home Park had a single entrance on a road called Wagon Trail. Taylor McFadden parked opposite the entrance on a narrow, tree-shrouded lane off Southworth Road. His nerves were shot. He was bone tired, but he was afraid to close his eyes, afraid he would miss Kyla Phelps if she left her house in the mobile home park.

Last night, in the parking lot of The Dive, Perry Walters had put Kyla's canvas tote in the back seat of her car Leaning against the Nissan, he had kissed and groped the woman while his little boy was alone in their apartment and his wife was doing her patriotic duty somewhere in Germany.

Taylor had followed Kyla in her Nissan Altima to Live Oak, a little town outside Austin. During the three-hour drive from Houston, he had tried to formulate a plan for how he would confront Kyla Phelps. The smart thing was to call the cops and have her arrested. But Taylor still could not bring himself to make the call. He had a score to settle first.

During the long drive, he had considered faking a carjacking. The prospect of ramming the Altima, and then pointing a gun at

Kyla Phelps's head had been almost irresistible. He had also considered forcing her car off the road, and then tormenting her before telling her who he was. Curiosity, though, had taken over. With each passing mile, Taylor had grown more and more eager to find out where Kyla Phelps was going.

When she had taken the Live Oak exit off Interstate 35 South, Taylor had backed off, but keeping the Altima in his view. He had backed off even more, though, when Kyla turned onto a two-lane blacktop named Southworth Road. Cautiously, Taylor had followed her.

In a quarter mile or so, the Altima's brake lights had come on, and the vehicle had made a right turn onto Wagon Trail and into the mobile home park. To avoid detection, Taylor had continued down Southworth. The road soon came to a dead end. Tucked in a grove of live oak trees was a rustic cabin. Lanterns glowed on both sides of the front door, lighting the porch and the wooden steps. Thinking that the cabin was the kind of place Hannah would love, Taylor had made a three-point turn, and then headed back to Wagon Trail and the mobile home park. The Altima was parked at 1113-C Wagon Trail.

In the early morning hours, Taylor had considered breaking into Kyla's house after she went to sleep but had decided that was too risky. The house might have an alarm system. Instead, he would follow Kyla until the time was right, and then he would pull the revolver out of his waist band and point it right between her eyes. If he thought about Hannah writhing in pain on the filthy pavement, Taylor thought he could actually pull the trigger.

Taylor rubbed the back of his neck, trying to untie the tension knotting his muscles. Picking up his phone from the dash, he tapped *Photos*, opened an album he had labeled *Hannah*, and then selected his favorite picture of her and Cass. It had been taken by a professional photographer at an amateur barrel racing competition in Burleson. Taken mid-race, it was an up close and astonishing image of Hannah clamped astride Cass. She wore a black felt hat, a white shirt with black stripes on the cuffs and collar, dusty black boots, and a fiercely focused look on her face. She and Cass had just cleared the left barrel in the clover leaf. Hannah's left arm was fully extended, almost shoulder high, her fingers clenching the leather rein. She was leaning slightly forward, her left knee inches away from the rim of a faded black barrel. Castaño's broad, muscular body leaned toward the barrel at an impossible angle. His rear feet had dug into the ground as he circled the barrel, disappearing into the dirt. His eyes, black as coal, were locked on the second barrel in the cloverleaf. Hannah and Cass had won the competition, beating the second-place winner by a mere five-hundredth of a second.

Taylor's cell phone rang, startling him. *Chirp*. He was so lost in thought that it took him a moment to realize that it was Ben's ringtone. He answered the call immediately. "Hi, Ben. It's Mac. What's up? Are you okay?"

"I've got some more news. It's about Kyla."

Exhaustion brought on momentary confusion. "She's not there in Houston, is she?"

"I don't know."

"What's the news?"

"Two detectives came to talk to my dad early this morning. The fat man told my dad that if he knew where Kyla is that he needed to tell them right then and there. He said Kyla's life is in danger."

Instantly, Taylor's mind began to race. Her life was in danger? Did the cops know that he had tracked down Kyla Phelps, that he had followed her from Houston? How could they know? It was impossible. He hadn't told anyone. His mother and Hannah both thought he had been in training all last night for his job at Walmart. He had told them that he was driving to Marshall today to meet a guy about team roping together.

"Mac, are you there?"

"I'm here, Ben. Sorry. What else did the detectives say?"

"That there's a man looking for Kyla. He told my dad to warn her, and to make her turn herself in." Words spilled from the little boy's mouth. "The other man … not the fat one … said that the bad man and Kyla hijacked a car together."

"They hijacked a car?" Taylor gathered disjointed facts and pieced them together. "Did I hear you right?"

"Yeah. Kyla and the bad man hijacked a car. A girl got hurt real bad, just like what happened to your friend."

Taylor paused, untangling his thoughts. "Did they tell your dad the man's name?"

"I wrote it down and hid it in my shoe," the boy answered. "But I don't even need to look. It's Wylie Thorp. We were right, Mac."

"We sure were, Ben. And now the cops know it."

"They showed Dad a picture of Wylie Thorp's mug."

"It was the man with the ponytail, right?"

"For sure. I looked at the picture real careful before my dad told me to go to my room."

Wearily, Taylor again examined the fragments of information. The police were doing their job. They knew who pulled off the carjacking. They knew who ran over Hannah. Had they actually arrested Rylie Thorp and were deceiving Perry Walters? Were they just trying to scare Kyla into turning herself in? Or were they telling Walters the truth, and Rylie Thorp was trying to track Kyla down to shut her up?

"Ben, if you see Rylie Thorp outside your apartment, call 911." Taylor spoke firmly. "Do not open the door. Call 911 immediately."

"Okay."

"Promise me, Ben."

"I promise.

"The cops are right," Taylor stressed. "Rylie Thorp is a bad, dangerous man."

"What about my dad, Mac? Should I tell him?"

"Yes. It's time to tell your dad." Taylor spoke urgently. "When your dad gets home tonight, tell him everything. Tell him about me. Tell him our secret. Make your dad understand that Rylie Thorp is a dangerous man. Tell him how Rylie Thorp and Kyla Phelps nearly killed my friend. But don't worry, Ben. I'll take care of Kyla. I know exactly where she is."

CHAPTER 33

LIVE OAK, TEXAS

In the funeral home dressing room, Blair gazed down at the body of ten-month-old Elizabeth Christian. It was such a big name for such a tiny little angel, she thought sadly. The baby had died during the night of a previously undetected heart problem. Jay Lytton had embalmed the infant. The meticulous care Jay had given the procedure was evident. The baby's hands rested naturally at her sides, not crossed on her abdomen as with an adult. There was a tiny gap in the center of her Cupid's bow lips, and her lids rested like petals on her eyes. Blair had dressed the child in her christening gown. It looked to be a family heirloom. Lace trimmed white cotton. Puff sleeves to her wrists. And a lovely, heart-shaped neck.

This should not be, Blair fretted, aware of the beginnings of a headache. Children should live. Babies should not die.

Along with the baby's clothing, her parents had brought along her christening blanket. It, too, was white, trimmed in lace, and adorned with pale, pink pearls. Blair opened the blanket on the dressing table, and then gently slid her hands beneath the folds of the baby's gown. Cradling the infant in her forearms, she was reminded of how unnatural the infant's body felt. Elizabeth was stiff and cold, like a doll, not a child. Placing her on the blanket, Blair drew it nearly around her and whispered, "You are loved, little one."

In her office, Blair returned phone calls, and then ordered a spray of pink carnations with baby's breath for Elizabeth's casket. She was preparing to phone a vocalist when her cell phone rang. Recognizing the Houston area code, she accepted the call. It was the real Anna Mitchell. With so much on her mind, Blair had almost forgotten about the woman.

"Blair, I won't take but a minute of your time. I need a favor." Anna Mitchell explained that her partner's dad was a police officer. She had told him about her purse being stolen, and that a woman was using her name. "He said identity theft is a huge problem, so he wants to find out who the woman is. Would it be possible for you to get the license plate number off her car so he can do some checking?"

"Sure, Anna. I'll get back to you as soon as I have it." Ending the call, Blair immediately phoned Hazel. "Can you see Anna Mitchell's car from your house?"

"Yes. It's parked right across the street in her driveway. Why?"

"I'll explain later. I need her license plate number. Can you read it from where you are?"

"No. But I'll go to the front window." Seconds later, the woman said, "Okay, Blair. The tag reads HSV-2977. It's a Texas plate. And just in case you need it," Hazel continued, "her car is a Nissan Altima."

Repeating the license plate number, Blair wrote it on a notepad, and then jotted the make and model next to it. "What color is her car?"

"Charcoal gray or maybe black. I can't tell for sure."

"Thanks so much, Hazel," Blair said. "I'll explain later."

"Give my love to Brandi," Hazel said, sounding deeply concerned. "I know she's worried about Alli."

Blair telephoned the real Anna Mitchell again, reaching her voicemail. She repeated the information Hazel had provided, and then ended with a request of her own. "Anna, call me when you learn more. I really want to know who this woman is."

Aware of a growing headache, Blair massaged the muscles in her neck and rotated her head. "Oh, my precious Alli." The words had just left her mouth when her cell phone rang again. The instant she heard Charlotte's voice, she knew the news was not good.

"The doctor left an hour ago," Charlotte explained wearily. "I would have called sooner, but Butler and I … we just needed some time."

The silence that followed unnerved Blair. Why had Butler and Charlotte needed time? What had the doctor said? She heard a shuffling sound through the phone, and then her brother-in-law's voice. "Alli's leukemia is back in full force. Her oncologist is concerned that she came out of remission so quickly. That's not a good sign. Not good at all. He's even mentioned a bone marrow transplant."

"A bone marrow transplant?" Blair repeated. Immediately, she regretted the shock in her voice. The suggestion of a transplant of any kind seemed like a desperate measure. Was Alli's condition that grave?

In far more detail than Blair could absorb, her brother-in-law related the steps involved in a bone marrow transplant procedure. Her mind alternately accepted and rejected the information. She was forced to focus when Butler said, "If we have to go that route, we'll need to find a suitable donor. Parents are rarely compatible, but Charlotte and I will be tested anyway."

"What about me?" Blair's attention locked now on the importance of what Butler was saying. "Maybe I could be the donor."

Butler agreed that Blair should be tested. He would also arrange for Alli's brother to undergo the simple blood test. Siblings were often compatible marrow donors, but not always. Not wanting to press, Blair asked where the procedure would take place, if in fact a transplant was needed.

"The oncologist here said that the decision is ours," Butler answered. "He assured us that the specialists at Children's Hospital in Austin are well-equipped to give Alli excellent care."

"That's good to hear," Blair responded, her thoughts leaping to the logistical impact of a lengthy hospital stay on both Charlotte and Butler.

Before ending the call, Butler brought up the possibility of Brandi being tested. "I know how she loves Alli, and that she would do anything for her. But, Blair, if you don't want her to be tested, should it come to that, we understand. Brandi has been through so much. Don't feel obligated to put her through anything more."

CHAPTER 34

Live Oak, Texas

Brandi's plan was firmly in place. She would get another bottle of Safe-T Soap from the funeral home preparation room, hopefully tonight. She had already spoken with Dr. Westinghouse about her plan. "I'm ready to go in the funeral home again, but I thought I should get your opinion first." Her psychiatrist had asked a few questions, and then agreed. "Remember to record the experience in your journal, Brandi. If Blair has any questions or concerns, tell her to phone me."

Now it was time for Brandi to put the next step of her plan into action. "Mom, do you know when Alli is coming home from Houston?"

"I'm not sure. Charlotte and Butler are still conferring with the specialists there."

"If she's going to be there a while, can we go see her?"

"Sure. She would love that."

"So would I." Brandi closed her iPad, and then set her homework aside. "I talked to Dr. Westinghouse this afternoon. I told him I was ready to go inside the funeral home again. He thinks it's a good idea, if it's all right with you. He calls it exposure therapy."

Because no families would be present, they agreed to go to the funeral home after dinner. Brandi managed to eat a grilled cheese sandwich, but then she vomited when it was time to leave. Her mom was waiting at the back door when Brandi returned to the kitchen, carrying an oversized shoulder bag. "You look a little pale, sweetie. Are you sure you want to do this?"

"I'm sure," Brandi answered honestly.

They drove to the funeral home in near silence. Brandi was still processing the news that Alli might need a bone marrow transplant. That afternoon she had researched the procedure on the Internet. Finding a suitable donor was the first step. The screening process involved an ordinary blood test. Brandi didn't mind being stuck with a needle. It was just a little prick, and the needle and syringe were sealed in plastic until they were used. But the thought of undergoing a bone marrow harvest was horrifying. She would have to be hospitalized. A doctor would stab an enormous needle into her hip bone, maybe dozens of times, suck out her bone marrow, and store it in a jar. She would be terribly sore for days.

But I could do it, she vowed. I could do it for Alli.

Entering the funeral home through the same door as before, Brandi immediately oriented herself. The preparation room was at the rear of the building, behind the door with the hazardous chemicals warning sign. She followed her mom to the reception office. Harley Fox stood when they entered, and then asked Brandi about her trip to Washington, D.C.

"It was amazing," she answered. "I was so proud of my dad, but I'm glad to be home."

"Your mother tells me you're braving the funeral home again." Harley Fox smiled and winked. "I just finished turning on every light in the building. Oh, and I got you these."

The man handed Brandi a small box. "Paperclips?"

"Yes, you can leave a trail of them behind as you wander around."

"Like breadcrumbs." Brandi giggled. No wonder her mom liked Harley Fox so much. "Well, I'd like to stay and chat, but Gretel has a building to explore." She grinned indulgently at her mom. "No, I don't need you to go with me." She pointed to the doors on the far side of the foyer. "Those lead to the chapel, right? I think I'll start there."

Brandi crossed the foyer, pulled open a carved oak door, and then entered the chapel lobby. She remembered what Spencer had said when he was a little boy. "Aunt Blair, I didn't know your office had a theater in it." Soon Spencer would take a blood test. Would his bone marrow be a match to Alli's?

"Will mine?" she whispered.

Brandi pressed down her growing anxiety. She could not think about the hideous transplant procedure now. She had to find her way back to the preparation room, and she had to hurry.

She returned to the foyer at the front entrance. Her mom and Harley Fox were sitting in the reception area talking. They didn't notice when Brandi tiptoed across the foyer, and then slipped into the visitation parlor. Glancing over her shoulder as she walked, she crossed the large room, and then pushed open the door marked *Private*. She knew exactly where she was now. The hallway leading to the preparation room would be to the left. She took another anxious glance over her shoulder, and then shut the door behind her.

The back hallway was dimly lit with a series of night lights. The door with the warning sign was closed. Brandi turned the knob and pushed. Except for another night light, the space was completely dark. She ran her hand along the wall to the right, found a bank of switches, and flipped the nearest one. Light flooded the room. This was the dressing room. The preparation room was beyond the wide door over there.

Allowing the door to close behind her, Brandi removed a mask and gloves from her shoulder bag. She worked her hands into the gloves, and then looped the mask's elastic band over her head. With her mouth and nose covered, she took a tiny breath of air. She had to hurry. She could not get caught in this room.

One of the wheeled tables stood near the door leading to the preparation room. As Brandi neared it, she noticed a blanket bundled near the end. A doll's head appeared, and Brandi stopped to look. Who could have left a doll there? she puzzled. And why?

Unrestrained, a shriek tore from Branci's throat. She staggered back, her eyes wide with shock. *A baby.* It was not a doll wrapped in a blanket. *It was a dead baby.* Brandi's knees became weak. She felt as if her muscles were melting. She leaned against the wall to steady herself. *A baby. A dead baby.*

Trembling, Brandi backed away from the table, unable to avert her eyes from the bundle. She felt lightheaded, but she didn't want to breathe. *Germs.* They were everywhere — maybe even the germs that killed the baby.

Calm down, she ordered herself, turning away from the bundle. The soap. You must get the soap.

Shaken, Brandi slid the connecting door aside, and then turned on the light in the preparation room. She stumbled past the long, white tables to the counter across the room. The bottle of Safe-T Soap by the sink was nearly empty. She opened the upper cupboard and found bottles of shampoo, conditioner, a can of shaving cream, razor blades, a hairbrush and comb, but no soap. She opened another cupboard and found rolls of cotton as large as paper towels. Her pulse spiked when she opened the door to the cupboard on the right. The bottom shelf held at least twenty bottles of Safe-T Soap. Still shaking, she pulled a plastic sack from her shoulder bag, and then stuffed two bottles of soap inside it. There were so many. No one would notice two missing bottles.

Awkwardly, she shrugged off the shoulder bag, and then stuffed the lumpy plastic sack inside it. How long had she been gone? She had to hurry.

Lightheaded and shaking, Brandi rushed across the preparation room, pausing to slide the door shut as she had found it. The baby was an arm's length away. *A dead baby*. Again, Brandi averted her eyes, but she could still see the image of the dead child's face, even the tiny, little opening between her lips.

With a trembling hand, Brandi pushed open the exit door, and then stepped into the shadowy hallway. Anxiety soared inside her like a fever. She yanked off the mask, peeled off the gloves, and then dropped them into a large trash can. When she looked up, Brandi caught movement at the end of the hallway. Startled, she staggered back, bumping into the trash can and losing her balance. The bag slipped from her shoulder. Its contents spilled onto the floor. Bottles of Safe-T soap skittered and rolled across the tile.

"Brandi!" Her mom rushed toward her. Even in the dimness, her face was marble white, her eyes round with shock. "What in the world are you doing?"

CHAPTER 35

LIVE OAK, TEXAS

The drive from San Antonio took more than two hours. Heavy northbound traffic on Interstate 35 combined with a downpour in New Braunfels. Jamar slowed his vehicle to a crawl. Lenny was barely aware of the delay. Since leaving Worsham Services, he had been rehearsing what he would say if they got pulled over by a cop or a DPS trooper. He had settled on keeping his mouth shut and letting Jamar do the talking.

Lenny stayed in the car when Jamar pulled into a convenience store on Interstate 35 at the Live Oak exit. No one would recognize Lenny there, but he pulled the brim of his cap low, and then sank down in the seat as a precaution. The instant Jamar's car rolled over the county line, Lenny had violated his parole. But what choice did he have? He had to find his niece. He had to find Eden.

There was only one reason for Arlene's daughter to be in Live Oak. The trouble-making girl was spying on Blair and Brandi. Lenny's gut told him that Eden had been at the Alpine Haus the day he met Blair in New Braunfels. Eden had taken the picture of him holding the treasure chest out to Blair, and then sold it to the tabloid. He was sure of it. And if his own niece would stoop that low, then she would steal Jewell's album out of the treasure chest when Lenny's stuff was stored at Arlene's house. What kind of a person would then sell a dead woman's photographs to Wilson Rule?

Lenny retrieved his phone to study the picture Arlene had sent him. Eden was a scrawny looking girl with short hair dyed a mahogany color. "But she changes her hair color a lot, Lenny," Arlene had reminded him. "I'm not positive what color it is right now." She was dressed in black jeans and a black turtleneck sweater. What she lacked in jewelry, she made up for in makeup. Eden's face was as white as Dub Black's baking flour, but her eye makeup was mostly charcoal and black. She wore a matte burgundy lipstick and not a hint of a smile, completing what in Lenny's opinion was a rebellious, defiant look.

Arlene had begged Lenny to go to Live Oak and find Eden, breaking into tears as she ended their phone call. Jamar had been all too eager to go with him. "When we find that conniving girl, we'll snatch her up, and then haul her butt back here to San Antonio until her parents can get here."

Jamar opened the car door, and then handed Lenny a can of Red Bull. Popping the lid from a can for himself, Jamar took a noisy swig, and then fired up the engine. "What do you say we head on over to Wagon Trail and pay a call on that troublemaking niece of yours?"

Five minutes later, Jamar turned off FM 149 onto Southworth Road. The name sounded familiar to Lenny. On the left, a long driveway ended at a two-story stone house with six columns and a long front porch. The mailbox read *Lindquist*. Lenny's heart was pounding like a jackhammer when he realized that the cabin where Blair and Brandi lived was tucked in the woods at the end of Southworth Road.

Who was Eden visiting at the mobile home park? Lenny worried. Did she live there? And for how long? He tamped down the next question when his head began to throb. If things went sideways, he could end up in prison again. But if he didn't track down Eden, then Brandi's parents would make sure he ended up there anyway.

The map on Jamar's phone instructed him to turn right onto Wagon Trail. Arlene had phoned Lenny an hour ago to confirm the location of Eden's car. "Thank God, she's still in Live Oak, Lenny. Please find her."

Wagon Trail was a broad paved lane leading into a mobile home park. The sign read *Seven Oaks*. Up ahead, a man dressed all in khaki was walking a fawn-colored Boxer in their direction. The dog was on a leash and walked close to the man's side. Jamar gave the fellow a thumbs up as they drove past him. "None of these places has a garage," he commented. "We won't have any trouble spotting the girl's Nissan."

Lenny guessed the park had twenty homes in it, ten on each side of the lane which had been recently paved. The lots were large, and the backyards fenced. Each home had a private driveway for off-street parking.

When Eden's Nissan was nowhere to be found, Jamar made a U-turn, and then pulled to a stop. Lenny had a fit of panic. "Are you sure we're at the right place? How reliable is that tracking thing Herb and Arlene put on Eden's car? We gotta find that girl and get out of here."

"Shut up." Jamar put the gear in drive, drove a short distance, and then pulled to a stop next to the man walking his dog. Smiling, he lowered the window. The air was sharp and cool. "Evening, sir. Nice night for a walk, huh?"

"Sure is. How you men doing?"

"We're good. Handsome dog you got there. He's a Boxer, right?"

"Yep. Name is Hondo." The man glanced down at the dog who stood perfectly still, his ears erect. "I saw you pass by a minute ago. Can I help you with something?"

"I hope so." Jamar picked up Lenny's phone, and then tapped the screen. "I'm looking for this woman." He held the phone out the open window. "I could make up some story about why I want to find her, but I'm not going to insult your intelligence. The woman skipped bail, and if I don't find her, I'm going to be out some serious money."

"Is that right?"

"Yes, sir, and I suspect she's driving a stolen Nissan Altima. Black or midnight gray."

"A Nissan, huh?"

"Yes, sir. I have reason to believe she's living in your neighborhood." Jamar extended Lenny's phone toward the unsuspecting man. "Do you mind taking a closer look at her picture?"

The man stepped toward the car. "Sure. I can do that." He took the phone, and then studied the photo. "Hmm. She resembles a girl that's renting Jack Benson's home. Anna Mitchell is her name."

"Anna Mitchell," Jamar repeated, nodding his head. "You're right. That's one of her aliases."

Lenny sat dead still and speechless. Jamar was smoother than a snake's belly. Lenny didn't remember Arlene mentioning the name Anna Mitchell, only the name Kyla Phelps. The alias had something to do with Eden's dead husband Kyle Phelps, something sentimental, he guessed.

The man returned the phone to Jamar. "Anna's renting Unit C, but you won't find her there right now. She left a little while ago."

Lenny's spirits collapsed like a deflated balloon. They filled with hope again when the man said that they might find the girl at a place called the Stagger Inn. "A friend of mine told me that Anna is a regular there."

CHAPTER 36

Blair fought back images of the dreadful scene that had unfolded at the funeral home. The startled look on Brandi's face. Bottles of Safe-T Soap spilling from her shoulder bag and rolling across the floor. Blair shouting at her. "Brandi, what in the world are you doing?" On the drive home, she had been inconsolable. Blair had finally given up trying to make sense of it all.

How could I have been so blind, so naive? she agonized

In tumbling, disjointed phrases, Brandi had confessed that her decision to go inside the funeral home had nothing to do with exposure therapy. Recently, when Blair and Alli were cleaning the picnic table, she had overheard Blair mention a special soap used in the preparation room. With the trip to Washington looming before her, Brandi had become nothing short of desperate. And when she returned home from her trip, she had found out about Alli being in the hospital in Austin. "I knew she would need me to stay in the hospital with her," Brandi had sobbed. "But the germs, Mom. The germs."

Blair senses were on overload. She could hardly think straight. What should she do now? Pacing the living room, she felt weak-kneed and nauseated. Should she phone Dr. Westinghouse?

When Brandi appeared at the mouth of the hallway, her cheeks were flaming red. Her hair was limp and flat from what had surely been a painfully hot shower. She walked past Blair without speaking, took a bottle of water from the refrigerator and gulped it. Her hands were shaking. A white rim formed around her lips. She looked as if she might be sick.

Blair insisted that Brandi lay on the couch. When she complied, Blair went to the kitchen. She returned with a moistened towel, sat on the edge of the couch, and then pressed the cool compress to her daughter's forehead. "Try to relax. Take a breath. Just try to relax."

Brandi covered her eyes in the bend of her elbow. "I want to die, Mom." The white ring around her mouth had widened. Her lips were quivering. "I just want to die."

Blair cringed inside, knowing that at this moment her daughter meant what she said. "It breaks my heart to see you so upset, to know you feel so desperate."

"Don't tell me we'll get through this. I don't want to get through it."

"But we will, sweetheart. Together. We will—"

"What? We will figure out a way to deal with all this?" She lowered her arm from her face. Her swollen, red eyes flared. "What this time? Humor? Like when that stupid book came out. Don't you get it? I don't want to deal with any of this anymore." Words tumbled from Brandi's mouth with growing momentum. "And you know why? I'm not a normal kid, Mom. I'm crazy. I was raised by criminals, but I was too screwed up to know it. I'm *so* crazy that for nearly eleven years, I couldn't tell the difference between kidnappers and adoptive parents!"

The outburst shocked Blair. She could hardly speak. "Brandi, please. You were a baby when you were stolen. A two-year-old child. A defenseless child."

"People are reading that book, Mom. And people are looking at the picture of Lenny giving you Jewell's treasure chest. Everybody will know what a pathetic psycho I really am." Brandi jerked to her feet. She staggered when she stood, banging her shin against the coffee table. "I can't do this anymore. I won't do this anymore!"

Blair grabbed her daughter's hand, but she yanked it away. Her outburst was as surreal as the disaster at the funeral home. Her rage had erupted from deep inside.

"Oh, God," Blair muttered, hurting so badly she could hardly breathe. "I'm so sorry, sweetheart."

At the worst possible moment, her cell phone rang. Blair recognized the number. It was the real Anna Mitchell. She had to take her call.

Sternly, Blair told her daughter to lie back down. "Don't argue with me. Your face just turned white as a ghost." When Brandi obeyed, Blair said, "That's the real Anna Mitchell calling. I have to talk to her." Covering her daughter's lower body with a throw, she tapped her phone. "Anna, this is Blair."

"I'm glad I caught you. I have some information. The Nissan Altima is registered to a Herbert Stegall."

Blair plucked a pen from her purse. "Would you spell it for me?" She wrote the name on a magazine cover, and then repeated it. "Herbert Stegall."

"Right. Of Amarillo," she added. "My partner's dad is doing some more investigating, but I wanted you to know that much at least. I'll keep in touch, Blair. You do the same."

"Thank you, Anna. I will." Blair ended the call, and then sat staring at the name.

"Mom."

Brandi's voice, little more than a whisper, seemed to come from far away. Blair turned to her daughter, noting her puzzled expression.

"That name." She pointed at the magazine, her finger tremoring. "Why did you write down that name?"

"The woman calling herself Anna Mitchell is driving that man's car."

"Herbert Stegall." Brandi's voice quivered. She sounded stunned. Both hands began to tremble. "Mom, Herbert Stegall is Eden's dad."

An unruly sense of disorientation swept over Blair. *Stegall. Lenny's sister. Arlene Stegall.* The name had not even registered until this very moment. "Are you sure, Brandi?"

"Yes, I'm sure. I called him Uncle Herb. But why is that woman driving his car?" Brandi sucked in a quick breath, as if someone had startled her. "Eden! That woman, Mom. That woman is Eden!"

Blair felt suddenly weak, but her mind was working frantically. Had Lenny Bond's niece stolen Anna Mitchell's identity? Was Eden Stegall living down the road in Jack Benson's mobile home? Had the girl been spying on them? Had she been inside the cabin?

Brandi tossed the throw aside and sat upright. "The contact lenses. The black hair. The ring. She was covering up the tattoo. She was afraid I would remember it." Brandi's breathy voice grew strong with certainty. "It was all a disguise, Mom, so that I wouldn't recognize her."

"You're right, Brandi." Blair tamed her racing thoughts. "You were right all along. You never trusted that woman. And now she—" Blair chopped off the sentence. She had almost said that now a key to the cabin was missing. Was the key in Jack Benson's home or in Eden Stegall's purse?

Anger sparked in Blair like a lit match. "Damn that girl," she muttered. Furious, she picked up her phone and called Hazel. "Would you look across the street and see if Anna is at home?"

"I'm sweeping my front porch. I can see her car. It's in the driveway."

"Hazel, I need you to stay with Brandi this evening. Can you come right away?" When Hazel said that she would be glad to, Blair asked if she still had a key to Jack Benson's house.

"Sure. Do you need it?"

"Yes. I have to get inside that house. Brandi will explain when you get here." She ended the call, considered her options, and then called Manny Taggert. "It's Blair, Manny. I need your help again. Keep this to yourself, but I just found out that the woman living in Jack Benson's house is Lenny Bond's niece."

"You gotta be kidding me. Are you sure?"

Blair looked at her daughter. The white rim around her lips was gone. Her coloring was returning to normal. "I'm sure. Brandi figured it out. She's been suspicious of that girl since the day she met her." Blair stroked her daughter's hand, heartened when she did not pull away. "Manny, does Anna still come in the Stagger Inn?"

"Nearly every night," he answered. "You told me to get to know her. So that's what I did."

"I need you to make sure she's there tonight, Manny. Can you do that?"

"I can try. Sure. No problem."

"Call me on my cell when she gets there." Blair verified her number. "The minute she gets there. Okay?"

"You can count on me."

Blair's urgent tone was not lost on Manny, or on Blair herself. She could feel her heart rate rising. "Keep an eye on her the whole time, Manny. Don't let that woman out of your sight. If she leaves the Stagger Inn before you hear from me, call me immediately. I'm going to be inside Jack Benson's house."

CHAPTER 37

Taylor McFadden trotted in a crouch to an abandoned pump house. Breathless, he squatted in the shadows, peering across a clearing in the woods. Pale silver moonlight and a front porch lantern illuminated the empty driveway at 1113-C Wagon Trail.

His truck was still parked out of view on a narrow dirt lane off Southworth Road. He had watched the entrance to Seven Oaks all day, daring to drive past Kyla's house twice. The first time, her Nissan Altima was parked in the driveway, but the second time it was gone. Questions battled for space in Taylor's head. How was that possible? he worried. Had he dozed off? Even a few seconds could have been too long. Had he been watching the doe nursing her fawn under the live oak when Kyla wheeled the Altima out of the mobile home park?

It could have happened either way, Taylor decided. He was dead tired, so tired that he could hardly think straight.

Sitting on the ground with his back against the pump house, Taylor stared at the empty driveway. What if Kyla didn't come home tonight? he worried. What would he do then? He would have failed Hannah again, just as he had done the night of the carjacking.

Tomorrow Hannah was seeing the wound care specialist again. If she got the go-ahead, she would soon be fitted with a prosthetic foot. Taylor knew he should be with her, but he didn't want to. He didn't want to see her forced smile or hear her make another joke. "I really need another foot, Mom. I'm wasting perfectly good shoes." Hannah was going through what his mother called stages. "Taylor, that sweet girl is learning to accept that her life will never be the same again. She's digging deep, son. She's adjusting to her disability, and she will triumph. I know that because Hannah Rennick has a champion's spirit."

Someday soon, Hannah would sign a contract with CB Western Wear. Taylor knew it, even if Hannah didn't. She would start riding Castaño again, and then return to barrel racing. Hannah would soak up the attention. It would feed her competitive spirit. But every time she sat for an interview, every time she made a public appearance, she would be pressed to discuss the carjacking. With no other choice, she would begin her account with the words, "My boyfriend and I were on our way home from the mall."

Taylor sagged against the pump house, fatigue oozing from every pore. The heaviness in his chest felt like a stone. His eyes watered in the cold evening air. He heard the snap of brittle twigs behind him, and then looked over his shoulder, deeper into the woods. A deer, he figured.

A car turned onto Wagon Trail. Taylor leaned forward, peering around a sagebrush at the distant headlights. The VW sedan wheeled into a driveway, opposite Kyla's house. The headlights went dark. Where the hell was Kyla? Had he lost track of her for good? No, he argued. She would be back, and he would be waiting for her.

As minutes crawled past, the night grew chilly. Again, Taylor heard the rustle of leaves and the crack of brittle twigs. Something was moving in the woods behind him. What was it? A deer? A raccoon? A curious dog, maybe? Peering around the side of the pump house, he looked over his shoulder into the trees and the darkness. Seeing nothing, he focused on Kyla's house again, frowning at the narrow gate in the backyard fence. Was it locked? he wondered.

Deciding to take a closer look, Taylor scrambled to his feet. The revolver slipped from the waist of his jeans and dropped to the ground. Had his mom noticed that the gun was gone? No. She never carried it. It had belonged to her dad. She probably couldn't locate the cylinder release to load rounds into the chambers.

Wearily, Taylor bent to pick up the revolver. He was tucking it in the waist of his jeans when something hard slammed into his skull. His head erupted in blinding white pain. Stunned, Taylor dropped to his knees, his head throbbing with confusion and fear. A man loomed over him, his raised arm cocked. Taylor twisted away, but a pistol butt slammed into his shoulder.

A strange, cold fury filled Taylor's entire being. What the hell was going on? The man had come out of nowhere. Why had he attacked him?

With all his strength, Taylor rammed his throbbing shoulder into the man's groin. A cry exploded from the attacker's mouth. He doubled over in pain. His cap dropped to the ground. A thick, tangled ponytail dangled by the man's cheek.

Thorp. Taylor sprang to a half stand. *Rylie Thorp.*

Letting out a loud growl, Taylor rammed the man with his head and shoulders, knocking him to the ground. Clumsily Taylor pounced, pinning Thorp on his back, pummeling the man's face and neck with quick, hard jabs. Thorp twisted and bucked, trying to throw Taylor off. With impossible quickness, Thorp cocked his arm, and then slammed the gun into Taylor's temple. He cried out, and then collapsed forward, pinning the gun between them. Steel ground into Taylor's ribs as Thorp fought to free the gun. A deafening blast paralyzed the men. A bullet tore through flesh, and then lodged in a plank of rotting wood on the abandoned pump house.

◆　◆　◆

INSIDE HAZEL'S HOUSE, Blair flinched, and then backed away from the front window. That sound. It sounded like gunfire. She allowed the curtains to close. The crack, a single shot, had come from the woods. Odd, she thought, that someone would be firing a weapon near a neighborhood. It was completely dark, and there was only a sliver of a moon in the inky sky.

The Nissan had been gone from across the street when Blair arrived in Hazel's VW sedan, but she hadn't heard from Manny yet. The woman he knew as Anna Mitchell had agreed to meet him at the Stagger Inn at nine o'clock, five minutes from now. "Please, God," Blair whispered. "Help me. I don't even know what to look for in that house."

Hazel's coat and scarf were draped over the back of the sofa. The dear woman had insisted that Blair wear them to disguise herself. Hazel was clearly worried about Blair's decision to search the Benson house. Blair regretted involving Hazel by asking for the key, but all that really mattered was finding out for sure who was living in the Benson house. Brandi was certain that the woman was Eden Stegall.

"Oh, Brandi," Blair whispered, her stinging eyes pressed shut. Her OCD had spiraled out of control. The child had been so desperate to get to the Safe-T Soap that she had sneaked into the preparation room twice, wearing gloves and a mask. "She saw the baby," Blair moaned.

A clock chimed from somewhere in Hazel's house. The peal was as jagged as a thunderbolt, unravelling Blair's fragile nerves. She drew in a deep, quivering breath, and then cursed Eden Stegall as she exhaled. The clock ceased clanging. Her cell phone vibrated in her pocket, and then jangled loudly. *Beacon.* The ringtone she had assigned to Manny. Withdrawing her phone, Blair tapped the screen. "Manny?"

Music muffled the man's voice. "She's here, Blair. She just walked in the door."

Relief and anxiety swept over Blair. She stressed again that Manny should keep the woman busy. "And, please, don't let her out of your sight. I'm headed to the Benson house now."

"I've got your back, Blair. Don't worry." The man dutifully reviewed their plan. "I'll phone you the instant she leaves here."

"Thanks, Manny." Blair ended the call, sliding the phone in the pocket of her jeans with the key to Jack Benson's house.

Not wanting to be seen, she left Hazel's home through the rear door. A privacy fence outlined the small backyard, shielding Blair from view as she rushed across the yard, and then out the north gate. She emerged in a narrow clearing next to a wooded area at the edge of the development. The neighborhood had no streetlamps, only meager porch lights and lanterns. Keeping in the shadows, Blair walked along the edge of the woods, and then circled behind the Benson house. Seconds later, she was standing on the rear stoop, unlocking the back door.

Inside the silent house, she pulled a flashlight from her waistband, and then followed the beam down a short corridor. It intersected with a longer hall just ahead. Hazel had described the layout. Two guest rooms and the main bedroom were located down the hall to the right. Blair went left to the living room.

The roll-top desk Hazel had mentioned was on the back wall. Blair turned on a lamp, and then set the flashlight aside. The desktop was clear except for a notepad, a Sharpie pen, and a bronze paperweight shaped like a Longhorn steer. She opened and closed each drawer, finding them empty. Something shiny in one of the cubbyholes caught her attention. She slid it out, and then palmed the key ring in her hand. Rubbing her thumb over the cabin-shaped ornament, she cursed the lying thief who had intruded on their lives, and Lenny Bond for putting her up to it.

The main bedroom was dark. Windows on the far wall looked onto the woods. Blair turned on a lamp just inside the door. A suitcase lay open on the bed, its contents in disarray. A pair of black jeans, a rumpled black sweater, and a pair of inside-out socks cluttered the bed. Blair dug through the suitcase, careful to search the bag's numerous zippered compartments. Nothing. She searched the six-drawer dresser, but found only the usual assortment of underwear, sweaters, and a Houston Astros T-shirt.

The mirrored closet door stood part way open. Blair slid it along its tracks. The scraping sound unnerved her. The closet rod held only a few pairs of pants and two shirts hanging cockeyed on wire hangers. Blair ran her hand inside a pair of scuffed black boots lying on the closet floor. A carry-on bag stood in the corner. It felt empty when Blair lifted it, but she searched it anyway. She found nothing but dirty laundry.

The closet shelf held a carton of cigarettes and a tote bag from LL Bean. Blair gripped the sturdy canvas straps, and then dragged the bag off the shelf. It was jammed with unopened mail. Sitting on the edge of the bed, Blair plucked out a random letter. The envelope was addressed to Kyla Phelps at an address in Houston. Blair figured it was an alias the woman used. She thumbed through the remaining mail. It was all addressed to Kyla Phelps.

Setting aside the envelopes, she reached into the bag again, withdrawing this time a tattered white gift box, about three inches thick and twelve inches square. The lid was dented, and one corner torn at the seam. Curious, Blair set the box on her thigh, removed the lid, and then plucked out a thickness of crumpled tissue paper. It was a photo album, used and obviously cheap. Blair opened the cover, staring at the name and date penned on the inside page. Recognition struck with a sharp blow. "It's Jewell's album," Blair sighed. "Thank you, God. Thank you. This is what I was meant to find."

Blair turned the page. The first picture captured Jewell, Lenny, and Brandi at a beach somewhere. Clenched in Brandi's hand was a red, plastic shovel. Blair's heart ached. It was a shovel Brandi had been holding when Jewell snatched her from her sandbox.

Resisting the temptation to look at more pictures, Blair returned the lid to the box, and then set it aside. With angry anticipation creeping inside her, Blair thumbed through the remainder of the mail, glancing at the return addresses. One envelope was imprinted with a post office box number in Miami, but there was no company name. Blair folded black the flap, and then removed a check transmittal letter from *The Public Eye*.

"Damn you." Blair's voice was a croak. She grasped the bottom of the canvas bag, turned it upside down, and dumped the remaining contents onto the rumpled bedspread.

CHAPTER 38

The Stagger Inn was a freestanding wooden building with a tin roof, a narrow front porch, and warped oak floors from the front door to the back. Neon beer signs hung on the walls, and a coin-operated jukebox played a country song Lenny didn't recognize. The crack and roll of balls across the pool table in the back was a heartwarming sound. If his nerves weren't as tight as a fiddle string, Lenny would have felt right at home as he and Jamar made their way across the room.

The place was crowded, mostly with men wearing jeans and a work shirt of some sort. Lenny figured they had stopped off after work for a beer and hadn't gotten around to leaving yet. Two square tables had been pushed together to accommodate three middle-aged couples who were sharing a meal. Chicken fried steaks with cream gravy and baked potatoes. Cheeseburgers, pink and juicy and four inches tall, served with thick cut potatoes. Dub Black called them steak fries. Lenny figured the wedges had been doused with a chunky blend of salt, garlic, and red pepper. Dub never served skinny French fries, saying they were for little kids and sissies.

The patrons paid little attention as Lenny and Jamar made their way to the bar. Few gave them so much as a glance. Lenny noticed that when Jamar slid onto the barstool, he sat at an angle. His dark eyes casually scanned the room. Lenny sat with his back to the customers and the front door. If Eden showed up, he had to be sure she didn't spot him before he had eyes on her.

Smiling as she approached, a woman wearing a red shirt and snug jeans set a bowl of warm peanuts on the bar. "Fresh roasted," she said. Her lips were glossy red, and her smile was Texas friendly. "What can I get you, gentlemen?"

Jamar ordered a Corona and a cold mug. Lenny asked the woman to make it two. Worsham's no alcohol policy at work or on Worsham premises had seriously cut into Lenny's beer consumption. If he had his way, he would drink until Jamar cut him off tonight. Maybe a few beers would help him forget that he had violated his parole the instant Jamar's car tires rolled across the Hays County line.

The woman returned with the Coronas and two frosty mugs. She poured both at once, setting the bottles down when the head of foam was almost to the tops. "My name is Wanda. Do you gentlemen want to look at our bar menu?" When Jamar declined and thanked the woman, she smiled again and said, "Enjoy. I'll check on you later."

Lenny took a long swig of cold beer, and then licked foam off his upper lip. Jamar finished off what was left in the bottle first, and then struck up a conversation with Del, the bartender. Jamar's gaze shifted each time the front door opened. Lenny crushed the shell of a peanut and dropped the pieces on the floor with thousands of others. He popped the warm nuts into his mouth and chewed, listening to a Toby Keith tune on the jukebox. Now that man was a legend, Lenny mused, wishing the Stagger Inn was in Bexar County. This was definitely his kind of place. He was surprised, though, that his niece Eden liked hanging out there. He hardly knew the girl, but he figured her taste in music leaned more toward the ear-splitting kind.

The bartender stepped away to serve other customers. Lenny's nerves had just begun to settle when Jamar tapped his ankle with the toe of his boot. With a quick nod, he pointed to a woman returning from the direction of the restrooms. Lenny eyed the skinny, black-haired girl and frowned. She didn't look like Jamar's type. She sure wasn't Lenny's. The woman behind the bar, though, could eat peanuts in his bed anytime.

Jamar nudged Lenny again. "Is that her or not?"

Lenny set his beer down hard. Jamar was asking if the woman was Eden. Trying not to stare, he watched the girl swap greetings with a heavyset guy who obviously knew her. "Sorry to keep you waiting, Manny. I had to take that call." When the man she called Manny offered to buy her another beer, the girl pulled back a chair, and then sat with her purse in her lap and her phone face down on the table.

Lenny wouldn't have recognized Eden without the picture Arlene had sent. The girl was as thin as a pool cue and as pale as the talc the working man at the pool table was sprinkling on his palm. "That's her, all right," Lenny whispered, his nerves jangling again. "What do we do now?"

"That depends on what she does, doesn't it?" Jamar swiveled on the stool, picked up some peanuts, and crushed them in his hand. Casually, he reached for an empty bowl left by a customer, slid it in front of him, and then tossed the shells into it. The sight reminded Lenny of the way Jamar had squeezed Sylvia Reyes's hand until she flinched.

Lenny had promised Arlene that he would take Eden back to San Antonio and keep her there until she and Herbert could get there from Amarillo. Lenny intended to keep his promise. He had no choice but to trust that Jamar would do it without a commotion. He couldn't afford to bring attention to himself. For all he knew, the deputy sheriff who had arrested him for shooting Victor Rizzo was still on the force. Paul Dillard was a good friend of Blair. The man would get a lot of satisfaction out of placing the cuffs on Lenny Bond again.

CHAPTER 39

Nervous flutterings pricked Blair's chest. She had sneaked inside the Benson house half an hour ago, confident in Manny's and her plan. Nevertheless, she listened anxiously for the sound of a car engine dying in the driveway. The contents of the canvas tote lay scattered on the rumpled bed. Would Eden suspect that it was Blair who had broken into her house, pawed through her belongings, and then taken the album and the key to the cabin? Maybe. But she didn't care what Eden Stegall suspected. If she saw the woman again, Blair would threaten her with legal action. Then she would remind Eden Stegall that Manny Taggert was a friend, and that if she showed her face in Live Oak again, Manny would do more than invite her to meet him at the Stagger Inn for a beer and a game of pool.

With the album tucked under her arm, Blair followed the flashlight beam down the hall. In the living room, she eyed the Sharpie and the notepad. Impulsively, she scrawled a message. GET OUT OF TOWN, EDEN. DO NOT COME BACK!!!

Angrily, Blair yanked the chain on the desk lamp. The room went dark. Again, following the cone of light, she padded back across the living room and down the narrow corridor. The back door was just ahead. Blair quickened her pace, eager to get home to Brandi and Hazel.

"What's your hurry, Kyla?"

Blair shrieked and stumbled back. A hard hand shot out and slammed her shoulder with a bone-jarring blow. The man grabbed her by the neck, pinning her to the wall with excruciating pressure. He yanked a gun from his waist, and then pressed the barrel to her temple. Instinctively, Blair grabbed the man's wrist, dropping the flashlight and the album to the floor.

"Stop. Please. Don't." Her voice was a croak. She wedged her fingertips between her flesh and the man's fingers, trying to relieve the choking pressure. Blair forced herself to look at the shadowy face, her eyes wide with panic and pleading. "I'm not Kyla." The man pressed harder on her neck. Blair's heart pounded in her throat. Her voice sounded strange even to her own ears. "Turn on the light. You'll see. I'm not Kyla. My name is Blair."

The man slid his hand from her neck to her throbbing shoulder, pressing it against the wall. He inched back and flipped the light switch. They both squinted in the glare. Blair forced herself to make eye contact. The man was young. Stubble shadowed his boyish face. His eyes were bloodshot and sunken. His white shirt was soiled and wrinkled. Was that blood on the collar? More smears soiled the sleeve. The hair near the young man's temple was matted with blood.

"Where is she? Where is Kyla?" The man jammed the barrel of the revolver hard against Blair's skull. "And what are you doing in her house?"

"I was looking for that." Blair nudged the album with her shoe, her entire body trembling. "It's mine. She stole it."

"Where is she?"

Blair weighed her answer. The man had a gun. He clearly intended to harm Eden Stegall. "I'm not sure where she is. I saw that her car was gone. I sneaked into her house."

The man jabbed the barrel against Blair's head again, his arm and hand shaking. "Don't lie to me. You know where she is. You know when she's coming back. You wouldn't be in her house if you didn't."

Blair squinted in pain and gathering panic. She was trembling so violently she could hardly stand. But she must not panic. The man was not here to hurt her. It was Kyla … Eden he wanted. If she told him where Eden was, what would he do? The man had a gun. Did he plan to kill Eden?

God, help me, she prayed. What do I do?

The man reached behind him, and then turned off the light. Pale moonlight shone through the curtain behind him, but his face remained shadowed. His arm sagged, as if he were tired of holding the gun to Blair's head. When she spoke, Blair's voice was brittle with fear. "Why are you looking for Kyla?"

"She nearly killed my girlfriend." The man spoke in a neutral way, without inflection, "and she's going to pay for it."

"Your girlfriend … Will she be okay?"

"She'll never be okay. Kyla Phelps ran over her with a car. A doctor amputated her foot. She'll never be okay."

"I'm so sorry," Blair whispered. Her eyes were wide with fear and the urgent need to read the man's face. "We both have reasons to hate her. My daughter was kidnapped when she was a baby. She's home now, but the man who kidnapped her was just released from prison. I suspected that the woman living here is his niece. I was searching the house for proof."

"And you found it."

"Yes. I was on my way out when—" Blair's cell phone rang, the sound like a thunderbolt. *Beacon.* It was Manny. Eden Stegall was leaving the Stagger Inn.

"Don't even think about it."

The man jabbed Blair with the barrel again. "But it's—"

"Forget it, I said."

The ringing continued. "I have to answer it," Blair pleaded. "If I don't, he'll know something is wrong."

The gunman's hand shook violently. He was about to come out of his skin. If Eden walked through the door, would he kill her? She had nearly killed his girlfriend. Blair's mind worked frantically. "I have to answer it. He'll come here if I don't."

"All right. Answer it." The man grabbed Blair by the wrist, twisting it hard. "Put it on speaker. Don't do anything stupid. I don't want to hurt you."

Blair retrieved her cell phone, and then tapped the screen. Her throat hurt. Her heart hammered. "Hello." Her voice was little more than a whisper.

"She just left here, Blair. She said she was headed home. Is everything okay?"

Blair's mind raced. "Everything is fine … Paul." She forced herself to look the gunman in the face. Had he seen Manny's name on the screen? "Thanks for checking on me. I'll get out of here as quick as I can." Blair ended the call, praying that Manny had heard what she said, that she had called him Paul, that he understood she needed help.

With a trembling hand, Blair relinquished her phone to the gunman when he reached for it. "He won't come here now, but I'm supposed to meet him soon. Please let me go."

"I can't do that." Gripping Blair's arm, he propelled her down the narrow hall toward the bedroom. "I can't let you call the cops."

In the bedroom, the man stuck the revolver in the waist of his jeans, and then yanked the sash from Eden's robe. He tied Blair's hands behind her back, and then pointed to a chair in the corner. "Sit there." When the man began pawing through the contents of the suitcase, Blair worried that he was looking for a gag. "What's your name?"

"Mac."

"If you're looking for a gag, Mac, it's not necessary." Blair's voice was low and calm. "I won't scream. I got what I came here for. Now it's your turn."

CHAPTER 40

Brandi and Hazel waited nervously for Blair to return. She had left for Hazel's almost an hour ago in Hazel's VW, telling them not to worry. "Manny's got my back. He will let me know when Eden gets to the Stagger Inn, and then keep an eye on her. If she leaves, Manny will let me know right away." Hazel had made Blair promise to text them. "Don't let us sit here and worry." On the way out the door, Blair had joked that Eden Stegall was the one who needed to worry.

With Nixon in her arms, Brandi walked to the front window and looked out, watching for headlights on Southworth Road. It all seemed unreal. At this very moment, her mom was inside the Benson house all alone. What would she find? Proof that the woman was really Eden Stegall? Brandi had been suspicious of the impostor Anna Mitchell all along, but she had never suspected that she was Eden. The black hair. The blue contacts. The ring she wore to hide the tattoo. And years had passed since Brandi had seen Eden.

With each tick of the mantle clock, Brandi's anxiety increased. Nixon seemed to sense her nervousness and stayed unusually still in her arms. Why wasn't her mom home yet? What if there was no cell signal inside the Benson house, and Manny couldn't reach her? The last text Brandi had received had been sent from inside Hazel's house.

Desperate, Brandi called her mom's cell. It went immediately to voicemail. But why? Why didn't she answer? "I can't just sit here and do nothing," Brandi muttered. "I have to be sure Mom's okay."

Brandi turned away from the window, and then lowered Nixon to the floor. "Hazel, I'm going to let Nixon out, and then wait for Mom in my room."

"Okay, dear. Surely she won't be much longer."

Brandi walked toward the hall, motioning for the dog to follow her. "I'll let him out the door in Mom's bedroom, Hazel. The light is better on that end of the house."

In her mom's bedroom, Brandi disarmed the security system, and then waited by the door while Nixon lifted his leg on the trunk of an oak. Letting him back inside, she rearmed the security system. Over the beep of the keypad countdown, she whispered, "Go to Hazel. I'll be back. I have to make sure my mom is safe."

Slipping out the door in her mom's new bathroom, Brandi zipped her lightweight sweatshirt, and then picked her way around the end of the cabin. When she was certain that Hazel was not at the front window, she made her way up the driveway. Worry dogged her every step. Why wasn't her mom home yet? Had Manny Taggert messed up? Had he failed to signal that Eden was on her way home?

At Southworth Road, Brandi started jogging, her arms and legs pumping. By the time she reached Wagon Trail, the only entrance to the mobile home park, she was winded. She paused in the shadow of a live oak to catch her breath. Hazel's house was the last on the left, the Benson house directly across the street. Brandi peered around the enormous trunk, and then spotted Hazel's VW parked in her driveway. Wagon Trail curved a little to the right, making it impossible for Brandi to have a clear view of the Benson house from where she was standing.

Taking a deep, calming breath, Brandi stepped out from behind the tree, and then walked briskly down the street. She was almost to Hazel's house when she heard a car on Southworth Road. Glancing over her shoulder, she watched headlights appear on Wagon Trail. Was Eden coming home?

Brandi raced to Hazel's driveway. She ducked behind the Volkswagen, positive that she had not been seen. The headlights grew brighter with each passing second. "Oh, Mom," Brandi whispered, peering around the front fender. "Get out of there."

A thought whipped in suddenly. Maybe her mom was not in the house. There was no reason that she would have stayed so long. She could have left the Benson house through the back door and decided to leave Hazel's car in the driveway. That had to be it. To avoid being seen on Wagon Trail, she had left through the back door and had come out on Southworth Road.

The car continued its approach, and then slowed. When the Nissan pulled into the driveway at the Benson house, Brandi slipped out of view into Hazel's backyard. She emerged seconds later in a narrow clearing on the edge of the woods. She ducked behind a tree when a second car screeched to a stop behind the Nissan. Two men jumped out, and then rushed to the Nissan. One of the men jerked the driver's door open. The dome lamp lit the interior. The woman behind the wheel screamed.

Fear drove Brandi deeper into the shadows. The man was pulling Eden out of the car now. What was happening? Brandi froze, afraid to move, afraid to make a sound. Angry voices tangled and twisted. She listened intently, catching the argument in disjointed phrases. Eden shrieked when the dark-skinned man slapped her in the face. The other man grabbed her by the arm.

"You're going to get your idiot self arrested, Eden. Now let's go." Eden struggled to free her arm. "Get your hands off me. I'm not going anywhere with you, Lenny."

Brandi ducked behind a tree, shrinking back into the shadows. Her heart raced. *Lenny.* Eden had called the man Lenny. Thoughts collided in her head. Eden and Lenny. They were working together. He had told her where to find Jewell's album. She had sold the pictures to Wilson Rule.

"Why did I believe him?" Brandi whispered, dismayed and angry. "Never again. Never."

Out of view, Brandi peered around the live oak tree. The shouting had died down, but the argument had not. Brandi had never heard Lenny yell at anyone. "Don't you get it, Eden? You've been had. I promised Arlene that I would—"

Brandi couldn't hear the rest of what Lenny said. Eden was shouting over him, cursing him to his face. The other man gripped Eden's chin, and then smacked the back of her head against the car window. "Stop lying. You sold those pictures to Wilson Rule. Not Lenny. And you were in New Braunfels that day, weren't you?" The man yelled in Eden's face. "Admit it!"

Brandi had never seen a fight, and it frightened her. She backed away, her heart pounding in her chest. Her mom was safe now. If she had still been in the house, she would have heard the commotion and run out the back door. Trembling, Brandi backed farther into the shadows. Her heel landed on something. She glanced down.

A glove?

No! A hand!

A scream tore from Brandi's mouth. Images assaulted her mind. Fingers white and limp. A dark jacket hunched up in the back. Hair stuck to a blood-streaked profile.

Brandi stumbled out of the woods, and then ran across the clearing. She tried to yell, but her throat constricted, snagging disjointed sounds. The dark man spotted her and pointed. Lenny released Eden's arm. "That's Brandi!" He raced across the yard toward the clearing, jerking to a stop when he reached her. "Brandi, what in the world are you doing here?"

"In the woods—" Brandi's stark white face twisted. She grappled for Lenny's forearm, her brittle fingers clawing at his sleeve. "My mom. She's dead." The sharp edge of terror splintered her voice. "Eden killed my mom."

CHAPTER 41

Blair had no idea how much time had passed since the man grabbed her, but it seemed like an eternity. She had gingerly begun what felt like the insane process of getting to know her abductor. His name was Mac, so he said. Blair didn't think he intended to harm her, but the gun made her incredibly nervous, and her hands were tied behind her with a sash from Eden's robe.

He was standing in the corner of the dark bedroom now, his fingers between the window trim and the edge of the curtain. The commotion in the driveway had subsided, but Mac continued to watch.

"What's happening, Mac?"

"I'm not sure. The Black man is still holding onto Kyla. But I can't see the other guy."

"Mac, we have to get out of here." Blair worked her hands and wrists, trying to loosen the sash. "You can't take on both of those men." He ignored her warning, and then let the curtain drop. "What's happening now?"

Mac stepped away from the window. "They're coming this way."

"Please, Mac. This could get ugly in a hurry. Let's get out of here. You can confront Kyla later, when she's alone." The young man dropped his chin. He was weighing his options. "You don't have to do it right now, Mac. It's too dangerous."

The front door banged open. Mac pointed the gun in Blair's direction, warning her to keep quiet as he crept across the room to the half-open bedroom door.

The argument that had started in the driveway continued. Voices in the living room tangled. Blair recognized one right away. It was Eden Stegall's. She didn't recognize the male voices, but one of the men was shouting orders.

"Sit your ass down, or I'll bust your other lip. You ain't messing with your Uncle Lenny here."

Blair ceased struggling against the sash. *Uncle Lenny.* The man knew Lenny Bond. Was he there to collect Lenny's cut of the money from *The Public Eye?* Lenny wouldn't dare violate his parole by entering Hays County to collect it himself. Or would he?

With soaring determination, Blair struggled against the sash. Was Lenny Bond the White man arguing with Eden? If she could get closer to the door, she could hear the voices more clearly. But she and Mac had to get out of the house. Was either of the men armed?

The coarse fabric dug into Blair's wrists, but she continued to fight against it. Suddenly, the sash gave way. Blair froze for a moment, no longer than a breath, and then jerked her hands free.

The revolver was in Mac's right hand. Blair approached him from the left, and then whispered his name. The sound startled him. Blair quickly covered her mouth with her hand, and then shook her head from side to side. *I won't make a sound*, she signaled. Grasping Mac's forearm, she pleaded with her eyes. *We have to get out of here.*

Detecting a faint nod of Mac's head, Blair braced herself when he raised the gun. Instead of putting it to her head, though, Mac tapped his chest with the barrel, signaling that he would go first. Protectively, he tucked Blair behind him with his free hand.

In an awkward tandem, the two squeezed out the half-open bedroom door into the narrow hall. Blair's screaming nerves magnified the sound of their breaths and the creak of the floor as they crept along, hugging the wall. Voices were more distinct now. Eden was crying. One of the men told her to shut up. The other said, "We gotta get out of here, Jamar." He sounded like Lenny Bond. Yes. Blair was sure of it.

"Brandi stumbled onto a dead man in the woods," Lenny said, his voice high pitched and thin with alarm. "Poor kid. She thought Eden killed her mom."

The nightmarish words sent Blair's heart into sudden shock. *Brandi. A dead man. In the woods.* What was Lenny talking about? Where was Brandi? Was she inside the house? Blair rejected the terrifying prospect with all her strength. It wasn't possible. Brandi was at the cabin with Hazel.

Voices in the living room grew loud again. Lenny sounded panicked. "Tell her, Eden. You tell Brandi the truth."

"All right, damn you. Lenny had nothing to do with the pictures, April. It was all me."

"Tell her why I'm here in Live Oak," he demanded.

"My parents sent him here to get me. He's taking me to San Antonio."

Blair tried to pull away, but Mac blocked her way. *Brandi was in the living room.* What had she been doing in the woods? My God! She had stumbled over a dead man.

Vaguely aware that Mac was tugging her toward the back door exit, Blair stiffened and backed away. He looked over his shoulder, his shadowy face questioning. Blair leaned in close, her whisper as jagged as her nerves. "I can't leave. Brandi is in there. My daughter." She leaned away, touched the gun, and then motioned to the back door. "Go, Mac. Please."

Mac shook his head. "No. Not without Kyla."

Tightening his grip on Blair's wrist, the man forced Blair to follow. She ceased resisting. What would he do when they reached the end of the hall? Did Lenny or the other man have a gun? There was a dead man in the woods. Had Mac killed him? *Brandi.* What was she doing here?

Mac crooked his arm around Blair's neck, and then dragged her out of the shadows. He pointed the gun straight ahead and shouted. "Don't anybody move!"

Voices went instantly silent. The room was as quiet as a tomb. Blair scanned the space in a frantic search. Then her child's horrified voice came from near the front door. "Mom!" She was huddled in Lenny's arms, her head burrowed into his chest.

"Brandi, it's okay. Stay close to Lenny." Blair's voice was a croak. "Everyone just do as he says. Just stay where you are. It's Eden he's after."

A strangled gasp rose from a dark corner. Eden was sitting in a chair, the Black man looming over her. Blair recognized him as the man who had driven Lenny to New Braunfels.

Mac stiffened his arm, training the gun at Eden's head. "Get away from her," he ordered the man, his voice a sharp knife of authority. "Get over there with them."

The man backed away, dodging a low coffee table. Blair stood perfectly still, Mac's grip still vice-like around her neck. Lenny held Brandi in his arms, muffling her whimpers in his chest. Eden cringed in a wing chair, tracked down by a young man who hated her.

"You don't even know who I am, do you, Kyla?" Mac was shouting in Blair's ear. "I'm Taylor McFadden. You pointed a gun in my face, you bitch. And you ran over my girlfriend with a car. Hannah Rennick. Do you even know her name? Answer me!"

"Of course, I know her name," Eden yelled, her voice shrill with fear and panic. "I'm so sorry. I didn't mean to hurt her."

"They cut off her foot!"

Blair gasped, twisting her head to face the desperate young man. "Taylor, please. You got what you wanted. Look at her. She's scared out of her mind. She confessed. If you leave now, I give you my word, I will call the sheriff. They will arrest her. They will take her straight to jail. Please, Taylor. My daughter is standing right over there. Look at her. She's scared. Please let Lenny take her home."

"I can't."

"Yes, you can," she insisted firmly.

Lenny cleared his throat, and then cleared it again. "Come on, man. Let me get this girl out of here."

"Please, Taylor," Blair begged. "If you're worried that she'll phone the police, she won't. Just let her go. I'll stay here. Brandi won't call the police."

Lenny stood perfectly still, his arms around Brandi. "Look, man. I violated my parole coming after Eden. I'm not looking to tangle with the law. Let me get Brandi out of here."

"Taylor, please," Blair pleaded, squeezing his forearm. "She's a little girl. Like Hannah was not so long ago. Let Lenny take her home."

The young man nodded wearily, his gaze locked on Lenny. "But Blair stays. I'm warning you, man. No cops. That dead guy in the woods … he didn't shoot himself you know."

Lenny released Brandi long enough to grip the knob and open the front door. Then he shoved her out the opening and followed. "Go! Go!"

With startling suddenness, the front door flung fully open. It banged against the exterior of the house. A dark form lurched to the side, out of view on the porch. Taylor twisted toward the racket, the wobbling gun held shoulder high. His sudden movement knocked Blair off balance. She staggered into the desk, jarring the lamp. The Black man ducked into the kitchen. Eden Stegall cowered in the wing chair.

Blair caught movement in the back hall. The muzzle of a pistol glinted. An agonizing instant later, Paul Dillard stormed forward. "Drop the gun!" The absolute authority in his voice ricocheted around the room. "Sheriff's Department. Put the gun down! Now!"

Taylor's eyes were wild with fear. He swiveled toward the shout, the gun still raised. Partway through the arc, Blair grabbed the bronze paperweight and hurled it, hitting Taylor in the face with a vicious crack.

Paul Dillard shot forward, shouldering the man to the floor. Manny Taggert burst into the room through the open front door. Eden Stegall stumbled toward him, and he grabbed her by the arm.

The struggle on the floor ended as suddenly as it had begun. Taylor went limp, and then released his grip on the revolver. Blair kicked the gun aside, trembling, her heart pounding in shock and relief. Paul shouted commands while he holstered his weapon. "Face to the floor! Now!" He cuffed Taylor's hands behind his back, and then rose to his feet, breathless. Blair dropped into the desk chair, burying her face in her shaking hands.

CHAPTER 42

Two Weeks later

San Antonio, Texas

Lenny Bond was surprised to find that, despite Tommy Lee Worsham being the boss, his office wasn't a bit fancier than Hortense Holder's. His oak desk and the credenza against the wall behind it both looked used. The upholstery on the chair where Lenny sat was worn on the front edge, but the frame was solid.

The instant he had gotten the message that Mr. Worsham wanted to see him, Lenny's stomach had twisted into a knot. Jamar had been pressing him to tell their boss about going to Live Oak and what had happened there. Lenny had yet to see the value in poking Tommy Lee Worsham with a stick. Now he worried that the man had found out on his own.

But how? Lenny puzzled. Blair had persuaded her deputy friend Paul Dillard to let Lenny and Jamar leave after the ruckus ended. "Paul, they were trying to stop Eden," Blair had explained, her hand firmly pressed against the man's chest. "Lenny violated his parole to help Brandi. Please, Paul. You can get their statements later." Because of Blair's intervention, Lenny and Jamar had been back in the dorm before midnight.

Lenny had spoken with his sister several times since that night. Eden was in a Houston jail. For now, her parents were refusing to bail her out. Their daughter was in serious trouble. Identity theft was the least of it. The girl had teamed up with a thug named Rylie Thorp and pulled off a carjacking. Now Thorp was dead, and a girl named Hannah Rennick had an amputated foot.

"What the hell got into that girl?" Lenny muttered. Eden could spend more time in prison than he had.

Pushing all that misery aside, Lenny pondered the possibility that the meeting with his boss had nothing to do with what happened in Live Oak. Maybe Worsham intended to brag on him. Even Dub Black had admitted that Lenny and the crew were doing a good job on the retaining wall, and Dub Black was one hard man to please.

Lenny stood at attention when Tommy Lee Worsham walked through the door. His attorney shuffled in behind him. Lenny extended his hand to his boss, managing not to flinch when they shook. "How's it going, Mr. Worsham? Nice office you got here." Nodding, he shook Monaghan's spongy hand. "Howdy, counselor."

Monaghan squeezed into a chair in the corner. The man's hips spread from side to side and bulged under the chair arms. When Worsham sat, Lenny followed suit, fearing that crumbs of hope for an attaboy meeting would soon turn to dust.

Without missing a beat, Worsham launched into the purpose of the meeting. "Mr. Bond, I don't usually meet with new employees so soon after hire, but something has come up." Worsham opened a folder lying on his desk. "I have a couple of letters here that we need to discuss."

Lenny swallowed hard. Unless Mr. Worsham was a kidder—and Lenny didn't much figure him to be one—the man wasn't fixing to read letters of appreciation from the head honcho over at the job site.

"This one is from your parole officer." Worsham tapped his thumb on the letter, gazing at Lenny. "Mr. Aleman and I spoke recently about a letter he received from an attorney representing Senator Myles Lakeman."

Lenny's stomach lurched. "Oh, hell," he muttered.

"The senator's attorney alerted Mr. Aleman to the fact that you were in violation of your parole." Worsham read from the letter. "The terms of Lenny Bond's parole forbid him from contact of any kind with the senator's child, Brandi Emerson-Lakeman. Despite this prohibition, Mr. Bond is believed to have provided or sold photographs of the child to author Wilson Rule and/or to a tabloid. Mr. Bond, though he admits to having had in his possession the originals of some of the photographs, denies having sold copies for publication and/or profit."

Lenny's knees had begun to bounce when he heard the words *parole violation*. Now both legs were vibrating uncontrollably, the heels of his work boots inches off the carpeted floor.

Worsham continued. "The reason I asked Mr. Monaghan to attend this…"

His boss continued speaking, but Lenny was incapable of listening. There was a train wreck going on inside his head again. Blair knew for a fact that he had not sold pictures to Wilson Rule or anyone else. She had overheard Eden confess to the whole mess that night in the mobile home, but she had allowed Myles Lakeman to sic his lawyer on Lenny anyway. Now he was about to get fired because of it. If he didn't get another job quick, Aleman would write him up, and his parole would get yanked.

"Mr. Bond, are you listening?" Worsham asked.

"Yes, sir. No, sir."

"Mr. Monaghan asked if there was anything you wanted to say?"

"Not guilty, sir." Lenny grabbed for words like a child after spilt M&M's. "Mr. Worsham, sir, I did violate my parole, but I swear to God that I did not sell pictures of Brandi to nobody. I wouldn't do such a thing."

Monaghan shifted his weight. The chair groaned. "Then what was the nature of the parole violation, Mr. Bond?"

The man stared Lenny down, as if he were a human lie detector. Lenny blinked. "Here's the truth, gentleman. The whole truth and nothing but the truth, so help me God."

Lenny spoke nonstop for five miserable minutes. He admitted to meeting Blair in New Braunfels to hand over the treasure chest and everything Jewell had squirreled away inside it. He told them about searching for Jewell's missing photo album, so that he could give it to Blair too. Finally, he told them about his niece Eden stealing a woman's identity and showing up in Live Oak to spy on Blair and Brandi.

"I promised my sister I'd go to Live Oak and get her girl, that I'd get her away from Brandi. So I did that. Eden is in jail in Houston, where she belongs." Lenny's brain began to wind down. He could feel it running out of words. "So, yes, sir. I did violate my parole, but I didn't know what else to do, given the dire circumstances I found myself in."

The two men exchanged looks. Lenny read their minds. *Can you believe this loser?*

Worsham slid another paper from the file. He leaned back in his chair, gazing down at the document. "Lenny, are you familiar with the term *mea culpa?*"

"No, sir," Lenny admitted, his mouth so dry he had no spit.

"A *mea culpa* is a formal acknowledgment of a personal fault or error." Worsham grinned, and then tossed the paper to Lenny with a flick of his wrist. "I would have that *mea culpa* framed if I were you. It's from a United States senator. Those clowns don't often admit it when they're wrong."

CHAPTER 43

Two Weeks later

Austin, Texas

Blair took the elevator to a cafeteria at Children's Hospital. At three o'clock in the afternoon, the tables were mostly empty. For the time being, only Charlotte and Butler were allowed in Alli's room. The child's immune system was severely weakened. The medical team was keeping exposure to a minimum. Although the procedure had not been scheduled, the decision had been made. Allison would undergo a bone marrow transplant.

Charlotte and Butler had decided on Children's Hospital in Austin, rather than MD Anderson. When Allison had first been diagnosed, they had chosen MD Anderson, in part, because Butler's sister worked there. She had been invaluable to them as they navigated the daunting task of caring for a child with cancer. Bethany had also lived near the medical complex and had insisted that Charlotte and Butler stay in her home. But now, Bethany had retired from nursing, and moved to Galveston.

Knowing that Alli would receive excellent care at Children's Hospital, Blair was enormously relieved to have her family close to home again. Now that the transplant decision was made, the search for a donor could get underway.

Blair had told Charlotte nothing about Eden Stegall or what happened the night she had sneaked into Jack Benson's mobile home. The near-disastrous confrontation seemed unimaginable to Blair now. But picturing Brandi in the middle of it all made it jarringly real.

Pressing the memories aside, Blair scanned the cafeteria. She spotted Taylor McFadden easily. He and Blair had talked on the phone several times since that night. She had spoken with Taylor's mother, too, a loving woman devoted to her son. Yesterday, Taylor had asked if he could visit her. "Hannah wants to meet you." Knowing she would be in Austin, Blair had suggested they meet at the hospital.

Taylor looked little like he had that horrible night almost a month ago. He was a handsome young man, his lean face stubble free. He wore a crisp, blue shirt and neatly creased Wranglers. The girl sitting beside him was lovely. No wonder, Blair thought, that CB Western Wear had selected Hannah Rennick to help launch its new clothing line.

Taylor faced some legal matters with respect to the gun, but the death of Rylie Thorp had been ruled accidental. The man had followed Taylor from Houston to Live Oak, and then attacked him in the woods. Thorp had been shot with his own gun in the struggle.

A detective in the case speculated that Thorp was actually after the woman he knew as Kyla Phelps, knowing that she could implicate him in the carjacking. The man had been a career criminal, a suspect in a home invasion, and the assault on an elderly Houston man. Few people, Blair figured, would mourn the death of Rylie Thorp.

Taylor spotted Blair and stood, his body language signaling his nervousness. Blair extended her hand. The young man took it, but then embraced her with his free arm. Blair was deeply touched and hugged Taylor tightly, patting his back until he released her.

"Blair, this is my girlfriend, Hannah Rennick."

"I'm very glad to meet you, Hannah." Blair sat opposite the couple, taking in their fresh young faces, and the aluminum walker pushed to the side. Hannah had been fitted with a prosthesis. According to Taylor, she called it her bionic foot.

"Blair, I know you need to get back to your family," Hannah began, "but I had to say thank you. Taylor and I owe you so much. I'm sorry you got caught in the middle that night, but I don't know what would have happened to Taylor if you hadn't been there."

Like Hannah, Blair had pondered countless what-ifs since that night. What if Taylor had attacked Blair, and then realized she wasn't Kyla Phelps? What if Manny had not picked up on Blair's signal that she needed help. *Thanks for checking on me, Paul. I'll get out of here as quick as I can.* What if Taylor had not consented to let Lenny get Brandi out of the house? What if Taylor's gun had discharged when Paul slammed him to the floor?

Taylor slid a saltshaker in front of him and began spinning it between this thumb and index finger. His expression said he was choosing his words. "Blair, I've said this already, but I'm really sorry about what I put you through. It was like something took over me. It was rage. I was so angry. I wanted revenge. I wanted Kyla Phelps to pay. And I felt so guilty about Hannah. I was out of control. I should have confided in my mom. I know that now."

"Believe me, Taylor," Blair said, her tone compassionate. "I am all too familiar with the power of guilt and rage. What do you think drove me to sneak into Jack Benson's house that night? Those feelings can propel us into some scary territory."

In their previous conversations, Blair had told Taylor about Brandi's abduction, doing her best to describe the breathtaking guilt she labored under for leaving her two-year-old child alone. She had done her best to describe the rage and fear she had battled when Lenny Bond, after his extortion attempt, had eluded police and fled to Mexico. Finally, she had explained to the guilt-stricken young man why she had sneaked into the Benson house that night.

"Taylor," Blair continued, "I'd like to say that you'll get past believing you failed Hannah, but that's not entirely true. The guilt, the regret, the shame. It comes and goes. It will be the same for you, Hannah, as you cope with fear and anger, and with the sadness you might feel about your loss. But, trust me, both of you will learn to work around the fallout from being victims of crime. It's the only way you can fully live the life God gave you."

To lighten the tone, Blair brought up the subject of Hannah's modeling contract. "I'll be watching for the ad campaign. Should I ask for your autograph now?"

Hannah laughed. Taylor put his arm around her and squeezed. His expression said that he loved the sound of the girl's laughter. This was the first time Blair had seen this handsome young man with a smile on his face.

"We don't want to keep you, Blair," Taylor repeated. "We need to get back to Houston. We have another stop to make this evening."

"Not another apology stop, I hope," Blair said teasingly.

Taylor exaggerated a what-can-I-say shrug. "When I was playing private detective, I came between a little boy and his dad."

Blair listened sympathetically as Taylor explained how he had teamed up with a little boy who lived next door to the woman he knew as Kyla Phelps, enlisting him to spy on her and to report to Taylor. He had even told the boy to keep their secret from his dad.

"My mom and Hannah think I need to make things right with Ben and his dad." Taylor grinned guiltily. "Mom loaned me some money to buy Benjamin James Walters a tablet at Walmart. I'm working there. I also have to pay for his Internet access for the near future."

"Hmm. That's quite an apology." Blair suspected there was more to the story.

"Ben needs to keep in touch with his mom." Taylor smiled again, mischievously this time. "She's a soldier in Ger-na-my."

CHAPTER 44

TWO WEEKS LATER

LIVE OAK, TEXAS

Brandi rested her head on the chaise cushion, and then closed her eyes to the warm afternoon sun. Her mom had covered her legs with a quilt before going inside to check on the cobbler. The reporter, Jason Hammond, would be there soon. Nixon, after completing his mysterious circling maneuver, curled at Brandi's feet, his weight anchoring the quilt in place. The tiny Shih Tzu leaped onto the chaise. Brandi thought Nixon looked annoyed in the seconds before he nestled his head in the folds of the quilt.

Martha Goode had brought Mitzi by yesterday after the welcome home party Hazel had organized. She was a gruff woman, but she had said goodbye to her father's companion with tears in her eyes. "Brandi will take good care of you until Allison gets home. Okay, Mitzi? The little girl needs you, and she's going to love you as much as Dad did." Allison didn't know about Mitzi yet, and Brandi could hardly wait to tell her.

Brandi shifted in the chair and grimaced. Her hip hurt like crazy. Sometime the pain shot down her leg all the way to her knee. The doctor had inserted the enormous needle into her hip over and over again, sucking marrow from deep in her bone. Harvesting, he called it. Brandi called the whole process bizarre and disgusting. All that mattered, though, was that at this very moment, Brandi's healthy cells were multiplying in Alli's bloodstream, and giving the wicked cancer cells the fight of their lives.

During her hospital stay, Brandi would pretend to be asleep, trying to calm the whirlwind in her head. So much had happened, and so fast. Images and sounds of that horrible night at the Benson house still tangled in her mind. Eden was in jail, and Brandi was glad. The girl she once thought was her cousin deserved to pay for what she did to Hannah Rennick and her boyfriend Taylor McFadden. Brandi liked to think that Eden was being punished for lying, too, and for betraying people who cared about her. She had stolen Jewell's photo album and another woman's identification. She had sold family pictures to Wilson Rule and to *The Public Eye*. Lenny had violated his parole because of Eden. He could have been sent back to prison. Had Lenny been told about the second letter her dad had written to his parole officer?

Since that disastrous night, Brandi had apologized to Hazel for deceiving her. "You're an honest person, Hazel, but I was not honest with you." Her mom had called sneaking out of the cabin impulsive and reckless. "When I'm finished feeling grateful and relieved that you're safe, I'm going to be furious with you." Brandi had told her mom that she was sorry, but she did not say what she was sorry about. She had wanted to say, "I'm sorry that man pulled a gun on you, but I'm not sorry for trying to protect you."

♦ ♦ ♦

BLAIR FILLED THE kettle with filtered water, and then set it on the stove to heat. A foil-covered dish of blackberry cobbler warmed in the oven. Al Finley had brought it by yesterday at the appointed time. The persistent man had told Blair that he was out of her favorite peach cobbler, but she didn't believe him. As much as she resisted admitting it, though, Al was right. The man's blackberry cobbler was amazing.

The refrigerator held leftovers from yesterday's fried chicken feast. Hazel had organized a welcome home party for Brandi that had lasted fewer than thirty minutes. "I know you're tired, Brandi, after the drive back from Austin. But we just had to welcome you home."

The guests had been waiting on the front porch. Hazel had retrieved the *Chin Up!* caricature from Brandi's room. Brandi's best friends, Nekisha Jackson and Stephanie Patterson, had presented the treasure as if Brandi had never seen it before. Then the girls led the small crowd in a hysterical rendition of *For She's a Jolly Good Cousin.* Paul Dillard had helped Brandi maneuver the porch steps. The child had faced the harvest procedure courageously, but her hip was still painfully sore.

The night before the procedure, in an utterly intimate moment, Brandi had asked if Blair believed in miracles. In a precious mother-daughter moment, she had asked Brandi for her definition of a miracle. "It's when something so awesome happens that only God could have come up with it." Then they had relived a number of extraordinary events, connecting them together like pearls on a string.

They had decided to give God the credit for the miracles that had happened in their lives. "I'm home with you, Mom," Brandi had said, adding teasingly that she was safe and relatively sound. "And now, I'm the only one in the family with bone marrow for Alli. How miraculous is that?"

Gazing out the kitchen window, Blair smiled at the sight of Brandi lying on a chaise. Gusts of a late fall breeze fluttered the edges of the quilt covering her legs. Nixon and Mitzi were nestled in the folds. It was through this open kitchen window that Brandi had first heard about the Safe-T Soap while listening in on Blair's conversation with Alli. Weeks before that day, Brandi had cut back on her medication. There were days, she had explained, that falling asleep in class had seemed far worse than worrying about germs and washing rituals. But the inadequate levels of the drug, combined with Brandi's anxiety over the trip to Washington, the sudden media attention, and Alli's illness had caused her washing ritual to spiral out of control. Desperation had driven Brandi to brave the preparation room twice in search of what she called the special soap.

The kettle whistled. Blair poured the bubbling water into a thermal pitcher, and then carried a tray of tea essentials to the picnic table. A car pulled into the driveway right on time. Nixon and Mitzi leaped off the chaise, and then bounded across the backyard.

Like before, Jason Hammond looked as if he had slept in his car. His jeans were wrinkled, his shirt hastily tucked. He introduced the lanky man with him as a photojournalist, referring to him simply as Bird. Blair introduced both men to Brandi. The dogs sniffed the men's shoes and pants legs, quickly lost interest, and then reclaimed their spots in the folds of the quilt.

Blair set a glass of tomato juice on a small wooden table within Brandi's reach, and then offered hot tea to their guests. Jason accepted, but Bird went right to work. To Blair, the task could best be described as fiddling with a camera and a slick new iPhone. Jason and Blair made polite conversation, and then Bird signaled to Jason with a thumbs up.

"Brandi, we have a surprise for you." Bird passed her his phone. "Your aunt is putting Allison on the line. Take a look at the video we just sent her."

Brandi tapped the screen, instantly grinning. "Oh, my gosh. Mom, look!"

Blair knelt next to the chaise. On the screen in astonishingly brilliant colors was a video of Brandi with Nixon and Mitzi asleep at her feet. The sweet little Shih Tzu's coat had been clipped to simplify care. Her big, dark eyes looked into the camera with an adorable expression. "Where a Shih Tzu goes," Martha Goode had said, "chuckles and mischief follow." Nixon was clearly unimpressed by his prissy companion, but his impeccable manners required that he share his space with her.

Bird explained to Brandi that hospital policy placed limitations on what electronics could be brought into Allison's room. "But my new phone has an awesome little speaker. I'll be creating another video while you're talking to your cousin. It will pick up every word the two of you say. Then you can both relive this day forever."

Brandi giggled. "This is so cool."

Seconds later, a weak, hoarse voice floated from the speaker. "Brandi, hi. It's me. I got the video. Is that Mitzi sleeping next to Nixon?"

"Yes. She's our house guest for a little while. Miss Goode brought her here yesterday."

"Neat." Allison's voice deflated even more. "Then where is Mitzi going?"

"To *your* house, silly."

Alli's squeal was weak, but the effect was electric. Brandi beamed. "Mitzi is your dog now, Alli."

"For real? Honest? Mom, is it okay? Mom's laughing, Brandi. Did you already know, Mom?"

Brandi giggled again. "Of course, she knew. Our moms always stick together." Brandi shifted on the chaise and flinched. "Oh, Alli, I miss you. I can't wait for you to come home."

"Me, too, Brandi. Maybe it won't be too long. Today my doctor said that our blood cells really like hanging out together."

Struck by unexpected emotions, Blair went inside the house, and then took the cobbler from the oven. She lingered by the window, gathering control. The transplant had gone smoothly. Chances of a cure for Allison had been dramatically increased, but she was still a very sick child, and sometimes sick children died, like tiny Elizabeth Christian.

Blair pressed down the distressing reality. Blinking back moisture that had gathered in her eyes, she picked up the dish of warm cobbler, and then returned to the backyard with a cheerful smile. Jason Hammond joined her at the picnic table.

"The girls are having a great visit, Blair. It's all being recorded."

"Thank you so much for making that happen."

He gave her a no-big-deal shrug. "I owed you, Blair. After all, you invited me here today for an interview, you got me entrée to your sister, and to Brandi's dad. I fly to D.C. tomorrow for a one-on-one with the senator."

Blair smiled. "I'm trusting you to write a beautiful story."

"You have my word." The young man eyed the dish of cobbler. "Umm. Blackberry."

"I have Blue Bell in the refrigerator. Homemade vanilla."

"I'll take it straight."

While Blair spooned cobbler into bowls, Jason produced a recorder, and then set it on the table. "Before we get started …" His tone suggested that an understanding was in order. "Just to be clear. I won't be able to include in my story every word you utter today."

Blair chuckled, flashing back to their contentious previous encounter at the cabin. "Understood."

Jason dipped his chin, and then raised a single eyebrow. "One other thing. That big guy with the claw hammer isn't lurking around here anywhere, is he?"

About The Author

LINDA AMEY IS A NATIVE TEXAN, living in Austin with her Boston terrier Regent. She proudly claims to have mastered spelling her maiden name, Brazendine, before finishing first grade. Linda graduated from the University of Texas at Austin, and then practiced as a funeral director for nearly twenty years. Linda and her late husband John served thousands of families at their Austin funeral homes.

Writing novels, while primarily intended to entertain her readers, is an extension of Linda's long-held desire to lift the veil that has shrouded her profession with secrecy. To that end, she takes her readers behind closed doors in a funeral home, interweaving scenes with myth-dispelling descriptions. Such insights are offered to allay the reader's uneasiness about funerals and the funeral profession, and to provoke thought about life, loss, and human worth.

Linda enjoys time with family and friends. After years of playing mahjongg, she remains an enthusiastic rookie. Her passions are reading, travel, and serving as a Docent at the Texas Governor's Mansion.

Made in the USA
Coppell, TX
18 March 2025